BY ABE ABDELHADI

ALL TOGETHER NOW

All Together Now

by

Abe Abdelhadi

for Scott Chapin

Chapters

1. The Beginning of the Middle   02
2. Well, I'm Here Now   24
3. What Would Frank Sinatra Do?   43
4. How's Your Joint, George?   60
5. Good Morning, Derduwan!   84
6. The Road to Canaan   105
7. A Funny Thing Happened on the
    Way to Denmark…   120
8. Don't Harsh My Zen, man   137
9. This is the Best Part of the Trip   156
10. May You Get What You Want   175

Chapter 1-The Beginning of the Middle

This story begins as these stories often do, from the middle. I am twenty-three years old and on the wrong end of an M-16 rifle. It's March and the year is 1988…

****

"I see a red door/and I want to paint it black…"

The Stones song marching through my head on that last night in the States was actually played by Echo & the Bunnymen. I was in my room, dreading this trip I was about to go on. Now Echo hailed from Liverpool, England and they were one of the reasons anyone of any real taste had a good 1980s. They owned the decade as far as I was concerned. At least they did in Los Angeles where I grew up and in 1985, I saw them play three nights in three venues; Universal Amphitheater, Pacific Amphitheater, and Irvine Meadows. They sold out all three places and it was hysteria as soon as they came on stage. Just so fucking epic. Ian McCullough even made smoking look cool. Lead singers can do that. Even though I was a drummer, I actually had all my pants cuffed and tailored because that's what Echo did. Much was made of their contemporaries, U2, the Smiths, and R.E.M. While I liked all kinds of music and bands, Echo & the Bunnymen were it to me.

The night before I left the United States for the Middle East, I repeatedly listened to a live 3-song EP recorded in Germany, alone in my room. It was Echo covering "Paint It Black" by the Rolling Stones, "Friction" by Television and "Run, Run, Run" by The Velvet Underground. If I didn't know the songs, I'd have sworn the band wrote them. They had that intangible quality that made me want to hear more.

My old college roommate and I lived in an old craftsman house in an even older neighborhood just outside of Los Angeles. I had these French doors in my room which I had open all the time, despite living on the first floor. There were bushes on the side of the house so no one could see from the street. The moon would shine through the bushes and splash onto the floor in my room. I could see their shadows move as the breeze blew. Because of this camouflage, I left the doors open all the time which was great because the jasmine wafting through town would drift inside that time of the year. That smell was peaceful to me. Always felt like I was home.

That night my room was dark except for my desk lamp. This was all the light I needed, especially when the moonlight fell in from the other side. I didn't sleep because I couldn't. I sat and watched the record go round and round and round, patiently waiting for the needle to lift so it would start over again. Shelly was on my mind. We had broken up two years before and back then she was as into Echo as I was.

The night we broke up wrecked me, and she did it in this room. I had never felt that way about anyone up to that point. If I was quizzed about it I couldn't tell you if it was love or I just got used to her. What stayed with me was how I dropped to my knees, burying my face into her stomach, my arms tightly around her hips and wailing as I begged her not to end us. I don't know why I was so overcome but I was. I didn't even know what was so lost that had me drop to my knees in that way. Frankly, we hadn't been very passionate as much as we dissolved into being really cool buddies and I knew it. For about six months, I even thought of dumping the whole thing myself a couple of times but was too lazy or scared and I didn't know which. So my grief came because maybe she just beat me to it. Petty, I imagine, but I was still hurt.

In the beginning, all we did was laugh and make love. After eighteen months, we were simply keeping each other company. Guys were coming onto her at our shows and at parties. That didn't happen in the first six months we were together and I think it's because she put out that "I'm taken" vibe. Maybe I thought it would get better again, maybe she *knew* it wouldn't. What I did know is that if she was gone for more than a couple months, she'd be gone for good. That was the sinking feeling that probably drove me to my knees that night. Could be why I was riding things out; I had never been very good at "getting back together" once much time had passed. A couple of girls had tried and failed spectacularly as I lost all interest. I was always excited by the devil I didn't know…

She'd regret her decision later and I would see it in the saddest way.

I played the Echo record over and over until dawn. The anxiety of my impending trip, was weighing on me. I somehow felt doomed. Funny thing about pressure, real or imagined, it brings the most random things to bear. Those weren't even my three "desert island" songs but it didn't matter because there weren't any three songs I wanted to hear any more than those three, and right now, repeatedly. Who knows? I listened, paced and played my own guitar along with the record. The light in my room was the only light on in my house. My roommate had said his goodbyes and split to his girlfriend's

3

house. I had a framed poster of the film "Easy Rider" in the darker corner of my room. Staring at it as I played my guitar, Peter Fonda had his back to me in the dark, looking like he was ready to turn around and say something significant to me. The field in the background looked like it was moving in the breeze, as though Fonda had the one secret that could save my soul. But he just stood there, his sunglasses over his eyes, earnestly searching an American landscape that was long gone with the movie tagline,

"A man went looking for America and couldn't find it anywhere."

I didn't always feel at home but I knew this was a good country. There were good people despite feeling out of place at times which probably came from my being a bit "arty" anyway. This was requisite musician behavior especially as a 23 year old working to find his place in the world. I was kind of a weird kid growing up. But I loved what America stood for; since nowhere was perfect and I was about to find that out.

I was wired and couldn't sleep so I went for a walk in the middle of the night, trying to wear myself out, came back and played the Echo record again and again. I still couldn't sleep and I was too wound up for jacking off to have the desired narcotic effect because I did and it didn't. Packing my bags should have worn me out enough to have a solid nap but not that night. Maybe I should have smoked a joint but then my dad would smell it when he and my cousin came to pick me up and I didn't want a scene.

My dad was religious like most people but despite any earlier tendencies I may have had toward a more pious existence, rock and roll and the West had become my true religion with my nascent decadence still under some tacit discipline. We all have something higher than ourselves to aspire to but I was prepared to live with the spiritual uncertainty a lack of faith could bring.

I was still up when my dad and cousin came to pick me up to go to the airport. Maybe that's why I had Shelly on the brain. Maybe I felt anger, mixed with self pity that no one would miss me, that she was part of "my life passing before my eyes" and there wasn't as much to show for that life as I wanted. The funny thing about that last night in the States was that I was playing that record like I was going to die.

Maybe I was.

Even though I had never really feared death, I still had no desire to go. Not to the Middle East anyway and not fucking now.

For me "fucking now" was playing in a band and working at a record company in Los Angeles, California. The sole purposes of which were to a) keep my dad off my ass because I was "using my degree" and b) to make connections and learn the music business so me and my band could avoid being screwed. Those stories were legend and I always kept the Badfinger story front and center; they let themselves get talked into leaving the Beatles label and signed various deals with several devils which left them broke despite several years of Top 10 hits and sold out shows. Two of the guys even killed themselves. That was a tale of what could happen if I lost focus and let others find clarity for me like it's a favor. There are no free favors. Everything costs.

Things were going well when my father tearfully asked me to perform this pilgrimage by taking my dead cousin back to be buried in his family's plot. It was to the West Bank of Jordan which had been occupied by Israel since 1967. I was not up to it in the least but my dad didn't really care about whatever would be for anyone's good but his. He was also a wildly manipulative man with habits bordering on the Shakespearean so he threw in a good old fashioned crying jag for good measure. I'm sure he meant some of it and he got the desired result so who was I but his son, to judge?

The poet once said, "Many a father begins as a king, but ends up as a king in exile". My dad was well on his way to an exile from us kids whether we knew it at the time or not, so not caring about his emotional state was something I was used to for a long time now. Moments are funny like that.

I am twelve years old and having fallen off a roof, I tore my arm open. I required over thirty stitches. With my arm in a sling, I took a beating as soon as we got home from the hospital. My mother had to pull my father off me. Spittle ran down his chin, catching his breath as he taught me a "lesson."

"We should have let him bleed to death!" He screamed at my mom, "Teach him a lesson when he dies!" I was twelve and the hospital visit cost a hundred bucks but I still don't know if it was the money or that I could have been killed and that freaked him out. I imagine I was required to discern this from the beating.

Dad couldn't go to Israel or the West Bank at the time because he was still on a green card with his own U.S. citizenship a few years away. Being there on a green card, the Israelis could have kept him indefinitely and on any whim too. In hindsight, I should have let him go as time in an Israeli jail may have done him some good and maybe cooled him out. But I didn't. Not at twenty-three, for it was my naïve hope that this small courtesy might finally get me that connection with my dad at last. Gratitude, however, was not a strong suit of his.

I told the band and my boss at the record company I worked at that I would be gone for a few weeks. My band had just gotten a manager and she was earning that potential ten percent. The write ups were just starting to show up in the L.A. Weekly and the Times. We were having the time of our lives. I was the drummer and wrote songs with our singer, Derrick, who was a real cool guy. He was an assistant to one of the busiest photographers in Los Angeles, while shooting his own art stuff on the side, so he did all our band pictures. He was real good. I wasn't particularly photogenic and even I liked the way the pictures came out.

We'd go out to clubs after practice, milking the local recognition for all the juice it was worth; networking for better shows, although we never dared call it that but we really treated the band like a business, saving our gig money in a joint account which paid for rehearsal space, demos and equipment. We met girls through his work, my work, the band; it was epic. A record deal was right around the corner, I could feel it. We had the world by the balls and our shows were getting better. What's more, the band was a family I had chosen to be in. We were in business together and we partied together.

Jim and I had met Derrick and Paul while I was a college intern at the record company I ended up working at, C.I.A Records, a label started by the son of an ex-Army intelligence officer. It stood for "Artistic International Conspiracy" but backwards so it was very spy-like.

Derrick had dated Julie, this other intern I knew, and she introduced us. I was a drummer and Jim, whom I had known for a few years, played bass. We were best friends and we always said we should be in a band together. We were always playing with other guys that we didn't like very much.

One day we said "fuck it" and decided to do our own thing. We started looking for a singer and guitar player and that's where Derrick brought Paul. Julie introduced us and we all hit it off immediately on a personal level. We still had to see if we could be a band so we jammed for a couple months in my living room. As long as we did it when no one was home, my roommates were cool with it.

Things were humming along okay when one night, we were practicing and Derrick was tired and we were just not clicking that night. We had been working on some of our own tunes. He stopped, took a draw on his beer and screamed, "Sire! The people are revolting!"

To which Jim and I responded in unison, "You can say that again!"

This was a Marx Brothers reference from a very old film and the small fact of him getting that, meant the world to me. Jim just thought it was funny. It seems so inconsequential looking back on it now but I felt like I discovered flight that evening.

We decided to be a band and we called ourselves "Mayan Tango." The name didn't come from any one of us, which made it more democratic. We were stuck for a name and Jim's friend, Rick, had just gotten back from Mexico where he saw a Mayan art exhibit and was inspired. Since we were drawing blanks and egos were rampant, it just made sense. So we were Mayan Tango.

We went from begging for shows at the worst places to getting weekends at some of the best clubs in Los Angeles within 18 months or so. We were drawing good crowds at our shows and opening for some pretty big groups like Primus and the Red Hot Chili Peppers. We worked fucking hard. We were not even close to what we ultimately wanted but the path was getting sweeter. People would think that it's one big step to success but it's a business fought by bloody inches as I imagine any business or something worthwhile usually is. We had to simply do it and live with tension and working to "making it." This was paramount above all else which made it difficult to just enjoy the moment for the moment's sake sometimes. Life is comprised of moments as events come and go but we will be dead forever. I wanted to learn to enjoy the moments.

Derrick and I wrote all our songs. Playing covers paid more but the point was to get a record deal, sell our songs and be rock stars, not playing "Louie, Louie" to fucking drunks in Orange County.

So going away at this time was a huge favor to my dad but it wasn't enough. He wanted me to cut my hair as it was down past my shoulders. I cut it but not all the way off. I wanted to grow it back faster when I got home, after all I liked it. It was my hair. He said it made me look like a fag. He had an odd logic that often left me wondering where I was supposed to be won over.

So here I was on the wrong end of an M-16. At twenty-three. In the desert...

****

We were crossing the border from Jordan into the West Bank. My cousin, Ali, and I have our dead kin with us. Ali's brother died suddenly at work in Los Angeles, from a heart attack at twenty-eight years of age. He seized up and dropped dead in front of an accounts receivables woman as he was asking after something of vital importance the point of which vanished when he died right in front of her. Her name was Hilda or Helga, I forget which but she was a plump Latina woman who was very nice to our family at the service we held in L.A. She hugged my mother in the greeting line who was also crying like it was her own child. Mom really did like my cousin.

There is nothing quite like the ashen faces death brings to a funeral. Even if people didn't like the person, they look like soldiers on a troop truck to hell.

Personally, I thought it was drug related. However, I would not have brought that up to my dad. Even thinking that would crush him; he may have been a hypocrite but he wanted to believe that the family was doing the right thing at all times. Dad paid good money to send his nephew back home to be buried with his father. He was my dad's brother-in-law, whom he respected a great deal. There were a lot of mandatory religious traditions but going back to the homeland to be buried wasn't one of them. If anything, it was a grandiose way for my father to show his family that he "raised his kids right," sending the oldest boy to handle "family business." The family opinion was all that mattered to him.

My dad left home at seventeen and met my mother in Brazil five years later. Of course, she lived there and she was a Catholic. They married and came to the United States in the 1960s, where my brothers and I were born. This kind of matrimony was very risky. I had grown up religious (before logic, women and drink got the better of me) and found that divergent philosophies can do as much damage to a marriage as coming home to your bride with a case of the crabs. There's a verse in the Bible about being equally yoked. I felt not enough people took it seriously.

However, being the eldest son, it fell on me to take the body back with Ali, my other, more alive cousin. Ali was not the eldest in his family as that distinction belonged to an aggressively annoying human being in the form of his brother. No one really cared for him due to an over indulgent sense of self pity and revenge on anything with a pulse that had the slightest tinge of paying him even a perceived insult.

He's a millionaire these days but I would never blame the money for how he turned out as he was that way when we found him. Charm and ethics can't be bought. He had a bad fallout with his mother so they weren't speaking and he was not speaking to the dead brother when his heart exploded. They had a fight for different reasons entirely. He had other failings in personal and business relationships with the family that left most feeling ripped off, betrayed, hurt or a combination of all three. He was not the least bit remorseful about any of it as it was "their problem." Those boys were born in Ramallah, 20 minutes away from their village where my father also grew up. Their mother still lived there.

So here I was this very American guy in the Middle East. There's an old joke with a punch line about it being different than the Mid West. I don't remember the joke itself but the punch line was so goddamned true.

We landed in Amman, Jordan and stayed with my dad's cousin, Roman, for 3 days but it felt longer. Hell, we have a dead guy with us so we had all the fucking time in the world! Landing in Tel Aviv was certainly allowed, but not advisable. We could have been held in a processing center for a couple weeks before they got around to us and things would not speed up because we had a dead body, not at all. This would have been an inconvenience if not a complete fucking drag. So Jordan it was and our gracious host, Roman, being politically connected, expedited our papers much faster than any traditional means would allow. Watching him negotiate, back slap and glad hand the local cronies was quite impressive and he liked to hand out Cuban cigars. I always knew that if you speak the tongue and wave some dollars around, "officials" in these shitholes give in easily. Of course it was our dollars he was waving but I was still impressed with how cheap bribery was here, what with the exchange rate and all. I wondered what else was easy to get through customs if one were so inclined. The fish does rot from the head. King Hussein's rule hinged on convincing folks that he was a direct descendant of the Prophet Mohammed. It worked, for the most part. People do whatever the hell they need to for control. A little bit of sacrilege? Perhaps, but my question was, "So what if it was true? Wasn't Mohammed just a guy?" Every religion has a version of that very question and no one likes to be asked much about it. Customs was no exception there.

Because I was wiped out from the flight, the Amman journey, and basically over all the travel, I was still in the proverbial coma. I believe Roman was a former Deputy Assistant Minister of Communication or something. This more than made up for the extra three days our visit took and was a wildly impressive feat, as feats go with martial law or bureaucrats in the Third World.

Amman was like any large city that you would find in Europe but without really any major point of interest that I can recall. It wasn't Mecca or Paris and Dubai was 20 years away. Maybe I was too zoned out. What I noticed about Jordan though was how everything was kind of incomplete looking if not just grimy. The smells ran the gamut of a "good block, bad block" scenario; some spots were lush and the powers of the city went out of their way to cultivate a lot of shrubbery. Other spots suffered from outdoor plumbing which smelled like the rot of old food and garbage. These were open sewers that ran parallel to the sidewalks. Not all but a lot of the buildings kind of had that "What were we thinking? Let's start over." vibe. Unfinished homes or mini malls dotted the streets in between homes that were lived in though I wouldn't even call those homes quite finished either.

I began to notice that every shop or business had a huge, framed portrait of King Hussein. God help me if I had talked shit about the King, man. I would have disappeared, as in fucking gone or more to the point, dead. I found this out when our erstwhile guide, Roman corrected me.

We were in a breakfast place when I had noticed this trend in royal portraiture and attempted humor, "Man, they must really love the King, here, huh?"

Roman turned to Ali and me, with his eyes squinted and "SSShhhh" was all he said.

I got it, thankfully, but when we walked outside of the café, he told Ali in Arabic, then me, "If you want a long, healthy life, it's best to say nothing about the King. It does not matter for your passport".

****

To cross into the West Bank, which was essentially Israel, with a dead body, was not something to enter into lightly. Security was no joke and this was before suicide bombing became a fad of a mentally disturbed contingent, that some would call freedom fighters. I got that they were fighting an oppressor but if I were dead then there'd be no freedom. At least that's how I saw it. The obvious points get lost on us when we're heated up. I also didn't think God or an Allah needed that kind of help.

My other concern was that the seventy-two virgins, they promised Muslims for their martyrdom, could be really ugly; they could look like my Aunt Fatima who was a dried up old maid with moles that had hairs stiff as speaker wire coming out of them and a headscarf to hide the fact that she was balding.

10

She lived with my parents in the U.S. and my brothers and I called her the "lump". Of course, this could be why they're eternal virgins to begin with. My aunt was no beauty queen and charm was not long on her list of virtues.

Roman rode shotgun in the ambulance with us to guide the driver. He wore a suit with no tie which, in Jordan, gave him an air of authority. While our papers were cheap, it meant we had to go through a specific checkpoint because that's basically where our bribe counted. We pulled up to a cinder block bunker in the middle of bloody hell. It straddled an open sewage stream and the smell was recognizable, which was a polite way of saying it smelled like shit, but thank God the water *moved* so the shit didn't sit still. I knew I'd hit bottom when such an observation made me grateful. Technically, we were still in Jordan but it looked the same on both sides of the stream, frankly.

The area made an average American trailer park look like Shangri-fucking-la. It was in one of the vast, undeveloped sections of the West Bank which was basically a no man's land. Humidity and dust clung to you like muddy mist as soon as you got out of the car. Our Jordanian host got back into the ambulance after we said our goodbyes and took off. Israeli soldiers took the body around to the back which was blocked to the public by guards. However, they did give us a receipt which, despite the professionalism, reminded me of an absurd comedy sketch.

Even Ali, who was not really one for sarcasm grimaced as he said, "Oh wow! A receipt!"

They would spend three hours on him, combing the carcass for plastic explosives before we get him back. He was covered with a sheet on a stretcher and we didn't get the coffin back. We didn't lift the sheet. It was a slow day at the checkpoint and we had faith...

The coffin came in handy for the funeral in the States as well as the flight. Muslims just wrap a guy up, say a prayer and slide him into a crypt. Israelis use the confiscated coffins to bury indigent Jewish settlers. The $3,000 it cost was dad's de facto contribution to the State of Israel even if he spoke no Hebrew. My father called such actions the "cost of faith" as he believed one had to do the right thing by faith when one could. Of course, like most people, the right thing was what would serve him best in the end sanctioned by God. It's interesting how God does that.

As we walked into the front of the checkpoint we got patted down for weapons and contraband. The place bore a striking resemblance to an

11

American DMV. The floors were of that soft, cheap, brown linoleum that was in my junior high school cafeteria. There must be a U.N. charter invoking the mandatory use of government-issue, light green paint so decreed by the international light green paint lobby. There were two men with M-16s pointed at us as benignly as one could point a gun at people. Tourism issues warranted a maintained feeling of welcome so one can't point guns menacingly at the tourists or locals. They scare easy. Without the guards, I would have thought I was back at my old high school except for the faint, shit smell creeping in through the walls, blown around by the ceiling fans.

The guards also took our shoes.

There is something subservient to removing one's shoes at gun point or doing anything at gun point. There is no real cool way of doing it without being in a vulnerable position (kneeling down is obvious but doing it while standing keeps one off balance and thus not cool) and they kept our shoes the whole time they dealt with us. This way, if we tried to run, they would have had an easier time shooting us. Our socks would fill up with dirt and sand and weigh us down.

As Ali and I were processed I had this sick "going to prison" feeling even though I knew this wasn't jail, at least not yet.

Then I hear, "You American?" My theory is that my longish hair and over coat betrayed me although I could have been European, too. But why would the Europeans come here when the south of France promised wine, cheese, and topless French girls?

I looked up and saw a very American grin, American teeth and all. The Israeli says, "I'm Liev…What's your name, man?" I tell him and then he asks, "Where you from?"

"L.A.," I answer proudly, used to having said that anytime I left home. Mentioning the state or country was not necessary when you're from L.A., man. "How 'bout you?" I asked.

"Jersey," he said looking around, "This was a fucking mistake…you visiting?" When I said that I was, he offered, "Whatever you do, don't live here, man. I mean it…"

At that point I wondered if it wasn't some sort of trick. I have read about tricks.

Frankly, I was also a little checked out right then, for obvious reasons, "Yeah, wow… no man, I *am* just visiting…" I nod in the direction of my dead cousin and pointing toward the back, "You know, stuff brought me here…Jersey, huh? Shit, well…what brings you here?"

"Fucking brochure those 'Right of Return' fuckers fed me, man. They show you a great time in Tel Aviv but then you get here…Milk and honey my ass, man. It's the middle of nowhere, fucking *nowhere!*" Liev shakes his head, "I haven't seen a good show since Springsteen at the Garden in '85," his grin long having vanished at that point.

I told him about the U2 show I saw at the Coliseum with the Pretenders having opened. Told him about the R.E.M. show I saw in San Diego in 1986 before they got real big. It was their last festival seating show and I saw it at the San Diego State gym.

He looked to one side as he'd been whispering the whole time, "As soon as this tour is over, I'm out. I can be a Jew at home. Who needs this shit, you know what I mean?" He was speaking of his tour of duty in the Israeli Army. It was in our moment of truth that Liev's superior appeared over his shoulder like a bad moon rising.

I suspiciously nodded my agreement as my shoeless cousin tapped my elbow and shook his head subtly, arching an eyebrow. Apparently, we were each fraternizing with the enemy. What both of these guys didn't understand is that we were Americans and not the enemy!

Liev was nothing more to me but a dude who didn't like it there. I was 23 years old and we were about the same age and we cared more about rock and roll and movies and art than we did for miniature dirt wars fought by the masses, energized by dead gods and fairy tales. I'm certain that in a conversation at a party, this view may sound venal and offensive, "But as opposed to what?" I thought. Religion? A practice that was so deep and worked so well that it was worth killing or jailing people for? I thought if it worked, there'd be no killing and those that believe in forgiveness could forgive the fact that I didn't get it.

So what makes me better off? Is art god, then? I had no answers but in my perfect world, nobody dies and everybody went to heaven, which I pictured to be a cool museum where the best live music would be played in the next room; everything from Brahms to Hendrix to Miles Davis to Echo and the

Bunnymen and not just because I liked it but because the world is better for all of it and the food would rock.

It's where I'd get between six and eight extremely hot professionals instead of seventy-two really ugly, un-laid chicks. Whatever I termed as my poison would be *my* chosen heaven not to be dictated by some dude in a tall hat and a dress. This would be a place where, if God did build it, he splits and lets us enjoy it because that's why the God of my design built it for his kids in the first place. But all my anger and inner dialog was not going to help change that day or what happened before. I'm learning to live with that.

I also came here for a reason. I had a dead cousin who just wanted to be buried with his father, in the manner of his religion and who am I to judge?

****

"Teenage Mary said to Uncle Dave/I sold my soul, must be saved/Gonna take a walk down to Union Square/You never know who you're gonna find there…"

There was a group of family members waiting for us as we got out of the bunker area and on to the main highway. The road was paved but still very dusty because this area had no real plants to speak of. The dust blew easily and the humidity made it worse. It was desolate as the wind spread more desert upon us which clung to our sweat.

The military escort transferred the body from their jeep to the waiting ambulance one of my uncles had contracted. The soldiers were very polite and professional. Liev was one of them and he did the cool guy nod thing that guys give each other when they're trying to be subtle. The Arabs didn't quite ignore the Jews but were pleasant without kissing a bunch of ass.

My Uncle Ayoub and a couple of cousins helped the Israelis with the stretcher. The ambulance door was closed and Ayoub looked at one of the Israeli boys and smiled sadly as he patted him on the shoulder with an attitude of patriarchal humanity versus oppressed and the oppressor. I was strangely comforted by that even though the moment was brief. There seemed to be a tacit understanding between some in these two camps that they did what they had to do to get along. Neither side here was kingmaker, but simple errand boys, sent by the grocer to collect the bill as the poet once said.

Ali kissed my Uncle Ayoub three times on the cheek, "Assalamu alaikum," he said. "Alaikum salaam," Ali returned the greeting. I spoke next to no Arabic but I heard this all my life so I could at least say that even though I was resolute in the non-religious aspect of my life. My uncle kissed me three times too. I felt relieved by him in a strange way, having just met him but I guess his attitude toward the Israelis gave me a bit of hope. I was used to this side of the family exhibiting contempt and derision but not him. He was different and I felt a connection; I could see it in his eyes.

Everyone was dressed in khakis or jeans with windbreakers or sweaters. Ayoub, however, was in a floor length duster, kind of like the white ones the sheiks wore, except his was brown and wool, not silk. It still looked cool with his keffiyeh around his head, setting him apart from the others.

There was definitely a mixed feeling because it was obvious we were not on vacation but all were glad to see us safe, just the same. I had not met many of my father's family before except for the handful of cousins or the occasional U.S. visit by one of his brothers or sisters. My Uncle Ayoub had never made these visits but was genuinely glad to meet me as all they had were pictures of his brother's sons. We all hugged and kissed everyone on the cheek three times, exchanging "Assalamu alaikums." It's just what they do.

Having gone to Brazil without complaint, I made many excuses the several times my father made his trips here. I thought that I couldn't deal with an entire family of *him*. Of course, I was a kid and never knew my uncle was not like his brother at all. He actually went out of his way to make me feel welcome, although I spoke no Arabic and he spoke zero English. In the end, he would prove kinder to me than most of those who spoke my language.

A good friend of mine lost his father when he was ten years old. I see that it still affects him as a grown man. While no one ever really gets over it at any age, at ten our fathers are fucking heroes. Custer, riding high on his trusty steed, before the Indians turn him into a pin cushion. Paternal perfection frozen in time…

The American Indian was always made to be the bad guy, with history being written by the winners. If my own dad died when I was ten I would have glossed over his shortcomings completely, revising a history that couldn't exist given his disposition. He'd have died a winner, forever young. He wouldn't have gotten a good running start on destroying the hero's image which only ruins as life forges on or if I wasn't a student of history.

We tend to forget the good things people do. My father did some good but I always had to reference his past or hear it told by someone else to catch a glimmer of that good. He always had this near consistent animosity toward his sons. Ayoub was different but then maybe I was the third party source for his own kids.

My paternal grandfather sent my mother a platinum cross as a wedding gift when my parents got married in Brazil. Not a very Muslim gesture I suppose but he was welcoming of anyone coming into the family and especially if they were able to provide grandchildren. My father reviled this gesture for what he considered weakness and worked real hard to be the asshole his own father was not. He attributed his father's "lack of successes" in life to such weak hearted folly. My father never spoke to us in Arabic unless he was cussing at us. He usually spoke to us in Portuguese, which he learned in Brazil or English due to laziness. I found that this was common among the half bred children of Arabs of which there were quite a few, especially in our family. It was just something I learned to live with.

It was because of this lack of instruction, in speaking Arabic, that I recognized only some of the words of grief or reverence for a God I'm not too sure gave a shit to begin with. Here, on the roadside, there was the animated, Biblical wailing that one is used to seeing on TV in news reports on the Mid East. The men were choked up pretty bad and some were outright bawling. 28 years of age is awfully young to die and the few women that came (my aunt, Mahmud's mom, elected to wait at home) were openly screaming something in Arabic, with hands in the air to God that I'm sure was a combination of praise and rhetorical questioning.

Another car skidded to a stop next to the ambulance. It was Ali's asshole older brother, Adnan, who went by "Eddie." He was late but made a big production of demanding to see "my baby brother!" In his tradition of being a selfish prick, he couldn't even ride in the cars with the rest of the family.

He approached our side of the ambulance, hands waving, "If you don't let me see him, I'll smash this window open!" He had picked up a good sized boulder, popping it out of the dirt, from the roadside. It was bigger than he thought and further in the ground, which made the gesture less smooth and thus less macho than intended, but he somehow made it work. I chuckled but held it in. I think he said his thing in English for my benefit as he knew I didn't speak Arabic. The driver hurriedly opened the door, with the look on his face that said this was *his* van and not some company, so he'd better do what he's told, lest he pay the damages. As the door opened, the smell of death wafted into the desert wind for an unholy scent. My cousin lifted the sheet, facing the stench head on and wailed and it was very dramatic. If I liked him at all, I'd have felt some pity but I did not like him and felt fucking pitied out.

It was moments like these that made me regret not speaking the mother tongue so I could say, "Hey shit head! You couldn't talk to him when he was alive? Yeah, when people die, 'sorry' won't work, asshole!" or the pithier "Nice play, dickwad but he's dead already!" I was curious if these nuances would hold up in translation.

I believe as Ali and I watched this play out we both felt the same way. Mahmoud had been with us for about a week and he was still dead. Moreover, he'd been gone for almost two weeks and what's more, we have been doing all of the heavy lifting and I know Ali and I just wanted to be done with this shit because frankly, I was wasted tired.

But this tragedy was still fresh for these folks so we let it go. They needed closure and I knew making a scene with Eddie would make the situation worse. There was a bigger purpose than my feelings, to be sure. There is something uncannily natural about burying the dead. You don't ever really get over loss but there is no mistaking the overwhelming sense to get on with living. We want to live.

Mahmoud and I weren't even particularly close but I didn't really dislike him either and yes, I would miss him. At first I was here because it was my duty or a feeble attempt at trying to be the man my dad expected me to be. But then the whole thing just got to me. I have always processed death long after the fact for some reason. I never really worried about my own death for that matter. I have had enough situations to know that wasn't mere macho rhetoric.

I was sixteen years old and I worked at an ice cream store, in South L.A. and it was 1981. A harmless looking, black street guy came in to buy a cone. I looked down at the cash drawer as I took his money to make change. Suddenly he reached his hand into the cash! I grabbed his wrist and as I pulled him to

17

the floor, he pulled out a gun and aimed it at my head! The gun's make was lost on me but I backed away about six feet like I flew, with my hands up quickly. He said, in a low voice, "You dead, motherfucker!"

Oddly enough, I was calm as a cow in New Delhi and I simply thought, "This is it," nearly overwhelmed with the peace only an "I don't care if I die" feeling can bring. But after a blank stare for what seemed forever, he only took the money and ran out. I calmly walked into the back where Mike was washing dishes and told him we were robbed. I even showed him the dropped ice cream cone. The idiot even had ice cream stains in the drawer with fingerprints. We called the cops.

I wasn't upset and never got upset. To this day it doesn't even register as anything other than an interesting thing I used to mention at parties to impress girls...

Another gust of wind kicked up some dust and my uncle took control of the situation, clearly being the patriarch of the family in these matters; he walked over to the ambulance, eyed Eddie and shut the doors with a look and nod that said, "It's time," gently nudging him aside. He motioned for all of us to get in the cars, "Yallah!" he said authoritatively. We headed toward my father's village and followed my cousin in our grim caravan with my other uncle riding shotgun in the ambulance.

This was 1988, the height of what the Arab world called the first *Intifada* or uprising. I always felt like an alien space guest when heritage or what I knew about Arabs came up in conversation as a kid in the States. I wasn't very good about anything not American or of the West. Brazil always felt better for some reason. Maybe because it was not the Middle East, I don't know, but fitting in was paramount when you're 10 and 12. I spoke of it like it wasn't really my background but alas, it was. I felt like I was just telling the story of another people or even recounting a movie I had seen, feeling more American than anything else. But I knew the history and dug the food and that was as feeble a connection as an adopted kid finding out that his real father was a war hero.

My dad's family lived in the West Bank for hundreds of years before Israel became a nation. That happened in 1948 after the hideous brutality of WWII and the Holocaust. It wasn't hard to get the U.N. Partition of 1947 turned into a mandate for the birth of a nation. At the time, like it or not, Palestine was a territory of Great Britain and not its own country. As I grew up, the Arabs always seemed to enjoy the shock in talking about the brutality of the Birth of Israel. Israelis didn't like hearing it either but it was brutal; very American Indians being butchered by the white man sort of thing.

However, I could never find anywhere in history where a nation was birthed with cooperation and a handshake. The entire western hemisphere was ripe for this. "Sure, come on in and take us over! We'll get a pot of tea on!" was not anything I ever saw in history books which were written by the winners. They told a certain kind of truth as we all do to fit an agenda. Is that desire to gloss over history ever absent? I did it in my most mundane conversations about everyday life all the time so why not an entire civilization when the stakes are high? Someone wins, someone loses, and the winners get someone to write it down.

So we drove through the east end of the West Bank. The streets didn't look too dissimilar from anything I have seen in Mexico or the Bahamas. Again, a lot of that half finished look with light blues, yellows, oranges, and bad green or brown trim that had a tendency to not match the buildings which began with a purpose only to be left for us to guess what the fuck they were. There was no beach and I quickly noticed as in Jordan, the absence of exposed feminine flesh.

The women didn't wear burqas but they dressed modestly with pants fitting loosely if they wore them and the sleeves were long on blouses or sweaters with no short skirts and painfully, no cleavage. Lots of women wore the embroidered traditional Arab dresses. Even the advertising screamed Islamic rule but not Sharia Law. The Israelis would never allow it; not in the Territories. One billboard for tennis gear showed a happy couple dressed in tennis wear from the 1800's or something. The man had on long, white pants and a long sleeved sweater and she did as well. Swimwear sales were not making markets in this part of the world and I doubt there was an Arabic word for "lingerie."

We continued on through Ramallah which was like a ghost town at this hour. It was a full thirty degrees colder too. I was told to bring clothes for the cold because it could be like Chicago at times. I almost didn't listen, thinking, "It's the fucking desert, man!" I'm glad I took the advice. The place was way above sea level, much higher than Amman.

Because of the conflict, the towns closed up early. Jerusalem, Bethlehem, and Ramallah all had curfews. Certain towns were open for business from ten to twelve noon, two to four, and so on. But between the curfews, a mid east version of the OK Corral, complete with the student protesters showing up with rocks and the big, bad Israeli Army appearing with M-16's, rubber bullets and riot gear. Even with the rubber bullets it still looked very "David & Goliath." This imagery in the world media fueled as much. Liberals jumped all over the stories as it resembled the Kent State massacre, the Hippie Movement, Civil Rights, and pretty much the entire 1960s. Left leaning Europeans found something else to needle and dislike the "imperialist" U.S. for. Interestingly, it was the first time I can remember sympathy or empathy of any kind, for Arabs. Finally, albeit briefly the terms "animals" and "Barbarians" took a rest.

It was like Yasser Arafat went to a New York publicist, "Look, Maury, I have this image problem, see?" having adopted a Brooklyn accent. "The world thinks we're a bunch of goons...anything but! We're good people! People of the earth, religious people, you get the idea...but we have gotten a bad rap over this terror thing."

"Look Y.A. (because a good publicist always uses your initials) what you need is a total concept makeover," of course Maury is chomping a cigar as good publicists are wont to do. "There is nothing more guaranteed to piss people off than to have students getting shot...but they gotta be real now! No shipped in, professional rabble rousers you understand? None of that Al Sharpton bullshit! That leaks out and you are fucked. You read me?"

Of course, Yasser being the image whore that he is, has his concerns but is still very interested, his assistant taking notes, "Well, Maury, there have already been so many deaths and they're just kids and..."
"They got Nixon good with this shit! Don't you remember Kent State?" Maury puffs triumphantly, his tie lying at the top of his belly, bald head gleaming in the neon glow of his office.

"That was you?" Yasser is impressed and upon Maury's approving nod, noticing the autographed Abbie Hoffman picture behind him, becomes ecstatic, clapping his hands, "Done! When do we start?"

Maybe it wasn't quite that orchestrated and I doubt Arafat knew any publicists in New York that specialized in PR for protesting.

I saw a body on the side of the narrow two lane road we got on, charred beyond description. Man or woman, I really couldn't tell but the smell of old, burnt flesh came through the car window. I asked Ali and he shrugged, "Collaborator."

He went on to explain that a collaborator was someone, usually an Arab, who for whatever reason, acceptance, ethics or lack of, money, it doesn't matter, spied for the Israelis. Now, when the Arabs caught one, they took a tire soaked with gasoline and threw it around his neck and set it on fire. Of course, this was after he has had the ever living shit beaten out him with bats or crowbars. This tire trick was called a "necktie." Sometimes, they'd just set him on fire after the requisite tortuous thrashing which was the real punch line to the exercise. One thing that was a constant was that they were always burned and they were always left on the side of the road until the locals or the Israelis would pick up the mess. Made a statement. Not sure if the boys in marketing came up with that as a calling card but it was catchy, if not conflicted.

Welcome to the West Bank.

We got to the village and my uncles guide the ambulance to the mosque where the services were to be held in about two hours. The driveway was broken concrete as this place was built largely through western donations which had been re-directed out here sometime ago. Several of us lifted the stretcher out of the ambulance and moved it into a room where the local cleric was there with another guy who I believe was the preparation guy or something. Man, did Mahmoud stink. Technically, it's a sin to leave a body unburied this long as you're supposed to be buried as soon as humanly possible as in right the fuck now but God forgives air travel and border crossings. Religion, being a method of instruction, instructed this because people fucking stink when they're dead!

We went to the house and ate before going to the service. I was surprised at how simple the building was. Except for some religious stuff in the front, you wouldn't really know it was a mosque. It kind of looked like a really big, half finished tract home in California with random cement chunks in parts of the yard where plants or lawn were supposed to be. Here I see that most of my heathen family (except for Ayoub and another cousin) stood in the back with the women in the foyer. Apparently, they were as inconsistent as my dad and they didn't even know their own prayers. I subscribe to the ideal that if one bothers to claim a faith, said one may want to have a working knowledge on how it all works. One should know their respective religion's "dominus e pluribus unums" and that sort of thing, especially if claiming superiority is what one is into.

Now I was in back because I was not a Muslim. I was invited to pray by one of my cousins and I declined politely. I was no hypocrite or at least I tried to be as little of one as possible.

After the prayers and some cleric officiated, my cousin was carried on a nicer, religious stretcher through the village streets. There were probably about 200 people who made the 100 yard trek to the cemetery. It was an overcast day and there were people clapping, chanting with more wailing and calling to Allah for sure.

The graveyard was interesting because rich or poor, everyone pretty much had a crypt. I'm not sure but there had to be an "indigent crypt fund" or something for folks without relatives in the West. The space was pretty huge for a small village of 3,000. They slid Mahmoud into the crypt next to the one his father was buried in. They had a big piece of land for that immediate family. The workers came out with fresh cement right away. The women stayed and bellowed, consoling his mom who was on her knees, wailing with her soft, plump hands in the air, grinding her knees and embroidered dress into the dirt. Her face was completely soaked with floods of tears that were splashing off her cheeks onto the ground like rain mixed with the spit that only grief can produce. At times I thought she was suffocating, her mouth hung open wide for long stretches working to take in air before a moan could be emitted, evolving into a banshee's wail then she'd do it again.

I also thought I was cried out but apparently I wasn't. I'm certain I was feeling her loss more than anything else as I was numb for a few days until that moment. Ali opened up, letting loose his sobs as he and his brothers were holding their mother with an almost instinctual precision. It was as if this act had been passed down for generations and I suppose it had, if I thought about humans being human. Even Eddie suspended the feud, the memory of which was absent here and joined in.

Culture be damned because there is no sound like that of a bereaved parent burying their child. No sound on this earth. This was her youngest boy, the baby. It's like hearing a gun cocked in your direction or a dying child giving

22

out its last gasp. Few sounds stop your heart like that. It made my chest hurt. This was not the first time I heard it and I would be naïve to think it would ever be the last. The world is imperfect and shit just happens, and I was in the fucking Middle East where I just saw a burned up dead person.

Suddenly and with familiarity, the "I didn't really care if I died" feeling came upon me. So there's that.

Chapter 2-Well, I'm Here Now…

I slept until around noon the next day. Not like me at all but I was exhausted. I don't really remember all of what happened after the funeral as the evening came. Looking back on the time, I remember spending some evenings at the homes of some of relatives and folks who knew my mother and father when they all lived in Brazil together. Most of them were good people with very pure intentions, as good people, anywhere, are prone to have. As for that immediate evening I draw a complete blank, even now.

My uncle and cousins had been downstairs since dawn preparing and selling two head of sheep for the day's income. They fed this entire village with the couple hundred head of sheep they raised. Other farmers and growers did the same for the other food groups; chicken, beef, vegetables and a few bakeries which made pastries and pita bread, stuff like that. This was something they all did 5 or 6 days a week, funerals notwithstanding…

My aunt Samira fed me scrambled eggs, some leftover grilled breast of chicken, yogurt on a plate drizzled with olive oil and parsley with hot, fresh pita bread. Pita bread there was lumpy and soft, like a big, flat Semite biscuit. I wasn't able to speak to anyone in my uncle's house except my cousin, Ajazi, who spoke Spanish after some time in South America. Since the rest only spoke Arabic, they were very nice, nodding and smiling a lot; the food was good so I had no complaints. Even though I spoke an L.A. version of Spanish, Ajazi translating for us was better than nothing.

Samira was Ayoub's wife and was kind to me regardless of a language barrier. I was trying to be at peace with these people and shame on me for thinking "these people." It's just I never felt like I belonged and maybe my dad was such a fish out of water in America he had to be who he was to survive. To curry his favor though, I would sometimes over-compensate for an "Arab-ness" that I did not possess. I was always the first to greet visitors to the house, shake hands and put an unnatural enthusiasm into what Arab words I did know. It was never good enough. Maybe my father should have taught me some Arabic, but he preferred to put more energy into criticism. After all, if it got fixed, it can't be criticized. My brothers, being smarter, would dodge out and sneak off to play outside or go into their rooms and watch cartoons.

Samira didn't seem to care. Her smile said I was family and the pictures of me and my brothers on the bureau with her kids said I was hers. Maybe she loved me like my mom loved my cousins.

My cousin Sam dropped in that morning. His name was also short for something longer in Arabic. I knew him pretty well from Los Angeles. He was around twelve years older than I was. When I was a kid, I always admired him because he just so fucking *cool*. Cool as the other side of the pillow cool, this guy. He always drove an amazing car and always had a hot model type chick with him. I would say he was one of the few role models I had in my actual family. When I was younger, he was someone whose life I would have liked. It was only as an adult that I found his confidence came from a good amount of family money.

He went to college at UC Berkeley up in Northern California. We were at one of our cousin's weddings when I was twelve and Sam brought this blonde with him. Her name was Kelly (how perfect was that?). We were horny, adolescent geek boys in absolute awe. I was twelve years old and pimply, in a suit that was wearing me, fantasizing about the belly dancer and Sam was living it, THE LIFE man! I thought your 20's would be a hundred years away. Boy, how time flies.

"Waky, waky, my son!" he announced as I was being fed more food and coffee.

As Sam waltzed in, I was smiling a lot at my aunt who benignly smiled back. She was asking me if I had a girlfriend back in the States through Ajazi. I was feeling uncomfortable with the translation as Sam came in. Thank God for timing.

"What's up man?" I said as I got up to give Sam a hug. Good guy. We didn't get much conversation in the day before; it was an intense day. He said the usual assalamu alaikums to my aunt and other cousins.

"Get dressed, dude. We're going into Jerusalem today," he said. He clapped his hands enthusiastically, the business of living commencing immediately.

Sam and his nine brothers and sisters jetted back and forth between here and L.A. Theirs was one of the more prominent families from this village. They had business in the Territories, California, and New York. Sam, being the youngest, had the good fortune of taking time to "find himself" while he was getting paid by the family running business that already existed. He started a restaurant in Jerusalem called the Dome, which he ran with two of our cousins who handled the bulk of the duties while Sam traveled, even though he pulled his weight when he was in town and the investment was largely his.

BAM! Sam's hand smacked the table, "Check it out, I got my uncle's Mercedes! He's in L.A. and said we could use it to show you a good time while you're here," he said, beaming. "Finish up and let's get going…we have to leave Jerusalem before 6 tonight to come back. That's curfew."

"Cool…alright." I said as I finished my coffee, "Gimme a minute."

The sweet ride in question was a fully restored, fudge brown, 1963 Mercedes-Benz 300 SE with tan leather interior and a sunroof. Not exactly unique but may as well have been a Rolls Royce around here. While the offer was generous, there would be massive hell to pay if we wrecked the car or got it confiscated. That would suck.

I knew Ali would want to come as well, but I also knew he was stuck acting as buffer between his mother and brothers. He and his other brother were consoling their mother as she wanted to know for certain if Mahmoud died from drugs, which was the cruel rumor. That should never have gotten to her ears but people can be such assholes. Just because my dad ignored it, didn't mean no one had heard it. It's inherent in people to feel that "the rumor's always half true." If the boys had half a brain, they'd deny it even if they did know for sure. He's dead and they can't fix it, so fuck it, it's done. Eddie was forbidden, at least for the time being, in her home. The brief reunion at the funeral was not an invitation to forgiveness. It was odd how they parted once she regained her composure at the burial and then escorted back to her home where she held a reception. She sat on pillows in a corner and cried in a near fetal position. She had kneaded several dozen Kleenexes into mulch and the debris covered her coat like dandruff. That much I remember from that day.

Meanwhile, Eddie was in Bethlehem with some cronies that he hung out with. One guy was someone that my family knew, Abdul-Lateef. They were behind an antiques store, loading crates into a truck. There were around 15 or so crates and once they were loaded, Eddie smacked the side and yelled, "Yallah!" The truck took off, headed for Lebanon. Apparently, Eddie had developed a very healthy heroin trade. He'd ship it in from Afghanistan then cut it in Bethlehem behind this antiques store. Then it would go through Lebanon, Syria, and finally into Europe; that's where the money was and the borders were way easier to navigate. Risking the U.S. wasn't worth it. The Israelis were less intense with the Christians than with the Muslims so their policing that area was more for show. Even though they were Palestinians, the Christians just had this whole, "we're just kind of watching" vibe even though it was to be their home too, technically, if they ever got a Palestinian State.

Since I was here for awhile, I may as well do something. I didn't fly 18 hours to turn around and go home. I came for a shitty reason but I'm here now so I may as well make the most of it and see things. Sam was as great a tour guide as one could get. He knew the area, spoke English, Arabic, Hebrew, and Spanish. He made things fun and liked to party. Spanish worked here because of the many returning expatriates who spent time in Central & South America doing business and learning the language. Spanish was the number three or four language there, next to English. Sam chatted with my aunt and other cousins while I got changed.

Arab extended families could be fucking huge. My father's family, alone, numbered into over 500. This phenomenon occurred because first cousins could marry. It wasn't exactly right but it's just what they did. In fact, Sam was married to Nina, his first cousin on his father's side with Kelly having fallen off, long ago. I grew up with Nina in L.A.; good girl. Even though two thirds of the known world engages in this cousin marrying practice, I was never quite comfortable with it. That may have been because most of my cousins were pretty ugly.

Secondly, the families stay tight and had lots of kids. Cousins and cousins of cousins are regarded as uncles and aunts if they're older. That being said, Sam and I don't necessarily share the same aunts or uncles but because his dad and my dad are cousins, we get the same family privileges and favors.

So this Mercedes we were to procure belonged to his mother's brother, who also knew my dad and his family and whom my father regarded as family; having helped most of them get into the U.S. in the 1960s. They loan huge sums of money to each other, indefinitely and always pay it back. Kind of like the Mafia but with falafel and shawarma instead of capicola and prosciutto. However I always felt the Italian chicks to be much, much hotter if one were to compare notes.

****

"I knew it musta been some big set-up/all the action just would not let up…"

The Mercedes started out real rough as it badly needed a tune up. As we got going, the irony of this Nazi go-cart in the Middle East was not lost on me, not one bit.

We drove into Ramallah, to see one of Sam's brothers, Jamal. He had been married several times to American women and they didn't take. They were hot but that didn't really help a whole lot as marriage is a tad more complicated than a high school prom. I remember this kind of thing was always fodder for the Arabs who really were hung up with this shit. "See, American women have too much *freedom.* You have to marry an Arab, if you want to be happy. She can't go anywhere. She will shame her family because nobody will marry a divorced woman.*"*

This became more happy horseshit as the 90s dawned in America and my female cousins would contribute to the divorce rate with gusto and re-marry Arab guys who were not asshole Bedouin fuckheads. Russians, Americans, the French, they all had a shot at joining our family.

All this silliness was why I never got too hung up with a girl's past. She could have fucked the Chilean National Guard as well as the San Pedro Longshoremen's Union, during a cocaine-fueled, whisky bender and I wouldn't really care as long as she didn't cheat on me. Right *now* is all we have, isn't it? Enjoy the wine now. Enjoy the food now. Take in the perfume that wafts from her hair...*now!* If she's there because she wants me, well then, who am I to question a past I had nothing to do with? If she wanted to pose naked in a magazine, my letting her wouldn't have entered into the equation.

As we drove into Ramallah, it's clear that the road and sanitation departments did little else in addition to not existing. The streets were full of pot holes that would be called canyons anywhere else. There's a lot of stinky, milky water to splash through as there were no real gutters to speak of. There were some unpaved spots in street where the waste from sidewalk scrubbing kind of sunk in but that was about the extent of the gutters and not by design. People just crossed the street at will and would slap the hood if we got too close. Sam would scream something in Arabic at some and laugh at others, trying to explain what was going on at the same time.

Sam parked the Benz and we walked a couple of blocks to Jamal's shop. We almost got run over a couple times ourselves walking back down the same streets. I stayed close to Sam because frankly, I didn't look like I fit in. As we made our way, I could see the looks I was getting; some were friendly of course and others not so much. They had no idea what I was and I could have been a collaborator for all they knew. I nodded a lot to passersby and shop owners standing in their doorways. It was the same cool guy, expressionless nod I gave Liev at the border.

We got to Jamal's shop. It was a shitty little store front next to what was trying to pass for a hotel. The funny thing about it was that there was probably enough cash in the safe to buy Ramallah several times over. Jamal was a money changer who doubled as a travel agent, in the old-school-Bible sense of the word, Jesus flipping tables in the temple type stuff. Like Sam and the rest of his family, Jamal was back and forth too. At this point, I have American dollars that I needed swapped out. In the Territories, I would take a chance paying with dollars. Paying with dollars could get you robbed and shekels were wildly unstable at the time, so I got a bunch of Jordanian dinars which were backed by Saudi oil, which was backed by American dollars. This irony, like a Mercedes in the West Bank, was not lost on me either. Ramallah was more together than what I have seen so far in the Territories which wasn't saying much. Even though it had that old world European feel, the place was still not even close to gentrified. The last 20 years or so of increased fighting certainly could not have helped which partly could have explained the shitty public plumbing.

Jamal jumped out from behind the security glass and gave me a hug. He was a full 20 years older than I was and I guess he was just excited to see me grown. I haven't seen him since I was in tenth grade.

"How you been, man?" he asked. Arabs that live in the States for any length of time say "man" a lot. It fit in with their use of the word "boy" which they would call each other, in Arabic, all the time but not in a malicious way.

"I've been great, dude." Something that will never go away, being raised in Southern California, especially Los Angeles, is liberal use of the words, "Man," "Bro," or "Dude." I will always be proud of that.

Jamal got serious, "Sorry about your loss, cousin...it's good you made the trip". He was very sincere. "Your dad and me always got along." Everyone liked my dad, except us kids. He could really charm people so I had to give him that. There was an album that came out around that time called, "Everyone Loves the Pilot, Except the Crew" by Jon Astley. Although I don't remember him coming by the house, this guy may have known my father.

Jamal continued, "He really helped us out in the 60s when we first came to the States…you need anything, just let me know, man." His eyes leveled at me. "I know you got a one way ticket… so when are you leaving?"

"Don't know yet…everything was kind of rushed, I…"

Jamal snapped in, "Look, I can get you a six day lay-over in Copenhagen for the same price as a one way, straight to the States! You ever been?" he smiled.

"No I haven't…I guess it's cool," I was searching my mind for a "yes."

"Done! I'll set it up when you're ready. You are going to love it, my God! The women, the food, the beer…the *women*. You repeat this shit, I'll deny it!" He punched my arm, laughing.

"Right on. Thanks a lot. I really appreciate it." I couldn't believe I was here and I was actually enjoying myself. Jordan was such a culture shock and I wasn't settled with all the chaos. But these guys weren't my dad to be sure. That realization always saddened me a little as I wanted so much to like my father. I had stayed away from this cooler ilk of my family for so long, that I forgot who these people were. Maybe even as a small child, I felt there was too much to reconcile and just could not separate the two factions.

I had almost zero interest in anything Arab. In college, they'd show "Lawrence of Arabia" and I could not care less. Last thing I wanted was to follow the lead of my geek ass cousins and these good guys didn't come around enough. I did have a tinge of guilt over this but I somehow chose to ignore it.

We shook hands on Denmark then Sam and I walked back out into the street which was buzzing with vendors and people in and out of shops. Cab drivers asking if we needed a taxi, buzzing in my face like hornets, until I began making swatting motions to indicate, "Back the fuck off". Still, I stayed close to Sam and maintained the "I'm cool but don't fuck with me" sort of thing. The smell on the streets of old milk and the day's washout of the meat and produce shops was accumulating as the town was getting ready to close down for curfew. Ramallah had a university as well. There, the operating hours were 12-2pm then everything shut down. It wasn't always this way but because of the Intifada it had become so.

Everyone nearby got all they needed here now or they'd have to go to another town that was farther, to beat their curfew. We stopped at a shawarma cart which was kind of like this hot dog cart I knew in New York, at Broadway and 45th. But the guy sold shawarma in fresh pita bread. Pita bread there was not like the anemic shit they make in the states. It's thick and fresh. Chicken, beef or lamb, the guy had three rods full of fresh steaming meats and you could breathe in the spices and black pepper. I actually felt aroused by the smells. He was wearing a bomber jacket and a keffiyeh, *the* Arab headgear. Sam and I each got a lamb shawarma and poured fresh yogurt, tomatoes and chili peppers on them from the condiment tray he had. He sold us Cokes in these cans with Hebrew writing on them. It was like a reality dream. I was still full from breakfast but this smelled so goddamned good, I'd gladly risk the fate of the gluttony for more of this taste.

After the shawarma, we drove to Jerusalem which was half an hour away. I was in a food coma and as we moved toward the town, the architecture changed a lot. It was more a European and Mediterranean hybrid from all the hands that built on it before. More stuff seemed finished or more together. I saw a more modern version of the area than what was seen in the news or where we have been so far. Even Amman was pretty dingy, apart from the downtown areas. I commented on this and Sam said, "We come from peasants, man, farmers…In Jerusalem, you'll see more modern behavior."

I eyed him, "What modern? How?"

"Well don't get carried away but you'll see couples on dates without chaperones…getting ice cream… you know, like that." He chuckled, "It ain't Manhattan but it's good to see…The Christians come here too and they're more like the Europeans, anyway."

"Christian Arabs, you mean?" I asked, checking for clarity.

"Right, you know, they're less hung up, with a little more leeway. Especially in Bethlehem." Sam grinned.

We get to the main street down from the Dome of the Rock. It's packed, just like Ramallah, but with a different sort of energy and definitely more cosmopolitan. Driving lanes weren't that adhered to here either as we were getting screamed at by cabbies with hairy arms flailing at anything that annoyed them, pedestrians, other cars, buses. The buses really gave off a black smoke every time they started from a dead stop. But the city really had a hum that was vibrant as opposed to people just rushing around to get groceries like Ramallah. People jammed the roads and like everywhere else, the shops would close for 15 minutes for prayer. A cleric could be heard on loud speakers throughout the city. Everyone had to stop, even if praying was not your thing and they did this five times a day.

"We'll park in back. The front's a fucking zoo." Sam observed. "We can walk around awhile and see stuff. I'm still packed, but if you get hungry, we can eat at the Dome."

I looked at Sam blankly, "Dude, there's no way I can eat till tomorrow. I had breakfast and that food in Ramallah was fuckin' plenty." I took in the exotic bazaar we were driving through. The modern and the poor mixed easily as they navigated the different vendors and a small fight broke out between a fruit salesman and a teenager trying to steal an orange or something. A small crowd gathered to either watch or break it up. An Israeli Jeep passed, ignoring the fracas and Sam waved; they waved back.

"You know those guys?" I asked.

"Me? Nah, but whatever. May as well be cool about it."

Sam takes an alley, sloshing through some garbage and more of that white, milky water. He parks behind The Dome which was his restaurant and we walk through the back. The kitchen was buzzing and it was clear that OSHA wasn't on the clock in this part of the world; the cooks and busboys were wearing sneakers and sandals, smoking and just basically cooking like one would cook at home. We go through to the front and our cousin who runs the door looks up and smiles. He's wearing suit pants and a white shirt as the host but the place was pretty casual. His name was Amir and he knew who I was. We shook hands and he spoke English as well.

"How has everything been, cousin?" he asked.

This was Sam's place. It was the only business of the family businesses that was his from the ground up. He got the idea because no Burger King, McDonald's, or *any* other international chain would set foot in the Territories.

They were afraid that not only would the Arab locations get bombed but that there would be massive repercussions on a global level because to open shop in the Territories would be viewed as supporting Israel and the Jewish occupation as opposed to creating business which it would have. While Israel called Jerusalem its capitol, most of the world did not. This included but was not limited to Arabs. It was easy to see how opening up shop here could get dicey.

Sam was a fucking genius because he designed the logo to incorporate the dome atop the Dome of The Rock, which was down the block. Now, extremists who would hit this joint for blasphemy could easily blow up a sacred Muslim site on accident. Then they would risk getting hosed out of their share of, if not all of the seventy-two virgins. No straight to heaven, no collecting $200, no passing "Go," just a massive ass fuck in hell and denied the divine for eternity. Harsh!

The Dome was only a burger and pizza joint that also served fried chicken and resembled any one of thousands of places in any college town in the States so it wasn't exactly a sacred temple. But this place was different, funky. It had three floors. From the street, you walk right into the third floor but the second and first floors were below the third floor in the basement which was very deep. Down there the walls were concrete or the foundation, basically. This was pretty unique to Jerusalem; there were so many different styles of architecture from all the different conquerors through the centuries where some of the other towns had a lot of newer developments that were still incomplete.

Also, Sam fashioned the place after what the young Arab kids wanted which was a piece of the West. There was some paneling with Palestinian flags but also Manchester United posters and some World Cup posters from '82 and '86 with the German and Mexican teams featured. They were curling up and stained from the grease and smog in the air. The tables were these wooden picnic type tables you'd find in a park.

Because we'd occasionally chat over the phone, I had previously sent him dozens of records for his juke box; CD's were still a ways away. He had speakers through all three floors and pool tables on the second floor. Also, there was a dumb-waiter; a portable elevator that sent food and soft drinks to the lower levels so that you didn't have to come all way back upstairs. The only drag, war notwithstanding, was that there was no alcohol sold. Zilch. Verboten. Muslim countries were drier than the state of Utah during the Prohibition of the 1920s.

All the kids were either American or Western Civilization wannabes but mostly wannabes. They wore Levi's, what cool sneakers they could get their hands on, grew their hair, wore over coats, and listened to jazz and rock n roll. The Dome was the place to be if you were young, Arab, relatively sophisticated, and quite bored. People came here for a brief respite from soldiers, guns and drama.

"So you like?" Sam gestured like a gracious host in an old time movie.

"Yeah, man…I do." I was happy for him, "Great tunes." I smiled.

"Yeah I got these records from some fag in the States," he laughed. "He made me blow him first though…fucking prick."

"Fuck off!" I laughed. "The curfews hurt you at all?" I knew this was the Middle East but overhead was overhead. Thank God for family money.

Sam grimaced, "Yeah but what to do, you know? The situation will get worse before it gets better I guess." He had no idea how true that would be.

Within a few years, this entire struggle was near to bringing centuries old tensions to a close with a real and possibly lasting peace. Palestinians and Jews working together in as an imperfect world as one could find but it was working! There was even an airport in Gaza. My father would later land there to visit family and he was overjoyed that such progress was being made. Then in 1995, an assassin's bullet would shoot the whole thing in the ass, along with Yitzhak Rabin. A lone nut, rabbinical student would be held responsible with very little investigation. How fucking original and straight out of the Lincoln/McKinley/Kennedy primer. Garfield? He just got shot because the wrong dude lost his job.

Sam formally introduced me to the "staff" which included cousins and other assorted folks, same guys from the back when we came in, some just doing odd jobs for extra cash. Couple of the guys knew my dad and that was always nice. It was nice for people to know who I was in advance of my arrival. I'd not heard much or anything of them. It was kind of like being famous.

It was here that I realized that I just now thought of Shelly and how she didn't seem to matter at the moment. What dawned on me was how long it had been since I really cared. It was like a sudden rush of hope hit me because it felt like a century had passed. I was caring less. This was a good thing.

I am saddened by death and the passing of time. I saw fire…

I also enjoyed that people could say my fucking name! Even the Israelis could say it and they weren't assholes about it, either. There was none of the "what kind of name is that?" or "where's that from?" bullshit. Everyone here knew where it was from. As though I would choose this name if it wasn't given to me? I got into so many fights as a kid. Before the sixth grade, I had more fights than Muhammad Ali and he chose one of those names too. I never knew why the Nation of Islam guys would pick these names for themselves when I'm sure, being black in the United States of America was enough of a pain in the ass.

Sam was eager to show me Jerusalem. I suggested we take our time as I would be here awhile. He said, "Yeah, well things change fast here, man. You're not careful, you could spend the next two weeks in an Israeli prison or stuck at home, staring at your Aunt Fatima, which I guess is worse." He chuckled.

We had to be careful about moving into the Christian quarter, we were eyed constantly and the Jewish quarter was very much off limits. Seriously armed Israeli soldiers lined the borders between the quarters. We had to show proof where we lived or had documentation for any visits. We went to the wall of the Mount of Olives.

I asked Sam, "Hey, man. Can we go in there?"

Sam's eyes rolling and his massive face fart was part of my answer, "Dude, I know you don't feel like it, but we're Arabs. At least Arab enough to not be allowed tourist privileges in a Jewish holy site. Really?" He shook his head, smirking.

"Shit, take it easy. Just asking."

We weren't going to hurt a fly but of course, there's no way for the Israelis to know that. Muslim name on my passport was all the "security check" these guys needed. Then we went to the Dome of the Rock. The guards out front were Israeli and they checked our IDs and they were assertive too; no ID, no entry, no catastrophe. Not on their watch as it was the last thing they needed to go wrong. They didn't want Jewish settlers blowing the Dome up as that would not go over well, obviously.

"Where are you from?" the soldier quizzed. He was stern and not at all friendly.

"United States," I answered, eyeing him directly. "Like my passport says."

Sam, feeling the tension, piped in speaking Hebrew. This was impressive as no one else in my family did. He said something to the guard as his partner looked around. The guard loosened up and let us through.

"You have to be a little gentle with these guys." Sam explained. "They're jumpy enough without a lot of attitude."

And the cooler heads prevailed.

We then went through the Muslim checkpoint and they let us in. Cameras were expressly forbidden in most of the Dome of the Rock but there were lobby areas that could be photographed. It was all very art-deco looking but not anything that would look any different from a cool bar in Los Angeles built in the 1920's. I felt a little shallow in that observation but that's how it felt.

However, the underneath was breathtaking as there were acres of *underneath* and the entire place was comprised of catacombs and tunnels, lined with ancient gold leafing and ornaments that were tough to categorize by time or place since I was not an expert. It just looked really old and mysterious. No photos here, period. The Muslim guards could take my camera and expose the film if I shot anything. This would be some years before digital cameras were even thought of. I'm sure they took to smashing digital cameras just as energetically later on.

We saw the praying areas. There were several and the main Mosque was huge and very ornate with different murals representing the many stories in the Quran. Everyone was praying in lock step with each other, bowing, sitting up and bowing again. They were all saying the ancient prayers for forgiveness and atonement. Sam and I agreed that we had to get back as the curfew would be on us if we weren't careful. We walked through a lush, gorgeous green park which was a nice detour from the buzz of the street. There was a big stone sign that said, "Please Pray for the Peace of Jerusalem" in English. Was it the Arab way of asking for help from the Universe or the even the West? Maybe some grieving parent put it there. God knows they could use a little peace, I thought.

Once back on the street, we went back to the Dome, the restaurant this time and we saw quite a few American tourist groups. These were the Bible tours to the Holy Land. They had guides and paid Israeli guards with them, which was the clever thing to do on their part. Most of these groups were college kids, mostly white, some black but definitely suburban. The guides were a little older but not by much. I saw maybe five or six groups on the way back to the restaurant and I saw a couple of Latino and Italian groups too, but mostly it was various J. Crew catalog clones as one long, predictable centipede.

On the street, outside a shop, I saw this beautiful Arab girl who had this mane of thick, black, curly hair, down past her tits and huge brown eyes that were a combination of marbles and saucers which had a sexy doe like effect so I walked up to her and took her picture and she looked terrified. "You must not do that...my brothers!" she stammered as she seemed to be warning me. I felt awkward when all of a sudden…

Sam grabbed my arm and hustled me off. "Come on, man." We walked fast across the street, narrowly missing an oncoming cab and a shit smelling mud puddle. The cobblestones making any graceful exit kind of tough and as I looked over my shoulder, two men were questioning my photo subject and she did look a bit panicked. Sam just looked dead ahead and we kept walking.

"What, man? Why was she so freaked out? I only took her picture!" I was getting a little pissed. Still, no one came after me. Maybe my lady friend cooled those guys out.

"Dude! This isn't State Street on Halloween!" Sam was talking about the main drag at the University of California, Santa Barbara which was one of the best party schools in America. "This is the West Bank. Her brothers or her dad could kill you and the Israelis would figure the shit out after that fact. Now dummy up and be cool."

"Sorry," I offered without feeling. Between this and the Mount of Olives, it's never "I should have known better" because I *knew* better! I knew better and this was the part of *this* world that I always hated. I just got into the moment and I couldn't really do that there. Shit, I couldn't do it in the U.S. with my family either. Not everyone is "modern," ice cream and unchaperoned dates notwithstanding and I'm just visiting anyway so why was I so pissed? Maybe because this culture was what was expected of me and I outright rejected it in favor of the West. Yet I wanted approval for my choices from my family, especially if I proved successful. The approval from my family and living my own life really could not co-exist in the same brain and they weren't going to for much longer.

It was explained to me, that while I was there, I had two options. Because I failed to resemble anything remotely Arab, I was given a keffiyeh before we left my aunts' house. This was the traditional Arab headgear worn by everyone from the President of Syria to the Saudis (they have the fancier, imported silk version, of course where ours are fine cotton, which is still not silk, highlighting the difference between the sheep and oil families.)

Now, I was not about to wear this with my long hair as I knew it would make it matted and gamey. So I did what the other, dare I say more hip, Arabs did and I wore it like a scarf. At first, I didn't want to wear it all. I had about ten at home given to me by various relatives and my dad and would have brought them, had I thought of wearing them, which I had not. In fact, I only ever used mine when I had the flu and covered my head and throat to sweat out the fever.

Then Sam gave me two options.

"Alright," he said, "these are your two options…First, you can go without and with your Irish-New York Jew looks, you can wind up dead in an alley, stabbed to death by your own people, which would look real fucking stupid or second, you wear it and get hassled by the Israelis who are not as crazy about killing American tourists…then you're on your way and you live to tell your friends about your trip."

I gave this a second and thought if I wound up dead that it may as well look good. Sam was right; I'd look like an ass being killed by people with the same kinds of names as mine. Of course, they wouldn't know this because I speak zero Arabic so, "noooo!" choking through your own blood is pretty much "noooo!" in any language, choking through that language's blood. So the dopes who stabbed or shot me would think they did a very good job and served Allah and all that.

I opted for the keffiyeh as scarf and felt very fashion forward.

"History repeats the old conceits/the glib replies/the same defeats…"

As we passed the American groups, a couple of them saw me and Sam and thought it odd that we were wearing these weird scarves. I don't know how long they were there but one of the ethno centric American pricks sniffed, "nice scarf, dude." When I was a kid I had a lot of "temper issues." I got into a lot of fights because of the names kids call each other, specifically what they would call me. Whatever, I was twenty-three and grown. It felt strange being on this non-American side of the fence. Suddenly I didn't feel like a tourist and while not at all a local, I felt I had something over this little prick. So much so that I simply smiled at him, "It's cool, man."

One girl looked right through me though and I actually stopped breathing for a second. She was positively luminous. Jet black hair in a pony tail with dark blue eyes, clear as the Caribbean, set in a face that could be best described as pure art. God is a man and capable of, as the poet once sang, "Cheek bones like geometry and eyes like silk."

She smiled and the hustle of the street stopped completely. If I were to tell this story at party, I'd ask, "You ever been water skiing or wake boarding and wipe out with a face plant in the lake?" Because there's a split second that feels like forever. Time *stops* like you're dead and it takes a few seconds to shake it off, to get your bearings and realize that you can move your legs and arms. Looking at this girl had that kind of smack, a real pop! It was like I was in a vacuum and I couldn't feel my feet. I was completely still and this, I would find out later, happens about five or six times in a lifetime if you are fortunate. For me, it would happen once. And even though I thought I had been in love with Shelly, I have never seen anyone who made me feel like this right from the get-go. Not in my young life, anyway. This may be how people get married. No matter where you're at in the world or this life, nothing makes you feel safer and more invincible at the same time than that feeling.

"HOOOONNNNNKKKK!!!" said many cars as I walked into the jammed street. This one cab driver screamed, "Jahash" at us, but mostly me because Sam was still on the sidewalk, which meant ass or donkey. I think he said "goddamned" too, I'm not sure but I smacked his hood anyway and yelled, "Fuck you!" which always had its own unique, international charm. We moved past the groups as we approached the Dome, Sam joined me in walking the street to avoid the crush of the shops and people on the sidewalk.

Sam jumps in front if the group, opening the door to his place, gestures with his free arm, smiles and affecting a very fake, very funny Arab accent, says "Welcome my friends to the show that never ends, we're so glad you could attend, come inside! Come inside!" I'm certain the song lyric was lost on this Bible crowd, unless a former rock fan or stoner was in their ranks but I got a kick out of it. "Welcome," he said again, "to a piece of home, away from home. The very place for one, and all it is a place we call the Dome!" Clearly, he has done this before and as he would tell me later, tourists eat this shit up.

The head of one of the groups smelled the hamburgers and other fried delights, falafel, kieb and all the rest. Sam did serve Arab food, too. He wasn't stupid. Head guy heard the music and admonished his crew to follow. He introduced himself to Sam, his name was Tom and he noticed the special moment that I had with this girl who was one of his charges, I guess. Right away, I prayed for him not to be the boyfriend. Damn those pesky fucking boyfriends, husbands even! I saw her, she saw me see her and I think she liked what she saw. I know I did, so stay out of my way, dude!

The paid Israeli guards came inside and would take turns eating while the other kept watch. Sam couldn't offer them free food. It's not like American restaurants with cops. Here, that sort of kindness could get you killed and the lead Bible guy picked up their tab anyway. Of course, the girl I mentioned was in this group and thank God, not the group that kept walking. That would have sucked.

I'm sure we appeared imbalanced, especially Sam. "My cousin owns this place," was an obvious ice breaker but I was nervous. I knew how to talk to girls I wasn't really interested in. Sometimes, I grew into them later as long as they were cute to start with. Come to think of it, Shelly didn't grab me at first at all. In fact I met her while I was hitting on her friend. It was just that Shelly had a nicer ass which in the end didn't add up to a whole lot. But this chick was a *somebody,* man. How does one know these things instinctually?

Once inside, I could see the group relax. There was about twenty of them and the rest of the place was packed as curfew was about an hour away. The energy inside was wildly charged with the kitchen in high gear. I could hear burgers hitting the grill and chicken, falafel and fries dropping into grease. The smells instantly refilled the front of the restaurant. However, while whatever business was already inside could be handled, the doors closed in an hour with no exceptions. This was the reality of the outside world as lived in the Territories. This wasn't an Arab thing; the Israelis imposed these curfews because of the bombings and Intifada, so the protesters would violate curfews to stage the standoffs with Israeli soldiers. This way, as the logic was sold, civilians wouldn't get hurt, although many did anyway.

Sometimes the battle was held and nobody came while other times, it was pure bedlam. One couldn't blame the Arabs as they were, for all intents and purposes, occupied even though Palestine was never a country. It was a territory, kicked around like a Bedouin football by everyone and lastly, the British. Israel became a country in 1948 after a U.N. mandate. This is something I always kept clear, growing up and hearing the stories.

Now, keeping your doors open after curfew could mark you as a collaborator, if you weren't well connected, because that meant you were "cool with the Jews." I have already seen what happens to those guys so I was playing ball. No matter where we're at in the world, it helps to play ball. This is probably why, regardless of the culture, almost all sports deal with balls in one way or another.

Some of the group ordered right away while some went to the lower floors. One of the J. Crew guys called out that there were pool tables and others followed him down the stairs. Sam told them to send their food orders up through the dumbwaiter with cash of course.

I stood at the end of the counter.

This girl would eye me directly and tell me her name. This was good because my imagination needed a name for such perfection as I could not invent it and it was Karly...I told her mine. I still don't remember who spoke first but I'm glad someone did. The beauty of hazes...

"So what's this group about?" I asked. "Bible tour, right?"

"You could say that," she smiled. "You're not from around here, are you?" she held her fingers up in air quotes as she said "around here." They were pretty fingers and if she was trying not to flirt, she kind of sucked at not flirting.

"I'm on family business...so where in the States are you from?" I had to change the subject. I wasn't at all sure if girls found dead cousins appealing and suddenly, shamefully I felt self-conscious about being American again. I was feeling like I was better than this place. I always felt a bit of guilt over that.

"Central coast, California, closer to L.A actually. Ventura, have you heard of it?" She asked.

I told her that I lived an hour from there in Pasadena.

"No way!" she shrieked, then, caught herself, embarrassed. Grinning she asked, "So you know it, then?"

"Yep," I grinned back like a seventh grader.

Then I pulled an old school trick and got her food ordered before anyone else's. She was wildly impressed as it did have that "I'm connected" vibe. Sam glanced over so subtly that I barely noticed and threw a thumbs' up sign at his waist, so no one could really see it. That approval was better than any from my dad. A couple of Karly's girlfriends came over to get a table. She introduced us and asked if I would care to join in. So I joined in.

I knew this was a Bible Tour which meant Karly may have held a point of view that I had been very, *very* much over. Frankly, I had been on a pardon from the President of the Universe as far as religion went. But how many times in one life, does a goddess fall from the sky and in these God forsaken Territories on a trip I didn't want to be on in the first place? Dude, just shut the fuck up, pick a song on the juke box, have a cheeseburger, get a whiff of this girl's hair and even though it's a Coke, *enjoy the wine now...*

Chapter 3-What Would Frank Sinatra Do?

So Karly, her friends and I grabbed a table closer to the window facing the street and away from Tom and the group. Karly introduced me to Susan and Katie. Susan was very pretty while Katie just looked cranky. If she had a better disposition, she could have been way hot, but alas...no. We sat by the Israelis, one of whom eyed me directly while waiting for their food but not threateningly. I'm sure the keffiyeh masked any benign tendencies he would have liked to have seen in me. In his line of work, he had to be careful. The other stood by the door. These guys were over six feet, maybe 220 pounds of pure muscle and armed. They each had fists the size of a human head, so I doubt very much they viewed me as a threat. They were wearing khakis and black polo shirts with a company logo in Hebrew on them, probably a security company, definitely not army. I could tell they weren't looking for trouble, just wary of it.

The overcast day was beginning to give way to dusk and some of the street lights were coming on as businesses were closing up for the night.

"So you're from California?" the one named Susan asked. "That's what I heard you say."

"I don't like California. It's too weird." the one named Kate said.

"Oh Katie, what do you know? This is your first trip out of New Mexico! This is my cousin, by the way." Karly said to me. "Who hasn't been ANYWHERE!" she held her hands to her face to emphasize her point loudly.

"I like it. Cool stuff comes from there." I offered.

"So what are you doing here?" asked Susan.

After offering the same "family business" line, she blinked a little blankly then started in with some gossip that I feigned interest in with a series of facial expressions. This was part of their little test to see if I was alright. Girls do this.

"Well I think he's weird." Katie said finally after Susan's tale of witnessing not-so-secret petting between two of the Bible tours' most "chaste" participants in the back of the bus on the way home from Bethlehem the night before.

I kept the rest of the conversation light as I did not want to be subjected to the girlfriend tribunal this early in the game. Like a bunch of *Juliette Caesars,* they could vote thumbs up or down, "feed him to the lions, or spare him," I avoided that trap, man. The realization was made not long into college that "grownup" life was like eighth grade homeroom only with more money and more pettiness. It was not to be underestimated. I often found it vicious.

"So Katie, what was your major in college?" I figured getting this girl back on herself wouldn't be too tough, as she wasn't terribly aware, as much as self-absorbed. I wasn't sure if that was learned or genetic.

"Oh, it was journalism. Not finding a job though, which sucks." She said brightly, as she blathered on about her senior project, seemingly relieved that I cared at all, since I was paying more attention to Karly anyway. Susan seemed to be gearing up the next round of dirt to dish as she fiddled about her purse.

When the table was turned back to me, I talked about my old school, my job, my band and anything else that would keep our time casual. I stayed out of religion as they were on a Bible Tour for Chrissakes, so they really didn't need my opinion. We managed to avoid the politics landmine as that's always too big a discussion to be summed up at any one meal and people are weird. I found that if I disagreed with most, they would turn on me right away. It wasn't just me as I saw this with most folks. Vicious. So I stayed pleasant, goofy, and as charming as possible.

Karly slipped me her number on a napkin. I knew she had a thing for me, the girl's got taste. Her fingers briefly brushed mine and it felt like electric velvet.

She had to know I wasn't into the Bible thing, so slipping me her number was a nice surprise. I glanced down and saw the number was a California area code and sure enough, Ventura's 805. I figured if that Tom guy was anything to her, it'd be her place to tell me and not by slipping me a phone number. I was going to run with this and hoped I'd be seeing her on the rest of the trip at some point. I think she had the same feeling. I could see the corners of her mouth curl into a grin and she appeared to be suppressing giggles. Susan and Katie were not really looking at us. There's an unspoken vibe when people are trying to swap information. Karly's friends weren't stupid. They knew and were being surprisingly cool about it.

Tom started rounding everyone up, eyeing me straight away, "Alright guys; wrap it up! We got curfew and so do they!" referring to the restaurant. The Israelis re-engaged, getting back on their own clock and got ready to escort the tour back to their bus and hotel. The bus had just pulled up and one of the Israelis was on his shoulder mic to the driver who also had a guard with him.

"It was great meeting you!" Karly beamed. "I had a great time."

Smiling like a dumb kid, "Yeah, me too," I was sure there were a couple of mayors from neighboring villages wondering where their idiots were.

As she and her girlfriends were gathering up their things, we exchanged pleasantries, "Nice meeting you guys." I said to both her friends as Karly, standing behind them, held her hand to her face like a phone and mouthed the words, "call me" and I nodded.

Sam and I watched the tour get on the bus, walking through the gauntlet of protection they had hired.

After the Dome was cleared and we were done cleaning up, Sam asked if I wanted a beer. I looked around. "Here?" I asked.

"Yeah man, just be cool and don't tell anyone. I get it in Israel and bring it here…Shit, like the border guards care? You just can't sell it. I mean this isn't Mecca, so it's not like anyone gets lashes for beer but they could close me down and your dad will kick my ass. Turn the music back on and the lights off," he said.

We sat in the front as the night came. The lights from back in the kitchen were coming into the front as the crew finished cleaning up. Street lights glowed through the front windows on to the dark floors with the chairs making odd shadows. If anyone could see us, they couldn't see what we were drinking. Sam pulled out Maccabees Beer, an Israeli brew that had been around since the 1960s. He had a case in the walk-in refrigerator. This was a pale lager that was not bad at all. Because it had been awhile since I had a beer, I couldn't tell if it was really that good. I drank the first one real fast so it was good enough. An Israeli beer in Jerusalem, like a Mercedes here was not lost me either.

I loved beer. If anything, it had that unique quality that always made me *feel* American. When I drank with the guys, it was something that gave us unity.

The ritual of it was just so simple. I could see why drinking becomes a problem for some.

Despite being born in the States, I always had the feeling of being an outsider or different. It's tough when your parents had accents or ate "that weird food." I grew to appreciate the differences as I grew up but as a kid? I wanted to blend in badly; be named Donny or Michael, Keith or Bobby; anything other than my own name. As I grew up, however, I resented conformity and as such, I grew to appreciate that my parents didn't name me Roy. I would not have picked my background, truth be told, but now I wouldn't change it either. I learned to finally like me, at least for the moment, which is all any of us has. I truly started understanding what an American really was; a mutt, just like me. This was the running gun battle I had with myself most days; that fine line between gratitude and wishful thinking.

The other guys joined us for beers and this was a new feeling in watching these guys, because we never had liquor growing up in our house. Even the parties my dad held were dry. My dad's business partner would join us for dinner three or four times a week and he liked his beer. He grew up with my dad's big brother. My father would allow him the one tall can of Bud they picked up on the way home. It was to be left in the bag, in the fridge. He could drink it only at dinner but it had to stay in the bag as to not give the impression my dad was condoning this zenith of sins. I moved out at 20 after a transfer from junior college to university, where they had cheap housing so I started drinking and man, did I make up for lost time. I did that with pork for a while too. If that was illegal, I'd have been in jail long ago.

But these guys followed the Muslim religion like most Catholics do theirs; observe the major holidays and don't get caught doing anything really wrong as that's the unspoken general rule. Sam was not an exception as he pretty much was the rule. Not too different from my dad but dad would never be seen drinking. Dad was quite content raging along, cheating on my mother, sober as a judge which carries its own burden, leaving no margin for error.

He didn't think I knew but I knew. When he came to the U.S., he was selling door to door. Because the immediate L.A. area was saturated with sales guys and he could only hit certain neighborhoods so often, he'd travel. He and his partner would be gone for forty-five or sixty days at a time. The travelling in itself wasn't all of it because he treated my mom rather badly.

Being horny was my genetic curse. If I was gone for forty-five days, I'd figure something out, married or not. Shit, I've only been here *two* days and already

I'm looking for talent that won't get me killed by an angry, jihadist mob and I might even have risked the mob! I believed the main reason my parents got married was so that my dad could come into the U.S. hassle free. They made the best of it because it could have been much worse as it was for many such couples. Not exactly the makings a Shakespearean sonnet so no one could tell me my dad was always faithful.

"Cool chick," Sam smiled as he sipped his beer staring out into the surprisingly quiet street. "I thought sure you'd close."

"Here, with her on a Bible Tour? Are you high? That Tom dude makes friends easy though, huh?" I said brushing off the comment.

"Probably a virgin…" Sam said.

"Tom?" I asked. "Yeah he looks tight, too. It's obvious he works out. I think he liked you…get a number?"

"Fuck you!" Sam choked his beer as he tried to keep it out of his nose.

"Anyway, I won't find out here. But yeah, I got her number…I will definitely call her when I get home. Definitely," I said folding the napkin after looking at it again.

"Fucking Christians. Bossy as fuck and they didn't even tip." Sam smiled. "Your girl magically did, because I saw you leave money, you whipped mother fucker!" he said, chuckling. "Have another beer, man." He opened a couple more for the guys.

"*Yallah,*" Sam said to the remaining crew, Anwar and Nasser, meaning "hurry up," the rest was in Arabic, as he gestured to the chairs, which basically translated for them to have a beer and relax in the dark with us while Aerosmith played "Toys in the Attic" in the background. "In the *Attic!*" Sam screamed, shaking his head to the music, moving his feet off the chair in front of him for one of the guys who were laughing at the performance.

Two Israeli soldiers on patrol heard the music and peered in the window from the sidewalk. They couldn't see the beer but could only guess and laughed as they saw Sam rock out. One of the soldiers was especially animated and screamed as he made the "devil sign" with his fingers knocking on the window as he laughed while his grinning partner just observed. We all saw that and thought it was funny. I wasn't much of a metal guy and Aerosmith was rock and roll and not some goofy hair band, far as I was concerned. We all appreciated the brief camaraderie of such a simple act as the soldiers moved on.

This was how it went with humans being human. It's tough when the occupier can relate to people. It's tougher when the occupied can relate back. Either scenario may get us killed if we're careless. At this point, I felt what was fair or not was no longer the question. Palestine hasn't been a country for 3,000 years and Israel certainly wasn't going anywhere. It was a territory when Britain did what they did. Now these people have to deal with the consequences of such high end deals on a daily basis. It's their lives that change and not those of the deal makers but something was going to have to give.

Sam's kitchen guys spoke some broken English but we could talk and Sam helped out. "So, America…It is very rich, yes?" the guy named Nasser asked.

"Yes." I answered, waiting for the set-up. When I was a kid, this was always a prelude to a set-up by my cousins and my dad. By high school, I got wise.

"Why they keep helping Israel when the people, they no need too much help? He continued.

"More money and power I guess." At twenty-three, I only had so much history to fall back on.

"The U.S. why they against three hundred million Arabs for 3 million Jews?" Nasser pulled on his beer. "We would like to have peace. The world see how we are and then they understand." He said. "But you don't care. You are American. Not Islam. I know." He may as well have spit on me, too.

"You're right." I said. "I am American and I don't know why my country does…"

"See! Palestine is not your country!" Nasser cried like I was busted. Anwar tried shushing him but he'd have none of it.

Even Sam rolled his eyes, blowing air through his lips like a big fart and said something to the effect of "What does that make me, man?" in Arabic.

Nasser made a shushing noise at Sam and continued, "You are American first, yes? You are not…"

"Look, Nasser," I jumped in. "Like I said, you're right. You know what? I'm American and I'm not a fucking Muslim, either. But guess what? Neither are you!" Pointing at his beer as I cackled, "You're a hypocrite. I don't see you fighting Jews and getting beat up either. You work here and Sam pays you guys okay, and by the way, beer is not Islam so if you want to run and tell my uncles and my dad, then go fuck yourself!" Having exhausted my pique, I drank my beer. Echo and the Bunnymen came on. The song was "Gods Will be Gods." How appropriate.

We sat silent while Anwar worked at bringing down the tension and we talked about America's other attributes, namely women and money, something we could all agree on. I was fine and I could tell Sam was a bit relieved but Nasser could not be bothered. I didn't give a shit. I was ready to beat his ass. This precious, religious bullshit was always annoying and as it wore on me, my patience with it thinned. Christians, Muslims, I no longer gave a fuck. All these cunts were liars and I was no longer of the mind to be polite about it. Spent a lifetime doing that and felt, as a grown man, that if you were counting on me to be more polite than you while treating me badly, one could go fuck oneself and be sure to tip the innkeeper as I kick your ass out the door. So there's that.

The streets were quiet that night as the Mid-East version of the Hatfields and McCoys decided to take their night off. We could actually relax but the Dome was definitely closed for the evening and quiet, by no means, meant safe…

****

We finished up and walked out back. Parking the car in back was a precaution Sam was used to. This alley was long and took you around to the other side of two city blocks so it was like its' own secret tunnel. We got to the outskirts of town pretty quickly.

"Well, you'll hear about that little chat, I'm sure." Sam said.

"I doubt it. I bet no one else likes him either," I answered. "Right?"

Sam's silence confirmed my deeper suspicions about Nasser.

Driving home, the night was clear and the sides of the headlights lit the brush on the edge of the road. Sam took back roads as we were out after the curfew and did not want to get stopped by the Israelis or worse, other Arabs. I have found, under martial law, folks only react in one of two ways and that is to acquiesce or rebel. Not too much of a middle ground to be noticed, hence drinking Israeli beer in Jerusalem. It was a big chance to take but at one point, I guess people get so tired of the bullshit and there's that human tendency to push your luck until something bad happens. You keep getting away with it over and over until there's a fuck up. Then and only then does one learn their lesson, making deals with God, putting any macho bullshit or vitriol on the back burner until the next moral outrage. We humans forget pain quickly when we get ready to make fresh mistakes but hold onto it forever when moving forward is involved. I was as guilty as the next on that count, though it wouldn't matter in the long run.

"So how was your first real day in the Territories?" Sam smiled as he lit a cigarette. He had been here three months on this leg.

"Pretty cool, I have to say…a lot to see, you know?" I sighed. I was buzzed and it had been a long day, if not an intense couple of weeks. The recent episode with Nasser was not even registering as a blip on the radar.

Sam exhaled his cigarette, "Yeah…we'll do some cool shit for sure; let's just get home in one piece tonight."

Custer may have said it better.

"Shit man, not tonight!" Sam said smacking the steering wheel, cussing in Arabic as his headlights raced up a road block revealing the source of his frustration. We slowed down.

As my pants were about to require much in the way of laundering, I noticed that the road block was Israelis. I was relieved because I could see the Army trucks in Sam's headlights. I wasn't there long enough for such an informed opinion but a burnt up dead person left an impression so I waited for Sam's reaction. While he was cool about it, he wasn't thrilled and I wasn't necessarily orgasmic; all you need is one Jew to get nervous and you're as dead as a collaborator killed by Arabs, so who cares? Dead is dead.

We stopped and the guards came to the window. The main guy seemed cool and very mellow. Two guys had his back as the one soldier began in Arabic and smiled when Sam answered in Hebrew. He asked us to get out of the car. I opened my door to the soldier on my side and he let me out. The sergeant asked Sam for his keys and then in English asked us for ID and to take off our shoes…again with the fucking shoes. I swear to Christ, if cops did this in L.A. I would make a bloody fortune because I'd sue their ass with relish.

Sam and I stood on the paved road so as to not get sand in our socks. The soldiers went through the car. This took about 15 minutes while one solider had his gun on us, the rest hung out looking alert but bored by the routine at the same time. They probably figured us to be harmless and while not being an expert, I still thought that a strange habit.

The sergeant asked Sam, in Hebrew, what he was doing out after the curfew. He thought it odd that an American and an Arab were out this late, when it seemed like a good idea to be home earlier given the circumstances. After a brief exchange which included information about his being the owner of the Dome, the soldiers gave me and Sam back our shoes, I.D.s and sent us on our way.

"Man, that was intense." I said.

"Yeah, it went okay though, it could have been worse…Learning Hebrew was the smartest thing I could have done." Sam said lighting another butt. Apparently, the way this stop went down was per usual.

"Well, yeah. That guy seemed to loosen up after you started talking." I was genuinely impressed.

"You know that Arab saying, 'Learn another man's language and you learn how he lives'?"

My dad said it all the time; he knew four languages. Not bad for guy who was functionally illiterate. However, like a lot of Arabs, he would not learn Hebrew. His form of rebellion, I suppose. Me? I'm a big fan of the "know your enemy" or "when in Rome" philosophies. The Arabs that did learn Hebrew had a much easier time with the Israelis and that was a fact. More Israelis knew Arabic than the other way around and I always found that interesting. I knew a couple languages and would see Mexicans warm up real quick as soon as I spoke Spanish in L.A. I couldn't imagine it would be any different in the West Bank, people are people. Sam had the same effect on the Jew which also helps if you're both reasonable. Even with a cynics' view of the situation and the world at large, they both seemed to want to have a good night and see the wife and kiddies. We continued driving home. Sam lit another cigarette and said the soldier asked if I was Muslim.

Sam told him that I was not.

"You bummed?" I asked.

"Not really. You're no worse than me, I guess. At least you can admit it and act like you mean it." Sam quietly exhaled the smoke through his nose.

I was a little relieved because I knew Sam did not know my secret. When I was thirteen years old, I made a conversion to Christianity. So it wasn't as dark a secret like I was selling heroin to the kids at school or pork and hookers to Muslims. That would be a Saudi whisky bender in England.

But Sam was no Muslim either.

Being born into a certain family doesn't mark you. At the end of the day, we all pick our certainties while some of us may never have to fully defend them, save the occasional spat over Thanksgiving Dinner or a beer in a Jerusalem diner.

Sam dropped me off at my uncle's house, said he'd see me in the morning. He sped off in the Mercedes as he waved at Ali and his other brother who were hanging out on the porch. They were smoking as they had just wrapped up dinner and their mother had gone home. I walked up and greeted them and it looked like they had been talking a long time.

"How was the day, cuz?" Ali's brother asked.

"Pretty cool. Met a girl," I smiled.

"*Arab-ia?*" asked Ali, incredulous using the Arab word for "Arab."

"Nah, man, American," I said.

"Oh, I thought so. You can't do here like in the States, man."

"Yeah, we established that earlier today." I was referring to the camera shy, picture girl.

"Her parents would never allow it. Not without your father," Ali's brother offered.

"Imagine my disappointment," I grinned. If I had one gift, being a smart ass was it.

They had a chuckle over my beer breath and said something in Arabic which earned them a "fuck off" and a laugh in English. I said good night and went in.

Eddie pulled up to where he'd been staying with his wife and kids and they were asleep. He walked into the house, went down the hall and unlocked what appeared to be his own office and dropped his bag on the floor. He moved the stereo and opened the floor boards. There was easily a half a million dollars in the makeshift safe already. He opened his bag and pulled out ten stacks of hundreds, wrapped in plastic. He put them in the floor and sealed it back up. He went up the stairs and he looked in on his kids and then went into his room, undressed and got into bed. Not seeing their grandma has been tough on the kids and his wife, her own mother long since passed. His wife turned to him and asked him something, in Arabic, the tones hushed, almost conspiratorial but she didn't really know what was going on and Eddie made sure she kept her place…

As I walk in the house, Uncle Ayoub is the only one who is still up, he's watching TV, lying sideways on piles of pillows and smoking. These guys did smoke a lot. My uncle smoked his own hand rolled cigarettes. He carried a tobacco pouch and cigarette papers and he could roll one with one hand, lick it shut and light it in the middle of any task like it was a magic trick. I think he smoked 15 to 20 of these things a day and bear in mind these were not filtered. Half of the habits' addiction had to come from the rolling ritual. I knew this because I liked to roll things that weren't as addictive.

He saw me and gestures around the room indicating that everyone's asleep. I kiss him on the cheek, quickly and say goodnight in Arabic. It's one of the few things I can say but I also didn't want to linger too long, lest he made the beer discovery. He smiled and waved me off. I think he knew, but he wasn't like the others. He made that clear the day before when we were in the car and he held my hand like I was nine. He seemed to be not at all concerned with macho pretense. I watched him play with the younger children and he clearly felt that you could not love your kids too much. Family lore always held that he was more like my grandfather than any of the brothers. My dad must have been separated at birth.

Ayoub was just happy to have family around. That was always paramount to him and he was the only one who stayed there. He never left, not even to vacation. I suppose someone had to stay and guard the sisters and the sheep. All the brothers left to Europe, the U.S., or South America, to make their fortunes. The West Bank in the 1940s and 50s didn't offer much of a future for a young man, unless you were one of the oldest boys in an established family. Otherwise, you worked for someone else or your brothers. So his

53

brothers left. My dad couldn't leave fast enough itching to make his mark at seventeen.

Ten years later, Ayoub would be dead, having passed away during an afternoon nap. Never ill a day in his life…After all the tobacco was natural, I guess.

I went to bed and passed out quick. It had been a long couple *weeks* and the beers kind of got to me on that night too.

"It's quarter to three/there's no one in the place/except you and me…"

Sinatra's "One For My Baby" was playing in the background. Me, Karly and her friends, Susan and Katie, were playing poker and it was hot outside. The big, green, felt covered table was littered with cash, poker chips and whisky glasses. We were playing in a house which was an old, white Victorian number that I actually was surprised to find there in the Territories.

We were playing poker with several of the Israelis that I had met at the check point just two days before. The mood was tense as Karly had been winning more than her fair share of hands, if a poll were taken amongst the losers. It was funny how I already knew this but I sensed that one of the soldiers was pissed that she may have been using her looks to distract his buddy, Liev, the guy I met at the checkpoint, as he was also the guy who got us into this game.

Karly looked to one of the girls, then back to me, then to the Israeli, whom she just beat the worst after she'd been called. Her smile lights up as she put down four aces. The Jew exploded in anger and the table flipped over violently! He got his gun out but so did I! We blast away running out of this house. They were shooting their guns at us and I was hauling ass as I saw my uncle's Mercedes. My feet kept digging into the sand, making it hard to run. I felt like I wasn't even moving and while I was certain we were about to die, I kept thinking about the trouble I'd be in if I destroyed this car.

Karly was covering the both of us and firing away with a bag of cash in her free hand and a .45 in the other! As I ran up on the car, I could see that explosive charges were planted inside the wheel wells. White C-4 set to blow the car to pieces!

How did I fucking know this?

I dove under the car, the wind was blowing sand badly and I could barely see what I was doing but I dismantled the crude bombs made with sandwich bags.

Practically shitting myself as Karly was screaming at me to hurry up. She kept me covered but the Jews were coming fast, having already shot Tom and her girlfriends! These guys were heavily armed, pissed, and very serious… "fuuuuUUCK!!" was the operative word.

Finally, I got the charges loose and slid out from under the car! I got in the driver's seat, screaming at Karly to get in. She did so, shooting and cursing the whole time. Of course, it's in these tender moments that the car doesn't start right away, fucking Germans! I kept turning and turning the ignition and finally it started!

We peeled out, tires spit up rocks and gravel as the charges exploded behind us, blowing up whatever was left of the house, the Israelis and Karly's dead friends. Very Steve McQueen of me, if I may say so. We drove for a while; the windows were open and the warm wind started to calm me down. Our breathing slowed as the high noon sun bore down on us and the open highway. I felt like I was slapped hard, if not punched and just getting the feeling back in my face.

"So…where to?" I asked, feeling a little stunned.

"Beirut… I hear the beaches rock between wars, maybe even Turkey. I hear their beaches are even topless, hmm…" she purred. Karly leaned in, nibbled my ear and slid her hand over into my lap and rubbing my cock. She feels the erection, "Well hello, there!" she coos as she gently rubs on the outside of my jeans.

Somehow, feeling like this was an inappropriate time, yet grateful for the attention, I grinned nervously saying, "Well that was different…Too bad about your friends."

Seemingly, without as much as a hint of emotion, "Yes it is…But isn't that what heaven's for?" She unbuttoned my jeans, my rising progress gripped in her pretty fingers and before she goes down on me, she looks me dead in the eye and says "This is the luckiest thing about you right now", her liquid blue eyes disappearing into the back of her head as her mouth…

I shot bolt upright in my bed. I looked around. It was indeed quarter to three. Yeah, a dream, and I had a boner. My heart was beating fast. I haven't had that kind of dream since…fucking *ever*. Maybe the lack of visible female flesh and the excitement of meeting someone new and the beer got to me all at once. I was bottled up for a while by that point. Maybe that was it.

I dropped back down on the bed and tried to sleep but it was no good, even after I popped one off. So I got up and walked around the village. The rest of the house was sound asleep so I was real quiet sneaking out. Some of the porch lights were still on but it was clear the town was asleep as the homes were dark. A stray dog caught up with me and walked with me for a while before turning into what I assume was his house. He looked over his shoulder at me, bowed his head and went around back; I suppose he had a long day too.

It was so peaceful here and especially at night, not like the rest of the Territories at all. This place was so far removed that the last time Israelis were here or had *ever* been here was in 1967 during the Six Day War. They stopped to take a collective crap and coffee break in a café bathroom or something as the villagers hid in caves for the three days the Jews were here. What is it about Arabs and caves anyway? I guess they come in handy if you need to evacuate in a hurry.

I kind of knew where I was going and figured I could find my way back before sun up so I walked up the hill. I could see the lights coming from the different cities. I walked around past my other uncle's house and over to the pasture where Ayoub raised his head of sheep. They were just grazing, sleeping; they seemed peaceful. I wondered what they counted. The sheep have been in the family at least two hundred years. Not the same sheep but I got that.

Then I hiked over to where my grandfather was buried. He wasn't buried in the cemetery with everyone else. He was buried just at the edge of town in a crypt that was alone as he wished. My father actually had pictures of it which I thought a bit morbid, so I knew what I was looking for. It was on a big lot that he hoped the family would employ as time passed. At that point, it was just he, his wife, my grandmother, and my Uncle Jacob's dad's older brother. He would have grown up my father's business partner.

Uncle Jacob got blown to bits when he was eighteen years old. The British left munitions behind after the Second World War. Jacob and his buddies would go over to hang out and fuck around like teenage boys anywhere else.

They had done this before so it was only natural that my father, who was a six year old boy at the time, wanted to join in, driven by a six year-olds' curiosity. Hard to picture my dad at six and there were no childhood photos of him. Our family was too poor to have photos taken but as more money came into the family, photos were an indulged extravagance. This was probably why my aunt had hundreds of pictures all over the house. My grandfather had his first pictures done in the late 50s when he was in his 70s.

Jacob was my dad's hero but that day my uncle chased his baby brother back with a switch from a tree with my dad crying the whole way home. Jacob rejoined his friends and about an hour later, the explosions could be heard for miles and it wasn't just one either. My dad had said many times that it sounded like forever (his term and I was always surprised by the poetry of it). My grandfather and his neighbors took a horse and wagon to collect the remains of their sons. These men just seemed to know what happened as men like these tend to know these things. It wasn't like the cops or fire department had called the house or that the military chaplain dropped in. That too, proved to be a token of a luxury not enjoyed here in Derduwan.

My father told me this story quite a few times. It was his way of relating and I guess he wanted me to be nicer to my younger brothers as they were that far apart in years from me. Standing there, I wondered if Uncle Jacob did it on purpose. Maybe he wanted to die. Maybe he and his buddies had a pact because options were few here and eighteen is a dramatic age regardless of heritage, nationality or options. Or maybe, just maybe, this was the sort of horrible accident that keeps parents fearful of their kids ever leaving home. We'll never know but I once heard that having children was like setting your heart loose in the world with arms and legs attached to it. He died before my grandparents. I could never conceive burying my own child.

I never thought of this before or maybe I didn't want to. It's one thing to hear the story but here was Uncle Jacob, buried in a crypt at eighteen. He'll be eighteen forever. I wondered if that didn't massively fuck up my dad in some profound way. He was at a funeral for his hero at six years of age. Basically, Jacob was Custer without the horse or Indians.

I just stood there, contemplating my grandfather. He died at ninety-eight in his sleep. I was twelve at the time and as such, I did not get to meet him. The invite to come here from my father came when I was nine and I had barely got home from six months in Brazil with my mothers' family. I was not crazy about my dad, although I couldn't put my finger on why. As a child maybe I wouldn't because kids don't like to think of those things. Maybe because he never let me be a boy, I don't know and that night, it didn't matter. That night I had been a man for a while and I was fast creating a distance from boyhood.

But at nine, I thought my grandfather would live forever. I was torn about not going on the trip as I had an attachment to the perception of what "normal" grandparents should be like, at least by my American neighbors' standards or those set by sitcoms in the 1970s. That idea included grandparents that you visited often. Mine were thousands of miles away. Stories and pictures were not enough and I kind of felt less complete than my friends.

So at nine, I made the monumental decision not to go. My dad didn't have the heart to tell my grandfather I wasn't coming till he got off the plane. I was told he cried hard when he saw my father get off the plane alone. After all, I was his namesake or at least one of them. I always felt guilt about that. This was the projection of a man's guilt onto a nine year old. I was named after him as is the tradition for the oldest boy to be named after your father and not yourself. There were six of us cousins with that honor and eventually twenty-two and counting.

At the beginning of his career, Frank Sinatra was asked to change his name many times. Other Italians did it, so why not? He wouldn't even use a stage name, like Dino Martini had used Dean Martin. He famously said, "If I changed my name to Frankie Satin, like Tommy Dorsey wanted, I'd be singing cruise ships by now." There's something to be said for having vision without having seen the prize yet.

I have been tempted to change my name. It had come up a couple of times in my life; professional reasons or conflicts with my dad had me thinking about it more than I would be proud to admit. I could never bring myself to do it.

During the First World War, Palestine was then a British territory. It was not a nation so there was no black and white about it. Well, I guess there is if you want to dehumanize your enemy. My grandfather learned this first hand. Territories were property, pure and simple.

He was recruited with thousands of other young Palestinian men to fight the Turkish for the British as were the Jews of the region. They were told that doing so would guarantee a free Palestine (or Israel, in the Jews case) to rule as they saw fit. India would enjoy this hard won privilege some twenty-five years later by actually pressuring Britain as pressure was all they knew how to respond to. Grandpa was thirty-eight at the time when he was captured by Turkish forces and imprisoned with his men. This was a long time before the Geneva Convention or Amnesty International could even spell the term, Middle East. What's more, the Ottoman Empire was developing quite the reputation for brutality with the Armenian Genocide in full swing and nary a peep from the "developed" world.

My grandfather spent six months in a Turkish prison before he escaped with a buddy that he knew from a neighboring village back home. They walked back to what was then Palestine and it took them six months to get home. They worked as farm hands, farriers, roofers and whatever else kept them fed and rested. They kept walking just like David Banner in the Incredible Hulk. He made it; got married and started raising kids along with the sheep his father would leave him and his brothers. He and my grandmother would have fourteen children with her having been pregnant nineteen times in her life. She died when my father was thirteen. I don't think he handled that well and I doubt I would have fared much better.

My father always told me that I had my grandfather's temperament and that I forgave easily. He would say this with disgust as a way of highlighting my perceived weakness or what he considered a moral failing. Even though my grandfather never got rich, he was always the "go-to guy." He was the dependable man in the village. My dad said his father was as calm as a Hindu cow on the day he had to collect the remains of Uncle Jacob and the other boys. Maybe that's where I get it from, I don't know. I had never met him, only heard the stories. Are souls genetic?

There lay my grandfather. He lived like other men, loved and affected his family like other men. He died just like every man will. Like some men, he had a grandson he never knew, who was standing at his grandfather's grave. These men never got their Palestine and I doubt it will ever come. At least he died a happy, old man on his terms and not for nothing.

****

As I stood there, I saw the moon hang pregnant in the middle of the bright, starry night sky. I have never been able to put this together before and even as my grandfather lay dead in his crypt, he was helping me make more sense of who I was. This was a tall order at twenty-three but I knew that life was for the living and I wasn't going to waste it doing something I hated.

I walked back to the house as dawn was breaking. The porch lights in the homes in the hills of the village were giving way to the morning sun. It had been an interesting night; teenage wet dreams and Israeli beer having paved the way. I had never spoken of this night to anyone but it wouldn't matter in the long run.

I saw fire by a roadside and was struck by the sadness of death and the passing of time…

Chapter 4-How's Your Joint, George?

I slept in that same morning. Probably fell asleep around eight or so but the light coming into the window kept me drowsy more than actually falling asleep and I was too lazy to pull the curtain. I'd doze then awaken but not really awake and I was still in bed. The sun on my feet was nice.

I then went downstairs to see my uncle and others cousins, they were just hanging out with some customers and it was busy, lamb sales were moving that day. You could smell the fresh blood coming out of the kitchen which doubled as the cleaning area. Unlike the Scottish, Arabs won't eat the leftover blood. They'll eat the eyes, brains, stomach, balls but they'll draw the line at the blood. The space Ayoub sold meat out of was a concrete floor with painted green walls, same color as the walls at the check point. It wasn't like there was a health department and the Israelis could give a shit if Palestinians got botulism. There was a counter and he took cash so there was only a metal money box like the ones moms have at little league games in the States. There were two deep freezers that had maybe some meat left from the day before. With this many people to sell to, Ayoub only killed a couple of sheep a few times a week. There were no preservatives and he was good about "half off sales" when the meat sat frozen a few days.

They offered me some left over breakfast sitting on the counter by the cash till; dried Arab buttermilk, that are like rocks you could gnaw on as a salty snack or cook into a broth. He also had tomatoes, olive oil and yogurt with bread. I went into the side kitchen and heated up some pita bread and poured coffee. It was American coffee and the smell mixed with that of death or fresh blood was unique to say the least.

I chatted with a couple of the cousins in broken English as they were translating to Ayoub what I said about my life in America, what I had seen so far and some of how my mom and dad were doing. He smiled like he knew something I didn't. After all, he knew my father as his "little brother." Ayoub had a very sweet nature but when people translated for me, it was always hard to tell if I was coming off as intended. He asked my cousin to ask if I was looking to get married and smiled broadly when I said, "Not yet, I got time."

He told my cousin, "Yes, you do, but don't tell your father I said that." Then he winked at me while rolling another cigarette with his free hand, sipping coffee with the other. He was making smoking look as cool as Ian

McCullough did. Instead of wearing pleated pants and flicking the butt into an adoring crowd, Ayoub slipped his weathered, un-manicured hand into a leather tobacco pouch with a cigarette paper, rolling and licking in one motion. Then he'd screw the newly wrapped confection into his lips and light it with the same hand. It was a sight.

I washed up and went down to the coffee house a couple of blocks away. The houses all looked different in the daytime. There was no real uniformity, whatsoever. It was a small village and families would build homes as fast as their relatives could send cash; it was easy to see who was on point with their plans or not. There was a certain look to buildings when they took too long to complete. Even the new parts started to look worn and needed work again before finishing the whole thing. But this place was different than the big cities, it was cleaner. Folks here dumped out water at the sides of their houses as opposed to the street and there was a sense of permanence maybe because they didn't fear the confiscation of property by the Israelis.

Because property was still at a premium because of the seclusion, you could build a home and never worry about it being turned into a settlement for religious fanatics because this place was just too fucking far away to give a shit about. The valley it sat in made any considerable road work prohibitive cost wise. Although the saying, "never say never" was invented for a reason, most Israelis were pretty secular and hated that dollars were funding Jewish extremists. The attitude of most was less religion is best and the money could be better spent elsewhere.

As a result of this isolation, these Arabs, in this village, had a sort of removed hawkishness. They were more prone to demand that Arabs fight the Israelis. They were a little too quick to curse for cowards, anyone who was reluctant to do so. Of course, they constructed their views from a pussy-safe distance. Anyone can be an arm chair revolutionary when it's the other guy doing the dying. I couldn't take the brave talk seriously even at face value because it lost face. The odd thing about this village was no one here *ever* died at the hands of a single Jew. Not one. No one here lost property to Jewish settlers and they sure as fuck didn't throw rocks at armed soldiers. They could be here for months and never have to go into Jerusalem or Ramallah. There's a good band name for anyone shopping, "Arm Chair Revolutionaries." Their fans could call them, "ACR, man!!!"

The streets were cobblestone and cars rumbled as they drove on them. Been here a few days and I had just noticed it now. People here wave and smile or nod at you as you pass them. They were nice because they may have known your family or you may be related, which kind of was the same thing in that village.

The café was an old two story house from the 1800s that was converted in the 1920s. My grandfather hung out here and the locals knew him. The front windows and walls were removed so it had this open air vibe which was very cool. Everyone in the village knew it so there wasn't even a sign. As I approached, I could see the big doors opened out where walls used to be and the distinct aroma of coffee and baked goods like baklava and mammoul filled the air like jasmine. Folks sitting at the tables on the sidewalk and on the curb, in between cars said this was the right place. The sounds of debate, gossip and relaxation mixed together in a human way that was familiar and comforting at the same time, humans being human. At the end of the day, we all want the same things.

Make no mistake; this wasn't the East Village, two doors down was the village telephone operator. They were three guys who worked six hour shifts with no graveyard shift and they put your calls through. If you were too poor to have a phone, you could use theirs. But if you had a call to make in the middle of the night, well, tough shit whether you owned a phone or not.

I went inside and ordered. The coffee guy offered me American Coffee. His English was ok and I could sense some of the café patrons eyeing me and as I didn't want to look like a pussy, I declined and took the Arabic Coffee, which was a version of espresso. Why should I care what this guy thought but I did. Stupid, as this was basically thick, muddy grounds served at 400 degrees in an espresso cup with about four good sips in it, before you got to the bottom so I never cared for it. The caffeine was so concentrated the first hot sips came off like cocaine and gasoline. Adding cream or sugar was futile because then the mud stirred up like the bottom of a dirty lake and I took coffee black, anyway. It was taken black or one didn't take it. I was flying as it goes through the uninitiated like string through a duck while producing more piss than an entire liter of Coke.

"I know your father," said the coffee guy as he prepared my drink.

"Yeah," I smiled. "He's from here."

Failing to get the humor, my host said that he knew that. As I looked around, some folks waved and smiled benignly.

I got a copy of the English Jerusalem Post and looked at the middle of the paper first. It read like news read and reads still; housing is going up after being down, beef imports from Lebanon and Egypt were down, we have your inter-racial dating with another couple fleeing the wrath of their families for love, always a very little discussed yet dicey topic guaranteed to bring shame to the overzealous. This would be between Arabs and Jews and always wound up somewhere on page 17 of the "B" section. Some stock tips, sports, rugby and soccer mostly, then I perused the headlines; there was another story of students getting beat down, this time in Hebron. I could solve this whole fucking mess today. Arabs stop blowing up Israelis and Israelis stop taking properties that are generations' old and building settlements in the Territories then feigning shock at the reaction. Jews weren't there for 3,000 fucking years! If I could have given the Jews any advice, it would be to know that Arabs aren't going anywhere either, so quit taking what's left of their shit.

Arabs need to get over the past because Israel wasn't going quietly into the night and no, the Arabs will not "push them into the sea." Jerusalem? Neither one of them *really* needs it religious-wise anyway. Muslims have Mecca and where was Moses born again? Right, so they can share Jerusalem as they were both descendants of Abraham anyway, if the story was true.

I felt my Palestinian friends needed to understand a little gratitude. No one is in a dialog (read gives a shit) with or has their race preface the word, "question." The short list first would include the Basque, Kurds, the Irish and of course, the gran mal ass fuck of the ages, the American Indian! That their plight was referred to as the "Palestinian Question" should be cause célèbre for the body politic of this displaced group of folks and anyone who pretends to care. And that is because history is always written by the winners and always will be.

As I read the paper, my leg was twitching like mad. I couldn't see how these guys could have more than one or two cups of this stuff, but they would have as many as five or more, in one day and they live a long time, too. Amazing. My family drank this coffee like most of them smoked. My grandfather was 98 when he died. Many years later, his kid sister would die at 104. Still, I could see how terrorists or students got jacked up enough to fight *anyone*, just pour this shit down their throats. This coffee is to the Arab as Absinthe was to the French before they made it illegal and started losing wars. Comparing coffee to alcohol may have been an odd point of view but both changed your state of mind.

Ali walked in and ordered a coffee and sat down.

"What's the good word, cousin?" he said cheerfully.

I held up my coffee and paper, "In my element, man." I continued as I turned the page, trying to look casual, "You guys seemed to be into it last night when I got home." I was talking about his brother, Shipley, the good guy.

Ali drank his coffee. "Yeah, it's weird what comes up when people die."

Changing the subject, I talked about the day before and what a blast it was, the checkpoint with Sam and the soldiers, which was a little scary. Strangely, I failed to bring up Karly again because I didn't want a discussion on it. Ali could go either way depending on his mood but she was pretty much the highpoint of the day. I didn't want it tarnished with a discourse on what my father would say.

Ali pointed at my paper, "Nowhere else can a newspaper be as worthless as fast as todays' Jerusalem Post."

I know my expression was quizzical.

"Seriously cousin, give this a few days and you'll see. Things change fast here. Fifteen minutes sometimes." He was very solemn. "By the time it's made the paper, the story will change nine times."

Ali was still simply dealing and I could tell he had more on his mind than he was letting on. I wasn't exactly what one would call light of spirit either but I was more tired than anything else at this point. Maybe I was hopeful because of Karly? I don't know. Girls can do that to you. It was weird that I still felt out of sorts at all. I thought once we got this burial thing over with, I'd feel better. I was certainly over any jet lag but it had been a few days and maybe I just wanted to go home already.

Although Mahmud was closest to my age, it was Ali that I got along with the best of the four brothers. I always found Mahmud to be somewhat caustic and kind of a prick, although we never gave each other any real trouble. He always sided with my dad, if he was at the house during a discussion, being more Arab than American by a long shot. It used to piss me off because our discussions were none of his business, he just felt like he had to put in his say and he was five years older than I was. This made him an "elder" in his mind.

There was no sense of obligation, other than to my father, for coming. If I just got the call and went to the services in the States, I'd have been fine in a week. Dragging a body around through customs and dealing with this whole thing for the last couple of weeks did tire me out. But it wasn't *my* brother and I wasn't going to much miss the guy, even though I had nothing really against him either. He was always good to my mother so she really had a soft spot for him. The two of us got along okay if my father wasn't around.

Ali told me that our Uncle Dahoud or David (which was the literal translation), was having us over to dinner that night. David was the second boy in the family, behind Uncle Jacob. He made his fortune in Switzerland and Venezuela. He owned a chain of what could be best called dime stores in both countries. He cashed out, in a massive way, to an English conglomerate on the South American stores while he and his eldest son kept the Swiss properties. He had a wife in each of the three countries; Switzerland, Venezuela and the Territories. Each *knew* of the other but lack of proximity and continual cash flow into the individual households contributed to a lot of denial. While not quite a sultan, David was well off by most Arab standards so he done good as they might say in Texas.

I came to find that few men here had one wife by choice. The preference was more wives but it was a matter of economics because if you had the bread, you could have more than one bride. A bigger question would be, "who'd want more than one wife?" Up to this point in my life, one girlfriend was enough of a pain in the ass. Arabs haven't invented anything real useful since Algebra or the guitar so they had to do something with their time. Meanwhile, the British got the Rolling Stones and all that after the Crusades! Not all karmas are created equal. "How fucked up is that?" I thought.

I was apprehensive as I had not met Uncle David yet and he wasn't even at the funeral. Apparently, he and Eddie didn't get along either and he didn't want a scene. The two had some business dealings that didn't go well and Uncle David blamed Eddie for incompetence at the very least, not to mention the issues with his sister, Eddies' mom.

The afternoon was giving way to evening and dinner was at six. I had finished the paper, went home, cleaned up and shaved then met Sam and Ali at Sam's house. I saw Nina, Sams' wife and we chatted a little bit as I haven't seen her in years.

"How's it going, cuz?" she smiled as she kissed me three times. She seemed sad like seeing me reminded her of home. She wasn't making the treks back and forth with Sam as she was when they first got married. They had kids and decided to raise them here, closer to family and culture. While they wouldn't say it, they really didn't want their kids to end up like me although they had no real beef with me personally. It was just the *idea* of me that concerned them as far as their own kids went. It was a feeling I was used to.

"Going well, sweetie." I said. "No complaints, you know." What could I say in ninety seconds that would sum up the last couple of weeks?

Nina was here three years straight at the time with their two young boys. It's weird when you see people you knew as kids, all grown up with kids of their own. It was like we were all still 14 but they somehow came up with these kids. Maybe that feeling would pass if I ever became a real adult or even a parent.

The sun was setting as we walked over to David's house. Folks were on their porches or steps, enjoying the sunset and waving, saying good evening and all that, in Arabic. Dinner was coming on in many of the homes and the smells brilliantly crashed into each other as we walked down the street. People here all knew Sam and Ali who waved and smiled like Rose Parade princesses. Of course, I did not share in this celebrity. I was my fathers' son. But not for long; when I got famous, I may have come back and then they would have seen something.

Sam and Ali discussed some things in Arabic but I knew it wasn't about me. I could sense these people when they would talk and what it was about because they were comfortable or when they were gossiping about me. This came from years of that shit in the house with relatives or mom and dad as they both spoke each other's language. Fucking romantic and came in handy raising four boys who spoke no Arabic.

We get to Uncle David's house and it was ornate in a kind of gaudy, there's no-accounting-for-taste kind of way. It was a five story job with an elevator, which was cool. We went inside and were greeted by him and his wife. I could smell dinner and I did not realize until that moment that I had three aunts through this guy alone. This could make Thanksgiving a little awkward, if ever he was so bold and if the holiday were celebrated here. His wife spoke zero English and it was just as well. I didn't need to deal with any marital drama. David also spoke English and Spanish.

We went up the elevator which had this great cherry wood paneling with inlays. This was the most tasteful part of the house but like the rest of the place, had no discernible theme or real idea of what it was. Some of the inlays were Arabic writing and some were of horses or birds. I didn't read Arabic but I was certain it didn't matter. We had to stop at each floor. There were badly painted murals on the ceilings of the foyers of each floor and some had sayings in Arabic, made to fit the ceiling. It was mostly real bad Michelangelo wannabe type stuff; limbs were wildly disproportionate and the women had these strategically placed sashes over the naughty bits. God forbid we see tits or even (gasp!) pussy! The floors were solid marble throughout, which is pretty fancy even if this were in America. The railings were wrought iron. All the furniture was new but I wouldn't have owned it. Everything seemed hastily slapped together, like the murals. I was no expert but it didn't take a botanist to smell shit on a flower either.

We sat down to dinner after the grand tour. David gently grilled me about getting married, pretty much from the moment we sat down to eat. "Nice welcome to the homeland speech for you," I thought. Fuck "How are you feeling?" "How was your flight?" "Thanks for doing this," "Your father must be proud/grateful/happy," "It must have been a bitch dragging a fucking dead guy around." That would be too much as the only question on this enquiring mind was if I'd marry some Arab chick that I didn't know who probably had a real face for radio.

David asked, "Have you seen girls to like? Your father talk to they father, if for you." His English was not quite Sam or Ali's.

"I still have time, Ami." Pronounced "ah-mee," this was the Arab word for Uncle.

"The time she goes. You're old too fast then what to do?" He was looking down at his salad.

Ali was talking to my aunt, pretending not to hear and Sam was chatting with my cousins although he had an ear leaned in as if he was to referee indirectly.

Marriage was the farthest thing from my mind, especially the arranged marriage routine. These girls don't date. I was supposed to see a girl who's cute and tell my dad. He then tells her dad and if her dad liked me then he informs the daughter. If she's cool with it, then we'd begin courting which entails three to four chaperoned dates with her brothers, cousins and basically anyone you would never invite on a date, ever. Then we'd get married with the general idea being that we have zero idea as to chemistry until the honeymoon, having maintained some bullshit chastity rules that apply to even kissing. So if she fucks like a day old side of sushi, has odd looking genitalia or some chronic breath issue that's incurable with even the strongest mints or surgery, I am federally fucked as the U.S. attorneys' office likes to say. If the same holds true for her then she'd be as screwed as me.

I had some creative cousins who circumvented this pathetic ruse and figured out compatibility early so I had some examples. They'd sneak around in the middle of the night with their intended. I just wanted to play in my band and go back to work my cool job, deep thoughts notwithstanding.

Not my thing, man.

For some reason I was thinking about Shelly and the possibility of never seeing my dad again over her. Would it have been worth it if she didn't dump me? I always thought yes, if for anything, the decision would be made for me if my dad cut me off. While I didn't know Karly at all, lust does breed an odd familiarity which has befallen better men. Could Karly do the same? Break my heart? Would I allow it? Was I just a Greek tragedy?

Now, having said only some of this to Uncle David, sans the vulgarity and attitude, I made him smile, like I was the slow kid on the short bus headed to the skating rink. He looked at me blankly as he went back to eating. I had a feeling that this, plus my long(ish) hair, would make the rumor mill spin and spin concerning my "decadent" lifestyle and I thought "Good!" Glad I can entertain these people. That's what we Americans do. Most folks enjoyed drama because they had nothing better to do with their time and I was long done caring.

David walked us to the door after coffee and dessert, bidding us good night. The desert was vanilla halva over some pastry and the coffee was black and not Turkish, which went well with the desert. As the three of us walked back, Ali decided to call it a night. A gentle coaxing to hang out was rebuffed, so we confirmed plans for the next day and I went back to Sam's house hoping he had more of that beer.

"Sorry about that. But you had to know it was coming though." Sam offered.

We walked a minute, "Yeah, I guess but I figured I'm here to bury the guy's nephew, right? There'd be more to talk about or something. I'm 23 so why is it so crucial to get married? And who the fuck cares? I'm not his kid anyway and I got shit to do, man..." I sighed.

"Well, they don't really see it that way, you know?" Sam sighed. "Takes a village, that sort of thing."

"You can say that again," I said as I worked to keep my voice down. "There are two types of immigrants; you do know that, right? The first comes to America to make a new life, re-makes himself like David Bowie, on every new album, or something and the second comes to duplicate what he fucking left behind here. If that's so important, why leave?"

"Yeah, I guess there's that." Sam stopped. "But you can't get too hung up with shit either. You'll do what's right for you…Seriously, you're going to give yourself a heart attack and for what?" He looked around as he motioned me into an alley. He reached into his pocket, pulled out a lighter.

Flipping the lighter in his fingers, he pulled out a joint as he continued, "I mean, really, these guys still care about whose chicken is fucking whose chicken, for Chrissakes! Look man, it is what is. You're here now so make the best of it. At least you're seeing heritage. This is heavy shit. Americans think they come from 'Main Street.' Here you're getting the last five generations…You do get high, I assume? Mr. Rock Dude." Upon seeing my grin he pulled out a nicely rolled joint; great way to change the subject.

"You get this from the Israelis, too?" I still couldn't roll a joint to save my life so I always used a pipe.

Blankly, without eye contact Sam said, "Lebanon." With that, we fired up in the alley.

I never thought I'd see the day where I would be getting high with my cousin or any of my relatives for that matter. I took a hit, held it and exhaled, "Geez, that's nice."

I handed Sam the joint and he took his turn, held it. "Sure beats Mexican," he said as he exhaled. "Not that I have anything against our brothers and sisters south of the border, you understand…" he chuckled. I took the joint back with my turn.

We said no more the rest of that time. We took turns until it was all gone and we were more than sufficiently comfortable. The shit was smooth and here I thought Lebanon was simply where you went to have a good war. Beirut was the Monaco of the 1940s and 50s; royalty, movie stars and covert politicians vacationed, gambled, fornicated there and the beaches were pristine. Then, starting around 1961, when the Palestinian Liberation Organization (PLO) got started, everyone decided to run to or chase their enemies into Lebanon and it got wrecked, especially Beirut.

We walked home back to Sam's house. Nina and the kids were asleep. Sam went down into the basement and got beer. He kept a separate wine and beer cooler so that his parents wouldn't find it, nosing around in the kitchen. Nina never complained as she liked to tip a few back herself. That and bitching just wasn't her thing, anyway, even when we were kids. She was always a good girl.

The TV was on with the volume low. There was just the news on. More shit in Jerusalem was to be expected in the next couple of days as the elections of local authorities were usually met with cries of "sellout." Even though I was raised with the stories, I still had a hard time feeling total hatred for the Jews because I just knew they told their kids the same bullshit stories too. I kind of figured this out in tenth grade when I started digging into history. I knew they weren't really lies but some of the stuff was simply untrue like Palestine being a "country." Hate's a strong word, anyway.

Half my dad's family was in the same boat; either pacifists or pissed off purists, those were the choices, for want of better terms. It certainly wasn't a religious deal on either side of the argument really as much as it was about control but the powers that be used religion to exert it. It worked on the masses. One didn't have to be religious to want a homeland. It'd be a good idea to get religion out of it. I just thought these two sides had to make the most of it. They're here now and no one is going anywhere.

The little dark secret in the Arab world is they don't like Palestinians, not at all, not even a little, well, maybe a little, but very little. Palestinians were to the Arabs what Tijuana is to the rest of Mexico. Just above Egypt, who at least have a few more dollars and an actual country. Plus, they had that whole ancient culture thing going; Greeks, Romans, I mean Italians, Persians, excuse me; Iranians got away with a tad more because of their previous track record. Doesn't mean shit now but they still get some credit. Babylon, I mean Iraq, not so much; they're still Iraq. But Palestinians, forget it.

The Arab world loved to use the Palestinian/Israeli conflict as an excuse to cause grief to the U.S. and the Israelis and that's it. Truth is, if these Arabs ever got their way and "pushed Israel into the sea," the Palestinians would be next. I mean, if the Arab world really gave a rats' ass, why was there no push to give the West Bank to the Palestinians when Jordan was perfectly suited to do so? In 1967, Israel got it and then it became an issue?

When I was in college, Arabs in my class would catch up with me when they heard my name in roll call. Seems there was this Kennedy-esque family in Jordan with our last name and they were filthy, fucking, hog nasty rich. So these peasants would ask where my family was from as if we were one of them, like Beatles "them." Once I figured out the deal, I would say, "Save it man. My family's in sheep not oil," before they could even get it out of their mouths.

It got to where I hated being at a party and some blowhard, fucking hippie or Arab, who was not Palestinian, would blather on about the "evils of Israel." They would try and tell me how I didn't know the real deal because I wasn't really an Arab in the first place, given that I was born in L.A. So I'd watch their face go slack as I'd bring up the whole "Arabs-hate-Palestinians" deal. It was an excellent way to nuke an idiotic argument but I never went hunting for elephant in my underwear. I could back up the rest of the discussion, smile and go get myself another beer. When I did it right, it was impressive. The one blessing I had was I was quick.

The Israelis had an annoying sense of entitlement too. Any side agrees with you and all is well until you suggest a compromise. This was the problem and not just with Arabs and Jews but with most of mankind. I had met some cool Israelis but the government can be fuckers too. They were largely a secular society who gave into right wing asshole fascists, who would just as soon kill an Arab baby as any unhinged Arab would kill a Jewish baby. There's no one side that was better or right. They were all just a bunch of mislead fuck ups.

Wow. Stoned, man…

Sam came back upstairs and we popped open the beers and just kicked back. Sam was reflecting on dinner. He got quiet.

Then, "You're right about tonight, man…I…hmm," he started then stalled, closing his eyes like he was trying to remember something. "Sit tight," with that he went into the basement again. He came back with a big box. "Come here, I want to show you something. You remember Kelly, right?"

How could I not? Kelly would be the girl Sam dated when I was twelve when I thought Sam was a god and she was in my top ten "Greatest Hits Reel," along with the chick who played Lois Lane in the 50s T.V. version of

71

Superman, the *color* version to be specific. Sam pulled out Kellys' modeling pictures, scrap books she made for him, poems.

"Nina knows you have this?" I asked. After all, she knew who Kelly was too, everyone did.

Sam said that she did not. The box was simply marked "Sam's Stuff." I couldn't imagine any wife who knew of that girl would just leave that box alone but it's good to let sleeping dogs lie and that goes for lying husbands too.

Sam and Kelly were together seven years. His family tolerated her with a tacit understanding that he was just going through a phase and that he would marry the right way, when the time came. I had heard that too. He never told me that night if he ever stood his ground on her during those years. It didn't matter as he finally broke up with her when his father gave him the ultimatum. If he ever fought for her, giving in the last time meant he had lost forever as it was basically marry an Arab or else. With these people, "or else" meant getting cutoff and that meant the money too.

Unlike his attorney brother Mike or Jamal, who owned businesses apart from the family, Sam had no other means of income, at least not what he was used to so he caved and he married Nina. The thought of being separated from his mom and dad was more than he could bear, it seemed. He knew they'd do it too. They did it to Mike for 11 years before his divorce and subsequent pardon from the wilderness. I remember Sam and Ninas' wedding and looking back on it I can't say there was an emotional aspect, good or bad. He didn't seem too happy but I didn't really notice until that moment in his house.

So Kelly was off living her life in the States and here was Sam, crying in his beer in the Territories. I wonder if she would have been cool with the visits here as I didn't think she'd last a week. He never brought her over when they were dating, not ever in seven years. Why would he? He knew his parents, shit he knew everyone's parents, grandparents, uncles, and third cousins...Maybe she would have hated it. It takes a certain person to handle the life here even a little. The West Bank was not seen with a Eurail pass as one had to roll with it, head on a fucking swivel. Most of what the West saw on the news was true as there was splendid wonder mixed with very primitive, very difficult shit.

I grew up with Nina and I always found her pretty, but to leave your true love to please your dad? Fuck that and fuck your dad and mine too for that matter for even asking. My father and I recently had several arguments over the subject and I was quite ready to stand my ground whenever the time would come and I was actually quite comfortable with the idea of a permanent separation, so frequent were the threats of banishment. Shit, I've even dated several Jewish girls, if that meant anything. Get threatened enough with petty bullshit and I learned to care less and less and either I was going to give in or I dared the other side like life in an occupied country. I had a lot of pride and I found this to be a pattern, big or small; if you pushed the issue with me, you had to either be angrier than I was or armed. Those were your choices. While never quite proud of it, those were my circumstances…

I'm twelve years old. For a brief time one of my cousins, Abe went to my junior high school. I would often have dinner at their house as it was on my way home from school. His mother was my mothers' cousin from Brazil. She too had married an Arab who also happened to be my fathers' cousin and that's how they met so for all intents and purposes, she was my aunt as well and was accorded the same respect.

One evening as me and Abe were watching T.V. and waiting for dinner, his mother over heard me talk about this little Ecuadorian girl in my homeroom. Her name was Xiemena. She had jaw breaker sized brown eyes that glowed over her braces that she sheepishly covered with her lips when she smiled. As a twelve year old, this is goddess material. Her hair came clear to her ass and topped her forehead with bangs. She favored skirts and knee high socks and was always nice to everyone. Of course at twelve, all I could muster up was, "I really like her dude…" My aunt heard this and chided me in Portuguese that my father may have a thing or two to say about that. I challenged her and she dared me to ask him; my marriage was a decision he made for me, a foregone conclusion. I didn't stay for dinner.

I couldn't get home fast enough. My legs burned from near running but I was carrying books and this was way before backpacks for kids came into vogue. Dad worked late that night but I didn't move from our couch, I just watched T.V. to keep me occupied, feigning my homework which was neglected on the coffee table. When he got home I asked, "Who's Aziza?" He laughed so I asked again, saying "I'm not marrying her."

His eyes narrowed, "Who told you that?" He asked my mother who told him the news. Trying to suppress his anger (a rarity) he said, "What do you know? You're a boy!" As he said this, I got scared I was going to be beat but I held my ground. I was twelve, an awful age but fuck him...

"I like someone else. I'm serious," I scowled and I was.

He went into their bedroom and brought out a picture. Christ, she was ugly and she was my cousin, which could exponentially increase the odds of having some real stupid, real ugly, fucking kids.

"I won't do it." I said firmly. "When I do, it's because I love her...Don't you love mom?"

He softened, surprisingly saving my ass, I imagine but he didn't answer. I guess he figured at twelve, why have this fight now? It would not come up again for ten years and many girlfriends later. The stitches episode proved to be the last beating I took from him.

"You know something?" Sam was looking at Kelly's pictures. "I never cheated on her, ever." He handed me a poem. It wasn't very good, in fact it sucked. Alas, to poor Sam it may as well have been fucking Yeats, "But Nina? Shit. Every time I'm in the States. I bang the shit out of Mike's secretary. You know Heather?"

I said that I did. She's hot but still...and Nina? I think she deserved better as all good girls do.

"Don't do what they tell you, man. It's a fucking sham. I love Nina, she's a great girl. Good mom..." He trailed off as he was uncharacteristically sentimental. "But I'm not in love with her. I never will be and I think she knows that. She's not a stupid person. I just don't want to embarrass her, her family, *our* family."

"Well, I'm not here to judge, man." I said drinking my beer. "But you confirmed everything I ever thought about this arranged marriage business...Fucking peasants."

We had been whispering that whole time but I wondered if we were still too loud.

So far I got advice from an Israeli soldier from New Jersey and my cousin. Both were priceless pieces of third party information from people who dealt with enough and as such had no guilt. Liev didn't want to be there anymore than Sam, frankly. I got two great, unexpected nuggets of truth, kernels of wisdom. We kept drinking, Sam and I. Finally, I passed out with the T.V. on. I woke up on the floor around 6am to the sound of whispering coming from Sam and Ninas' bedroom. It sounded like my parents when they would do the whisper/argue routine. The lights were off and they were in bed but it's where they handled the heavy shit, away from us kids. Apparently, this was somewhat cultural or genetic.

As I quietly arose, I felt real stiff and wondered if Nina overheard our chat. They were speaking in Arabic so I wasn't sure. It was dark out as I walked back to Ayoub's house. He was in the shop, butchering the days' meat sales, having been up since 4 am. The lamb smelled good as it was being prepped but I stayed away from the side kitchen. God bless small Palestinian villages, you couldn't do this in L.A.

****

"What if no one's calling? God, then, must be falling..."

After waiting for them to do some business and family stuff, Sam, Ali and I finally got to Bethlehem. Bethlehem was cool because their curfew involved a late start and later finish but the hours ran straight through; unlike everywhere else that was only open a handful of hours at odd spots throughout the day. This was because Bethlehem, being largely Christian, had no real problem with the Israelis other than the whole occupation issue, which it kind of was and kind of wasn't. Even as Palestinians who definitely wanted a homeland, they were pretty forgiving of the "chosen people" and as such, the Jews were cool with them too. I did not necessarily find this a virtue as the Christians were basically waiting for the world to end anyway. Hence, they were willing to put up with a lot more bullshit because Jesus would eventually get here and fix everything as the story goes. Fuck that. But I wasn't going to fix it today either. But raising kids? Here? Being around a shit load of gunfire was a crap assed way to grow up.

We saw where Christ was born and that was cool. This was sacrilege to even ask after in our house, growing up but Sam and Ali knew it was something to see, regardless. It was history in the very least and Muslims counted Jesus as a prophet anyway. The Israeli guards who patrolled there weren't as intense as the guys in Jerusalem or Ramallah. I thought it lame that people could think they're better or could wish me death just because they believe differently than I did. As far as I was concerned, any real spiritual experience had been reduced to a bunch of fairytales that I was coming to grips with in terms of being a fucking fraud. A sham perpetrated by the powerful upon the weak and weak minded but that was just me because some folks got real hope from that crap.

At any rate, I wandered off from Sam and Ali who were busy haggling prices from a produce vendor. Bethlehem had a lot of tall buildings and the streets had more shade as a result. I passed by an antiques store as I went inside a café to grab a falafel sandwich and maybe some stuffed grape leaves even though I knew they never match my moms'. Even with my aunts making them here, my Brazilian mom's stuffed grape leaves kicked ass. I saw a guy in the café, eyeing me. Felt weird, like was he a spy? Then I noticed a ministers' collar and he was actually eyeing my keffiyeh. He was reading a paper. I ordered my food and as I did, I made eye contact with him. He saw me and acknowledged my "scarf" with a nod and he smiled. I pointed at the empty chair at his table, "OK if I join you?" It just seemed okay to do that.

"Sure…" he said with a tad bit uncertainty but he seemed to sense that I was harmless.

I sat, we shook hands and I told him my name. His name was Niven, like David Niven, the actor and he was probably about thirty-five. I asked how he got that name and he explained that his mother was Egyptian and that Egyptian Christians like western sounding names that separate them from Muslims and makes travelling the west a bit easier. She always liked David Niven and who didn't? So Niven it was.

After a few pleasantries were exchanged, he asked, "So what brings you to Bethlehem?"

I explained the story of how I got drafted by my dad and my cousin dying. I explained that I was glad to be learning a few things, "I'm meeting relatives I never knew existed." Trying not to sound dour.

Niven explained how he was from Nablus but lived in New York for a while. He came here when he was twenty-five, after having gone to seminary. He got married to an American girl he met while they were in school. She was an American photographer and her name was Sally. They had three kids but Sally died giving birth to their third child so he moved here to Bethlehem to serve in ministry. He seemed to be a pretty open guy and not at all bitter. Maybe he was simply all cried out and chose to live with it. What else do you do?

Then my food came. Niven smiled, "Go ahead! By all means, eat! …God is funny that way, you and me here now, you know?" he said, finishing his story.

"I guess," I answered hesitantly, sensing that a preach was coming and quite frankly blown away that he could still hold close a God that took his bride, the mother of his children.

"So you were born Muslim? I only ask because of the name but it's obvious from your story." Niven continued making it clear that America had affected his diction.

"I guess, technically, yeah. But it's weird..." I explain, with an air of conspiracy, that at thirteen I had defected and became a Christian. It was purely an intellectual decision as much as could be made at that age, which was not at all spiritual in hindsight as Christ guaranteed an entry of sorts into heaven and Islam did not. I told him how I sneaked around behind my dads' back, having gone to church and summer camps, regularly hiding my Bible like I had lived in an eastern bloc country. How as an adult, questioning my chosen faith stemmed from a desire to get laid but then graduated into more sophisticated fare including but not limited to; the validity of the Bible, Torah and Quran, Jesus actually writing anything, divine inspiration, God being sovereign and all the rest. It was a long list, to be sure while none of these discoveries were wholly original. That it was happening to me, given what I thought I knew, was like discovering I could fly. I was mastering new ways to think which involved challenging people. Being polite, feigning a "reverence" for a religion I no longer had held no place for me. If anything, maybe I'd end up spiritual.

By the time I was twenty-one I was on the fence about all this crap, working at a record company, playing in a band and enjoying the fruits of the flesh as it were. And here I was in the Holy Land, chatting about faith, whether Christian or Muslim with a minister. If we weren't here, I'd be thinking, "Only in America."

"Does your father know any of this? Of your conversion or now...How you feel? I guess your lack of direction, I mean?" Niven asked with some concern. "I'm sure he would be very disappointed...I believe in salvation. I would want my kids to have a relationship with Jesus. I think your father believes in his religion for you."

"Yeah, I suppose he would...don't know if faith is my thing, man." I said as I poured yogurt on my falafel.

"What do you mean?" Niven asked. "You're not an atheist are you?"

"Me? Fuck no. A swim in the ocean or hike in the woods tells you there's at least a God or something. I just don't know about God being in control," the dead bride was lurking about. I wanted to press him on it but I didn't have it in me. My belligerence stopped at the grieving of others. "I think he gets the ball rolling and we do the rest, like He drops you off at the airport but you still have to check in and get on the plane. Don't know which of you guys are right anyway and I'm not sure if I believe in hell either."

"Well," Niven paused, with an odd grin, "My friend, it all takes faith and without that, Jew, Christian, Muslim, you're on your own, not a good place to be…Even God won't go where he's not welcome." Niven said sincerely.

"Maybe we're on our own, anyway. Maybe, I don't know." I was reaching for a good metaphor or parable, if you will; trying to repeat my earlier point, hoping it would stick but it wasn't coming. It wasn't even breathing hard and I didn't care. Niven was a cool guy but in the end we live and die by what we believe, not what we're convinced of. The world proved that every day and eventually, it wouldn't matter anyway.

I see fire and I am saddened by death and the passing of time.

The minister chuckled, "Perhaps this is divine intervention, my friend…Maybe you're ready to come back to our side, avoid an existential crisis." This seemed to be an overcompensation, which I was willing to forgive.

"No thanks dude. I got early release for time served," I grinned. "It's funny, though. You said the same thing about faith my old pastor said. Seems to be the go to word with you guys."

"What, faith? Ah, yes, it's the go to 'F' word! The thing we 3 have in common, if not every other belief. How can they not? What would they have to teach? Faith is what makes belief in something outside our selves possible, provides vision." He nodded, implying people behind me. Sam and Ali were right there. The looks on their faces were rather expressionless. Then Sam said hello and the ice was broken. I introduced my cousins to my new friend. They shook hands and Niven said something in Arabic.

In the alley behind the antiques store, Eddie and Abdul Lateef jumped in a car and truck, respectively, and took off like their lives depended on it. The truck had another shipment of cut heroin. Apparently their partner ran afoul of a higher authority as everyone in the shop who had cut heroin for Eddie was dead; all had been shot with silencers as to not arouse the street outside. The place was soaked in gasoline with a bomb left behind for good measure. As Eddie and Abdul Lateef got far enough away, Eddie stuck his arm out his window. Abdul Lateef grabbed what looked like a calculator that had a key in it…

Niven excused himself to leave and we all exchanged farewells and shook hands.

"You make friends fast," Ali smiled. "Seems like a cool enough guy."

"He said you were pretty sharp in Arabic. Did you get that? Shit, got him fooled." Sam laughed and shoved me.

"Hey! Fucker!" I shoved him back, laughing, "I'm smarter than your Bedouin ass by a fucking long shot…"

Then

KAAA-BOOOOOOM!! BOOOOOOOOM!!!

I was rocked to my ass, falling hard. Sam grabbed a chair as he fell to his knees and Ali stumbled onto the deli counter, ass end into the dairy section. Juice and milk cartons popped and soaked him. The whole deli was coming down as the refrigerators and coffee machines were knocking over and a grease fire had started in the kitchen. The rest of the place was shaken up and stumbling as well. Parts of the ceiling fell in and you could hear glass shatter as it hit the sidewalk outside. People were screaming. The smells of burning buildings and flesh came fast and smoke was descending on the street and into our deli. Pure bedlam had gripped the place as it was sinking in that there was an explosion.

We righted ourselves and worked our way outside, squinting, coughing. It had happened two doors down and the newspaper would later confirm that it was an antiques store. The very one I had passed by moments earlier. It was blown out completely with everything in the store in pieces on the street including a few parts of a few people. Brick and rubble were everywhere. Flames were licking the edge of the building where windows used to be and folks who were in front of the store were immediately blown apart and there was blood everywhere and in large puddles too. The smell of burnt gunpowder and flesh had permeated the air and it was thick even though we were now outside. It was the smell of death, pure and simple.

Suddenly, as the buzz in my ears wore off, I could hear wailing and moaning and it was fucking biblical. I could hear the gnashing of teeth and it was truly hell.

Sirens and alarms had been going on for at least a minute and I only just started to focus after a couple of minutes had passed. Police and troops were moving in. As I stood on the sidewalk, my head on a slow swivel I saw a guy in a black jacket, sprawled across a knocked over fruit cart, his back was on fire but he was not moving. I saw the side of his face and it was Niven! I reacted before I could think and ran over to him. I skidded to a stop and in a panic, I started putting the fire out on his back but he wasn't moving. Later, I would remember a CPR class about that breaking a guy's neck or something if I wasn't careful. It's odd what comes to you in times like that. But Niven didn't move.

"Niven! Hey man! Shit! Oh my God! Can you hear me?" I knelt down and screamed into his ear. I saw blood coming out of it running down his face and he was still. He was dead. My arm jerked. It was Ali. Sam was right behind him.

"We get the fuck out of here, now!" Sam barked.

"But dude. He's…"

"Fuck it. We have to jam right now!" Sam was gaining his composure and control of the situation as he stepped into a small alley between two buildings. Ali pulled me away and we walked fast, following Sam. I was still in shock. Niven was a cool guy, a good man and a family man at that, not a soldier. Now he's dead? That fast? What the fuck? For what, I beg your pardon? There's no such thing as fair where faith is concerned and his kids became orphans. If any of those folks prayed to God at all it seemed He had something else to do that day. If I was one of Nivens' kids, I'm sure I'd end up atheist. I wasn't sure of my own name at that moment.

It felt like we weren't even walking. I don't remember my feet touching the ground. It seemed we glided the couple blocks to where Sam's car was. Road blocks were already being set up where we had just left. As we approached Sam's car, Israeli jeeps and Bethlehem police and fire trucks were screaming down the road. We slowed down to avoid suspicion. Common sense if you run and you're Arab, you're fucked, even if I did have an American passport. Shit like this puts that passport in "quotes" real fast. It could be a Muslim or a Jewish thing but regardless, we are screwed any way they look at it. Getting out of here was the smart move on our part but we still had the issue of pulling it off.

Ali motioned we duck into a church. "Just for a few minutes," he said. "When the emergency crews settle into the area, we leave." We sat in this old church. It was probably built in the 16th Century, I don't know. It was red stone, not brick and the inside walls weren't plastered but red stone as well. The stained glass above the Christ hanging from the front wall was sparkling with sunlight. Jesus was staring down at us, insisting it was our sins he died for. I don't know about Ali but Sam and I each had a ton of reasons why this would be ironic. Niven didn't have a care in the world anymore.

"Let me tell you about heartache and the loss of God."

15 minutes had passed and Ali looked over to us and nodded. The folks who were praying just kept praying, so quiet was our entrance. I'm certain that praying for peace was paramount to visitors. We got into the car and drove off. Sam found his way to Jerusalem and took the same back roads home as he did the other night. We didn't say a word to each other as he drove. I was in the back seat with the window open and I closed my eyes. The wind calmed me as it gently whipped my face and the sun felt just right. If I never moved again, that space was the one to occupy and I could have died right there. In the afternoon that stretch of highway looked like that place from my dream with Karly. I took a deep breath as I was not in the mood to be chased by Israelis and we had no guns.

Sam drove into the mountains and took a longer way home. Even though our village was pretty secluded, it didn't mean we couldn't get stopped before we got there or even chased. When we were talking about how this "ain't the States," we weren't just talking arranged marriages and ignorance. Democracy was at a premium when they shot or arrested you first and asked questions later. As for the Arabs, they can't even spell democracy for love or money and the Jews only apply it to their own. What's more, getting questioned or arrested, then released easily could have marked us for being collaborators. We sure as hell didn't want that either.

The mountainous road we were on was narrow and very high above Ramallah. We could see the town and since the day was clear, I saw Jerusalem and The Dome of the Rock. I lay back again and closed my eyes. The wind was my friend.

We got home and Sam pulled into our uncles' garage. We left the car and walked home. We still hadn't said a word to each other since we split Bethlehem. The three of us just stared straight ahead. I don't know if Sam or Ali ever went through anything like that before as they seemed to share in my shock, a shared experience that I wouldn't wish on anyone.

Understanding the day's events was just starting to sink in on our walk. Sam and Ali had kids and I can only imagine what they were thinking if we got arrested or caught standing too close to the explosion. I kept thinking of grandpa in a Turkish prison and wondered if we would fare any better in an Israeli jail 70 years later? If you're the enemy, history gets written by the winners and so would autopsy reports.

What the fuck was all this for? What was the point of blowing up an antiques store? Not a single soldier was killed. Not as though that would be preferable but shit, isn't that the point as opposed to blowing up your own? I guess Arabs don't count if they're not Muslim. And Niven did nothing to harm anyone. Where was God when this shit went down? I'm not whining but things like this did give me pause as to his omnipotence since it seemed to be flagging.

It's always the sideline guy or revolt groupie that says, "We have to support the uprising," or "We don't know God's mysteries and it's not ours to question," or some stupid shit like that. What do they know? They should get shot and then they tell us what that fucking reason would be.

I walked into the house and the news was on and my uncle looked at me and even though he spoke no English, he could see the look on my face. I'm certain it was blank as a chalkboard in a September classroom. I felt numb, my face felt Novocain numb. I don't think I could have told you the time if I looked at a watch. I had barely noticed that I have not said one word since I saw Niven dead in the street like an animal and that was a few hours past. For Niven, it was no more past, no more school, no more minister, no more wife and kids, no more sadness and the work to cover it up. It's all gone and that's too bad. He was a good dude.

My Uncle Ayoub motioned for me to sit by him. He held my hand and stroked it as I just watched the TV, like I was a little boy, just like in the car that first day. It seemed like the right thing to do and I was simply looking for familiar. My aunt got some food ready. Despite it being late and I knew they had already eaten, this did not feel odd at all. It was what I needed at that exact moment but they had to know I was not right. I said nothing as we ate. My other cousins seemed to be oblivious as to my countenance and I said nothing more either. I went to bed early even for here. I lay on my back and thought about everything. Why do we do this shit to each other? Why do we have to take sides? Why die? For the power grabs of the few? It wouldn't even matter in the grand scheme of things, not one fucking bit.

One year later, the Berlin Wall would come down and the Cold War and Communism would be over and dictators die. But many innocents died anyway and for what? For their country, a fucking wall? The views of a country change, like I change my own mind as a man does all the time and then what? Countries move on and you're still fucking dead...and dead? Dead don't change.

How many hundreds of thousands have died? How many more will die because it's easy to romanticize "serving your country?" Easy until the split second that finds me on the ass end of a rifle.

This will never end.

My throat was choked up and sore from holding it back then I wept and as it turned into abject wailing, I mashed my face into my pillow as to be not be heard by the family, until I fell asleep exhausted. I suppose that was the only logical response to a place that has lost reason but that would imply having it to begin with. So there's that.

Chapter 5-Good Morning, Derduwan!

It had been a couple of days since the incident in Bethlehem so the boys and I hadn't done much outside of Derduwan, the village I was staying in. Ali was hanging out at his mom's and I don't think she made the connection as to us being in Bethlehem that day, so she didn't ask any questions. Whether that was for her benefit or ours, I was never quite sure since she wasn't connecting with much after the funeral service. I'm not sure if Sam's wife said anything to him. I figured she may have thought it best not to bring it up, if she thought of it at all.

Alcohol and anti-depressants were making the same markets as swimsuits in this region so there wasn't a whole ton of help in dealing with or numbing down pain and grief other than to simply deal with it. So Ali's mom just had to grieve the loss the old fashioned way and that was round the clock wailing and kissing her dead son's picture. The house was a scene when I stopped in; people going back and forth with trays of food, different visitors, everyone barking out what sounded like commands in Arabic but were really just conversation of the topics of the day. It was chaos. Eddie was noticeably absent. I had only been there once after the service but I dropped by again. I didn't really want to but I knew that it was expected of me and she was really good to me when she stayed with my folks a few summers prior. My aunt's house was simple; the walls were lime green and there was a kitchen off to the side and a couple bedrooms. In the back there was a small TV that was on but no one was really watching it. Ali and his brothers grew up here. Ali was sitting next to his mother, on pillows, holding her hand. I hadn't seen Ali since the incident so we just the exchanged a look that belied a deeply shared experience like a war, that no one else besides Sam and I could relate to.

I said, "Kee fahk, amti," which was "hi auntie," more or less.

I went to hug her and she really needed to bathe. It had been days. She just grabbed my face, squishing it, like I was five and wailing, "Habibi. Habibi!" She kissed me many times thanking me for our journey in Arabic as she spoke no English herself. Even though I knew what she was saying, she made Ali make sure I knew of her gratitude and that I was "a good boy." She pointed to the pictures of me and my family and a photo on our lawn of me and her when I was in high school. I smiled benignly and her eyes flooded again, looking me in the eye, she bit her lip and let wail again. Maybe it was good that I came out here, after all.

Sam had to go into town and handle his affairs at the restaurant but he would come straight back home. We all just laid low. We all agreed that this seemed to be the smarter move. At any rate I was feeling a little better about at least getting out of the village as I was getting cabin fever. I had hung out at the café and read the paper on the incident. Apparently, Muslim fundamentalists had a beef with some Christians for sympathizing with the Israelis or so went the story. Sympathizing was a word that got stretched a lot in that part of the world not unlike the truth.

The next morning, Ali's brother dropped by my uncle's house to visit. Adnan or "Eddie," as he liked to be called, once he got to the States, was always looking for a fight to pick. He'd walk into a room with a grin but his eyes never smiled. He would find a seat but sit with a certain tension like he was ready to spring and for some reason; I felt it was always directed at me. I heard stories about other people he'd fight with, but it seemed like it was always at me and me alone. He fancied himself a bit of a flash with his dopey designer jeans which I always found to be the zenith of douchebaggery as I was a 501s man myself since the fifth grade and saw no reason to change. I wasn't dating Giorgio Armani so there was no need for his name on my ass. As for Levi? He was a badass and we weren't dating.

I was nine when Eddie came to the U.S. My dad helped all those guys get visas, green cards, whatever they needed to get legal. I always found it curious that some of these guys were pretty educated and here's my illiterate dad, navigating the immigration waters for them down at the Federal Building on Wilshire Boulevard in L.A.

Eddie had a real chip on his shoulder. But it was more than that; I always felt that he was capable of unspeakable, heinous acts. He was different than his brothers as there seemed to be something missing and though they all had dark features, his eyes just seemed black. Their father died when Eddie was 14 so he dropped out of school to start working to help support the three younger brothers and his mom. He went to work for Ayoub for a while, killing sheep in the mornings and then he went to work at a bank in Ramallah in the afternoons. He lied about his age but this was the West bank in the 1960's and iron clad background checks were nowhere to be found. As his brothers grew older they chipped in as to lessen the burden.

While he saved his cash, my father also gave him some money to come to the U.S. My dad had a soft spot for Eddie because of the loss of his father and being his little sister's kid. He also really liked Eddie's father who, by all accounts, was a very charming and funny guy and they had been in Brazil together for a while before my father met my mother. He was working and sending money home like my dad did with his dad. My dad couldn't catch a break it seems, because Eddie's dad was with my father at a party when he dropped dead of a heart attack at the age of 39 in Rio de Janiero. Sometimes I would think about this as I tried to absolve my dad of his sins. Death's a bitch but he made any sympathy real hard.

One can rise above bitterness, grief, anger and all the other shit that happens while one lived a life on earth or one can be a better person who empathizes with others but one can also be an absolute, corruptible shithead. Eddie seemed to relish in being the shithead.

At 23, I could empathize with his pain but I couldn't relate to how he dealt with it. Not with being vengeful and especially taking it out on me as a kid or any kid, for that matter. By the time I made that trip I was the same age as when Eddie came to the States and all he did was give me shit. He was 23 and I was *nine years old.* Knowing what I knew at that point, I would have gently suggested, "Date more mother fucker! Get laid! Have a pork sandwich! Have a fucking beer! Do anything but just get off my fucking ass!" At 23, picking on little kids was the farthest thing from my mind and I had an eleven year old brother.

But Eddie thought I was soft and not just me either. He thought all the American born kids were soft. Eddie thought that I had it too easy or I didn't know pain like he did. He suffered under the delusion the Japanese did before WWII and that was the Americans were all silly playboys and that was why they thought Pearl Harbor would be a goddamned cakewalk but they learned.

Eddie went out of his way to give me the pain he thought I required to become tougher and it would be years before he could see how well he did. He used to accuse me of being a sell-out because I didn't speak Arabic or look the part. He'd say that I was hiding my heritage and all the other self-righteous shit, ignoring my mom's background entirely. He wasn't exactly wearing a turban or riding a camel to work either. In the U.S. he assimilated fast, including cheating on his wife on a very regular basis and wearing shitty disco clothes.

Once, when I was ten he told me my grandfather died. He wasn't dead, of course but Eddie thought it would be funny. He waited till I started wailing and then my dad asked what was going on. Eddie laughed his ass off while my dad hit the roof. How was that funny? But that was who Eddie was, and fuck my dad for not banning the asshole from the house. *He said your father was dead and this was OK with you?* If anything, I would have expected some empathy given Eddie's situation but that's that I suppose. I had also taken a couple beatings at his hand as Arabs were fans of the "it takes a village to raise a child" theory. I swear to fucking God, if I ever had kids, anyone who touches them will die. I will take the whole village and shove it up their ass.

I must confess as a grown man, I wondered what it would be like to show Eddie how much he helped me to "toughen up." I haven't seen him since I was 17 and frankly, I always made sure to be gone when I knew he was to curse us with a visit. Maybe after making this trip for his family, he'd finally see me as blood or at least a peer. I wasn't expecting it to necessarily make me feel better but it would have been nice to get a thank you but I wasn't living for it. My aunt's gratitude and sweet tears were enough. Besides, he was avoiding contact with everyone since I got there. He was keeping himself in the house he owned there. By this time I had cultivated a healthy disrespect for some of my "elders." Eddie was definitely one of the elders I had zero respect for and while I was a bit conflicted, I was willing to be adult about it.

It was around nine a.m. and overcast when Eddie came up to the second floor balcony where we were eating at Ayoub's house. Ayoub had just come up from the shop to have a bite and some coffee to take a break. He smelled like the fresh lambs' blood on his apron and even though he washed his hands to eat, the blood was still under his nails. To describe this stoop as a balcony would be deceiving. It was really a glorified window sill that was not quite a porch but not much more than a partial outdoor room extension. This was by no means, my Uncle David's house.

Eddie said good morning and started talking to us in both English and Arabic just to be courteous. I ignored him, when he said "good morning" in Arabic, content to eat my food.

He repeated it in English saying, "It's not a good morning cousin?"

"It would be if I was suddenly down the street," I said.

That grin twisted and as usual his eyes were still, dark and quiet. "OK, I see…" he said. Eddie had a buddy with him, named Abdul-Lateef, who also knew my aunt and uncle. I had never even heard his name before but he did speak a little English. He was wearing designer knockoffs, probably from Iraq and even then, his clothes were faded and his sneakers had seen better days.

Maybe I started off badly, went too far. But I didn't feel I should display a fraudulent kindness just because his brother died. If the roles were reversed, I was sure he'd laugh at me for crying for my brother. After all he was supposedly an adult when we met and that didn't quite pull off so my lack of faith in his character had some credence. Moreover, I had just put my life on hold to schlep (a good Yiddish word) his dead brother half way around the world. One would think I would have that going for me.

"So cousin, I hear it got a little tight in Bethlehem the other day. Did you cry? Were you scared?" Eddie smiled with the expressed intention to insult.

"Here it goes," I thought which meant my shitty welcome *was* warranted. But how did he know? I was certain the guys didn't say anything.

I always had this tension when I was about to get in a fight. It was almost like kissing a new girl for the first time and while very different, there was electricity that went through me. I knew she wanted it and I seldom failed in that assessment. That same confidence followed me into a fight. I was always confident once I lost my temper because I was in control but I had to be angry to get to that place where I could beat someone and I hated getting angry. My temper was not one of my sterling qualities and I would scare people. I would always be depressed for a few days after. I didn't behave elegantly when I blew my top and would sometimes be embarrassed for what came out of my mouth. However, I must say in my defense that I never started a fight. I'd just make sure to finish it well, growing up like we did in South Los Angeles in the 1970s. Lately, Derrick, the singer in our band, was good at keeping me in check. Although I did manage to bail him out of a couple of scrapes after some misunderstandings at gigs. This usually would involve women, him being the singer and all.

I put my coffee down and reached for some bread. I could sense Eddie's eyes on me as I dipped it in my yogurt, "No more than you, I guess. Just like everyone else who talks shit in the States. They get here and run when the soldiers come just like fucking rabbits. Cute, fuzzy rabbits…at least that's what I've seen." I sniffed without looking up from my plate.

Eddie just stared and I could see his left hand squeeze his own knee as his right leg bounced up and down.

"So what brings you to breakfast, cousin?" I asked nonchalantly. I didn't take his physical cues too seriously. "I didn't know you were much of a gentleman…" That appreciation thing I thought might happen, got blown out I thought right about then. Pretty obvious.

I had a feeling it wasn't coming anyway as soon as Eddie opened his fucking mouth. He was such a coward and he could never do the right thing even if I had a gun to his kids' heads.

"You're not staying with Ali and your mom, are you? I was just there the other day." I smiled. I loved finally having something on this guy. Something that I could lord over with the same moral superiority that he thought he had with me all those years, except mine was real, "And why are you here? I don't recall giving you permission." After all, he did start it.

"Watch it cousin." Eddie warned, his right leg could churn butter at that point, "Don't make me embarrass you like when you were little…" as he trailed off, something seemed off. I think it was clear to him that I was no longer ten.

I looked up from my plate a couple of times. I eyed him directly, like I was armed, my voice still at a normal volume, breathing slow through my nose, I patiently asked, "You fucking high? How do you say 'fucking high' in Arabic?" I looked to his buddy, getting him in on this too; teach him to "choose your friends well," that sort of thing. "Lateef, is it? How do you say that? 'Fucking high?'…will you say that to my idiot cousin for me, please?" I had no grin. I was not kidding.

Lateef laughed nervously, "I do not know," his English was very formal sounding as they were given an hour a day in school with no time for slang.

Leveling my eyes at him, "Fuckin' A, you know. You fucking know," I was not smiling as I continued with Eddie, "You fucking little shit. Christ, you think you scare me? Fuck you, man. You're a joke." I reached for my coffee, "You rip people off or you're too stupid to do business with. Either way, it's not flattering, man. And while you could apologize, you won't because you're a fucking cunt." I sat back in my chair and sipped it like I was the President of the United States of Motherfucking Me and I wasn't done, "Great performance at the road side the other day. Really too bad the academy wasn't there. You could have won for 'best dipshit on the side of the road category.' That'd be neat."

"You called me what and what?" He asked like he was still the adult in the conversation.

Even though our voices were never raised and there was no yelling, tones are funny. My aunt and uncle spoke no English and even they could tell this wasn't going well. Ayoub said something that started with "Adnan..." because he knew where this was going as well-lived men tend to know these things and ended his piece with a warning sound, "Aagghhh!!!" or something like that and a phrase that I heard a million times from my father. This was after all, my uncle's house and he was going to command respect or the goddamned Arab equivalent! That of course, presupposes that one of the parties is respectful.

When Eddie responded in Arabic, I asked that he speak English. "What's the matter, you don't speak Arabic cousin?" He sneered.

Then this Abdul-Lateef guy pipes in with, "lish?" which rhymed with "wish" and means "why?" in Arabic. He obviously wanted to mix it up too because he did speak English after all. This was his chickenshit way of letting me know he had Eddie's back and I could give a shit. I may as well have been armed, what I would have done to that guy. Eddie started explaining in Arabic that my father failed us boys and all the other ungrateful shit I heard before and couldn't stand. I caught all this from a tone I was familiar with, it wasn't just simple paranoia.

I didn't understand everything but I knew Eddie which led to, "Fuck you, Eddie and your friend too." Calm as the Buddha at a statue convention.

"Cousin, I let that 'cunt' bullshit slide once because Ayoub's here! Don't think I won't beat your ass..." He was clearly operating from when I was ten, when this shit worked. But I ain't ten, no mo'.

"I won't think that. NOT AT ALL!!!" I exploded as I shot up out of my chair and shoved the table to one side, knocking over the remnants of our breakfast, grabbing Eddie by his shirt, popping him out of his seat, like the goddamned useless cork in the shit bottle of wine that he was and held him over the railing bent at his waist. This was done in one move and I even impressed myself as it happened, nerves at full bore. My aunt and uncle were in a panic and two of my cousins ran up the stairs as my aunt was screaming in Arabic and motioning like she was telling the firemen where to go. Lateef was surprised as he got knocked out of his own chair. I'm sure Eddie told him what a pussy I was; what pussies all the American cousins were, Sam included. Lateef, ass on the floor, was shocked at first but did nothing as my cousins clearly had my back. I just loved serendipity because I could not have planned this better. Never underestimate the element of surprise.

Then I could hear Lateef get up as the chair moved but Eddie waved him off, saying something in Arabic, but I wasn't sure if Eddie was taking this seriously yet because he regained that asshole grin like when he came in. His eyes got dark. But I was about to change that. It was serious and I had become a man.

"Take it back, motherfucker!" I growled. It sounded a bit disturbed to me. I was even scared when I thought about it afterwards with concerns of a latent mental disorder. I pushed on him so his back pressed against the railing. He winced and screamed in pain as his eyes welled up a bit, kidneys being sensitive to iron railings and the darkness in his eyes fading into something more human.

"Take what back? Are you fucking crazy?" Eddie was screaming. "I didn't say anything. You don't even speak Arabic! Get off me!!"

"Fuck you! And tell your boy to back off or I swear to fucking Christ, I'll drop your ass!" I was screaming in his face. Eddie had my elbows but my feet were hooked under the railing and gravity would serve me in the end. Lateef backed off after Eddie told him again to do so in Arabic. My cousins were watching and were ready to pounce, anyway. Nice to see I counted for something. Everyone had a grave sense that I was serious. That was a good thing because I was.

"Now apologize!" I inched him closer to the earth, his exposed back scraped the railing. A crowd had gathered to about forty or so.

"Nooooo! For what, man? Please! Have you gone nuts?" His eyes were watering and he was almost crying. He had kids and I felt like I'd be doing them a favor and would save them many years of the same bullshit if I just dropped his useless, Bedouin ass.

"FOR. WHAT. YOU. SAID. ABOUT. MY FATHER!!! ASSHOLE!!!" Each word carried several shakes that got harder and harder for emphasis. Of course, this was all done on a very primal level. All those pent up years, combined with these last few weeks, the bomb in Bethlehem, and Niven were just too much. He really did pick the wrong day. Man, if only this were the next week, I'd have been in such a better mood.

"OK, OK. I'm sorry!" He pleaded, spit on his lips as his back and kidneys were squeezed.

"That's good, dipshit. Now in Arabic!" I screamed with my own spit hitting his cheeks. Saying it Arabic meant they're serious. Anytime on the news, if some Arab leader said something in English, they *might* be serious but if they said it in Arabic it meant they were serious. It was a cultural thing and I didn't question it. This fact would have saved the U.S. 60 years of bad foreign policy.

It dawned on me in that moment, that my father was serious when he cussed at us in Arabic and bullshitting us when he said, "I love you" in English. I was overcome by a sadness that enraged me further when I realized that I was not defending my father at all but simply, finally glad to be doing this to Eddie. I got that this did not make me better than him. It just made us even.

"I said I was sorry, man!" Eddie screamed.

"IN. ARABIC!!!" How many shakes could he take before I set him airborne? That would be a great question on a math quiz. "To my father, by name or I drop your fucking ass right the fuck now!!!"

Eddie apologized in Arabic using the phrase "Abu," which meant "father of" then my name because I was the oldest. This makes it just a tad bit more humiliating because it's my dad, but *my* name. It was kind of like "say my name, bitch" but in Arabic. Rap was only a few years old at that point, but it seems those guys got it from somewhere. I made him say it again, then again and then louder for a fourth time. The crowd had gathered on the street below to about one hundred. Some were giggling, especially the women. There were some men who were walking their calves to slaughter or wheeling vegetables that stopped to watch the commotion. They were outright laughing, teasing Eddie who was by now trying to salvage some shred of machismo.

That village of 3,000 had only two cops and they had a combined age of three hundred years old. One was in France visiting his kids and the Israelis never went back there. Any incident, even with the magnitude of accidental manslaughter, would take days to sort through with memories in the Territories being what they were. Multiply faulty memories by an asshole who accidentally challenged gravity which will square or cube the sum, divided by it could have been an accident and it's easy to get an idea that I wasn't in the United States.

My knees were shaking from the energy. My Uncle approached, putting his hand on my back and quietly said, to me, in Arabic, "Halas, habibi." Now the word, "halas" had double meanings like, "you're done" or "finished," while "habibi," meant "sweetheart." Arabs don't usually say this to their grown sons or nephews unless they're especially proud of something or showing great empathy. Usually, it was said to babies or women who had the feminine, "habibti." I let Eddie go…

But I didn't drop him. He regained his composure and the darkness, albeit faded with being shaken, returned to his eyes. He wasn't expecting me that morning. He straightened his shirt as he shook off his fear and he looked at me like he was going to throw down, his fixed grin coming on his face like bird shit on a bus stop.

"Don't, man," I said quietly. "I'll fucking kill you."

Through clenched teeth, Eddie murmured, "We'll see…"

"I guess we will," I grinned while my eyes did not. I learned I could do that too.

Ayoub barked, "Yallah!! Imshih!!" This translated to "get going" or "get the fuck out," depending on the tone. He took Eddie by the elbow, ushering him out, waving his free hand in the air, screaming different cuss words in Arabic. I was at least familiar with these as my dad was glad to share those with us kids. Abdul Lateef followed after him, looking at me like he could kill. I returned the stare, as I would throw him over the railing and not flinch at all. He wasn't family, so fuck him! I looked to my aunt and two cousins but they were busy looking at the wretched refuse making their exit. Ayoub had his reasons to side with me; Eddie's mom was Ayoub's sister too and Eddie made no secret of the crap he pulled on me and others, openly bragging over the years.

Family could be strange because mine was not father of the year. Not by a long shot. He was a guy, for better or worse, who did what he had to do raising us boys and he pretty much sucked at it and mostly because he was not a good man. But what does it say about me to let this lifetime shithead run over my father with his cowardly bullshit and after all that was done for him and smiling the whole way like the chickenshit phony he was? He gave not one nickel to get Mahmoud's ass over here. Not a cent! So not on my watch, dick.

Even though I knew in my heart that it was more about me than any real family honor, I stood there at the balcony and looked at the small crowd as they dispersed to their homes, getting their days started, caring less and less, faster and faster. I didn't mind. I addressed the deserting crowd like a conquering hero because I thought it funny, "Well... GOOD MORNING, DERDUWAN!!!" I screamed without the slightest bit of sarcasm, shaking off the last of any jitters. Then I looked down at the corner two doors down. Sam was there and he was smiling with his arms folded then he waved and walked off.

As I got a mop, my aunt came back upstairs. I could hear Ayoub in the shop laughing it up with the customers, chatting in Arabic about the recent altercation on the stoop. I heard a loud "BAM!" someone must have slammed the counter with his fist, maybe doing an impression of Eddie, had I released him into the sky. My aunt tried to help me clean but I shook my head no. She sat and watched while my other cousin came in carrying a tray with coffee and a pitcher of water with glasses. I rebuffed his offer to help as well.

****

"I shouted out, 'Who killed the Kennedys?'/when after all, it was you and me..."

Later that day, Sam and I went to see Jamal. The timing seemed right to leave and get some air elsewhere. I was also ready to get that plane ticket to Copenhagen. The land of Hamlet was looking pretty good right about then. We went into Ramallah and after the requisite maneuvering through the traffic, shoppers and occasional loose dog; we parked behind one of the university buildings as the street was jammed. Calling the college in Ramallah anything more than a collection of office buildings would be deceiving but it was where folks went to school. Sam and me walked around and chatted. Dodging some milky puddles and making our way through the teeming bodies, trying to shop for food, I stuck my head into some of the shops and I picked up some scarves and Arab gold for my mom. I had tons of gifts to take back from the family but I wanted something from me to my mom.

We crossed the street to the Alhambra Palace Hotel. We went in and just dug on the vibe. It was almost all white stone. Built in the 1920s, this place was still quite the landmark despite its youth. Compared to everything else in the region, this place was a Holiday Inn, age-wise. The lobby and restaurant had old wood walls and huge overstuffed European chairs all over and even in the smoking areas. Frankly, I was surprised that it was still standing, given the circumstances of the last forty years yet it was a tad run down. We were in the courtyard which was lush with pines and fig trees. Jasmine shrubs were all over and the smell was intoxicating. I would always drive home at night in the spring and summer in Pasadena with the car window open. I'd then leave the window open in my room and the smell outside and our house would comfort me as I fell asleep.

Sam asked, "You smoke cigars?"

"Not for a while…" I didn't want to say it but I had pulled away from my father which, oddly enough, included cigars. He liked cigars, taught me about them. He would chew on one for what seemed like hours before he lit it. He'd walk around the store, chatting up customers, go to another one of his businesses, and then light up around lunch either before or after he ate. I liked the aroma but as I got older, I worked at carving my own niche out in the world, even if it did mean giving up something I liked. Then I thought about it a minute, took in a quick reflection of the morning and having defended the family honor which led to a "Fuck-him-it's-my-cigar!" moment, to quote the poet. "I'm cool if they're good, man," my little epiphany was had. Giving up on them had been such a poseur ruse in the first place.

Sam grinned, "You'll enjoy this." He asked the suited concierge if Mohammed was working the humidor and he was. The humidor was huge and the wood walls had absorbed an awful lot of cigars over the years. There's nothing like that smell. We went in and picked a couple of Cubans that you could actually get there. Mohammed was around twenty and wore a white shirt and black bow tie with black pants. He had 18yr old Lagavulin whiskey that he kept behind the counter for his friends and preferred customers. It wasn't permitted there either, so he poured it in espresso cups and while not quite Lebanese pot in an alley, it did hold its own unique charm nonetheless.

We sat in the smoking room, just off to the side of the humidor and puffed. It was more like a library reading room with fans in the windows turned backwards to blow the smoke away from the hotel. Cigars were an elegant pleasure I committed to in that for about forty minutes I wasn't going anywhere except for my chair with my cigar. This was unlike like cigarettes which one could smoke while taking a crap in the woods. We chatted about music, sports and Sam asked about my musical equipment. I told him about my '59 Gibson Les Paul and my '72 black Rickenbacker double bound S360 guitars and my Ludwig five piece drum kit with Zildjian cymbals which were still made in Turkey.

"It sounds like you really like the American guitars, eh?" Sam asked through the smoke curling out of his mouth. "How come?"

"I guess because anybody who I think is cool plays them. But you can really tell, man; the sound." Then I added. "Fact is I just write songs on them anyway. It shouldn't matter because I'm the drummer in my band but if the guitar is cool, you'll want to play it more."

Sam seemed genuinely impressed by this, "Well, it sounds like you know what you want. You talk like you know what you're doing."

"Well, I know what to do," I offered. "Dunno if it's the same thing as actually knowing what I'm doing." I held up my right hand in quotes and grinned as I put down my drink and reached for my cigar.

Sam talked about college. There seemed to be sadness as he expressed those to be "the best years in his life."

"So far, right?" I offered.

He looked up and said, "Yeah, so far." His face seemed heavy.

He talked about his kids; they were five and three at the time. "Yeah, funerals bring things into focus, you know? Fuck I don't know what I'd do if I lost my kids. Mahmud's thing was tough and even Bethlehem the other day." He shook his head like he swallowed spoiled food, "With all this shit happening and even comparing here to the States, I still take it all for granted and the whole thing could go up tomorrow. Today, even." Maybe the whisper argument the other night with Nina had something to do with these realizations.

"Yeah, man. I guess we just get stuck in our own little zone," I offered.

"So that was quite impressive this morning," Sam shifted gears, snapping out of his blues, puffing out smoke rings.

"I guess." I was not particularly proud of it. The sad side was dawning; losing my temper reminded me of my father, exactly like my father. But it was always nice to know I could kick ass if I had to. I'd rather be the asshole than the victim but a certain shame would always come on after the fact. During the rage, I was invincible, reflexes were sharp but it was a double edged sword, sadly.

"Remind me not to get on your bad side." Sam chuckled.

"You do know it was stupid, right?" I asked, staving off any gloating. "He could have been carrying a knife. Fucker could have stabbed me." Upon a quick deliberation, "He would have stabbed me. Wouldn't think twice."

"Yeah, but he didn't!" Sam offered cheerfully. "Whatever, man! He's a fucking asshole! He's had it coming for *yeeeaaaaars...*" Sam's head reeled back as he said the word, "years." Then he went on, "and what better guy to give it to him? What better situation? Here? That was fucking great." He just smirked, shaking his head at the thought, "Timing is everything." He sipped the whiskey in his espresso cup.

We finished and went to see Jamal. "Hey Cassius Clay!" This would be Muhammad Ali's former name, before his conversion to Islam in the 1960s. Interesting how he didn't call me Muhammad Ali. Arabs, on the whole weren't crazy about name changes. They thought it showed disrespect to ones' family. Jamal shook his head and smiled broadly as he came out from behind his money changer window, "Heard you kicked some ass today!"

I was a little embarrassed but news travelled fast, "Yeah, I guess...Hey man; I'm ready for that ticket to Denmark?" Jamal was overtaken with sudden concern which concerned me, "What? You look weird, dude."

"When were you thinking of leaving?" He asked. "Because there's rumor of a general strike, you know? Everything will be shut down...no curfews even." Jamal looked like he found a turd in his soup.

"I was thinking 3 days? You can still get me that deal, right? Copenhagen?" I asked.

"I am the deal, man!" he chuckled. "It's always good."

The problem would be getting out of the Territories in the event of a general strike. This would mean zero curfews and everything was shut down. It would be a good idea to book the flight for ten or eleven in the morning, that way if the strike went down, I would leave the house at 3 am, a full eight hours before my flight even though it was in the dead of night but at least I'd get there. Unless I was being watched, it was highly unlikely anyone would bother me. Maybe soldiers at checkpoints would stop me but they'd be cool being that I was an American with a passport. I could easily convey that I was just trying to get the hell out of there. All of this planning to travel just ninety minutes to the airport. This, sure as shit, wasn't L.A.

I asked why Tel Aviv, so Jamal explained, "If you get marked as a collaborator for travelling during a strike, they'll chase you into Jordan but they won't chase you into Israel," He said. "We also have to find you a cab driver that will do it and it could run $500."

This was 1988 money which was a lot, which led to, "Well shit, can you call in a favor? That's a lot for a cab ride, man."

Jamal said not to worry. They may not call a strike but he'd have it handled. So I booked the ticket. I had to get back. I had to resume my destiny as it were.

But I'm here now…

So Sam and I drove over to the Dome. He said that we should enjoy what time we had left, "You can't really explain this to people who haven't been…like telling a Martian what chocolate tastes like."

I agreed and even though I wanted to get back to L.A. and at some points wished I hadn't left at all, the concession had to be made that this was a very different experience than I thought it'd be. I was glad to have met some family that I should have met sooner. I was told so much different shit about this place by the media, family, church, whatever.

Had things been different, I would have told my brothers and other cousins to come here, regardless of the good, bad or ugly. I found out a lot about myself in a roots kind of way. Having people know who you were, without being the odd guy out was kind of liberating. I didn't speak the language, but this treatment felt familiar. Not perfect, just familiar. In the end, L.A. was my home and America was my country.

We drove into Jerusalem and after the requisite dodging of cabbies, and assorted cranky people, we parked in back of the Dome after taking a shortcut this time. We ate lunch and Sam had some office work to do so I went for a walk.

"Don't do anything dumb, man. This is no movie." Sam admonished as I left. He was right; there was talk of a general strike, Bethlehem was high on the list of concerns, the troops were visibly tense and this was the first outing I was taking without either Sam or Ali. That, coupled with a foreboding that anything's possible that could kill me or land me in jail without notice added to Sam's fatherly instinct kicking in. But fuck it. I was going to be careful but

I was going to be myself. Sam furrowed his brow after I let some air out of my face trying to affect a degree of machismo as I left the Dome.

I walked over a couple of blocks and the streets were packed. Jerusalem had just opened for the day but two hours goes by fast so people were out in force. Israeli troops roamed the streets but walked in the street and avoided the sidewalks. Periodically, an old woman would lunge at a soldier with a knife so they had to be careful. The soldiers tried to remain as neutral as one could here but it was tough. I was at that point very much over it and I wasn't there but a couple weeks.

I grabbed an English speaking cabbie and got a ride to Nablus. He asked if I was American.

"Don't I look Arabiya?" I smiled.

Omar, the cabbie, smiled, "No my friend, you do not. You look to the Jewish." His accent didn't get in the away of his English too badly.

I told him my name and showed him my passport, "There you go, man. See? Not 'to the Jewish'." The humor was lost on him as he smiled and told me to get in. It was a messy cab but he had a meter so good for him.

The ride to Nablus was a bit calmer than going into Jerusalem from Ramallah. The traffic was less hectic and the town itself seemed a bit cleaner as well. There were fewer cars but the streets were teeming with people, tents for the open air market with produce and meats and the smells of cooking. The restaurants were clashing with street vendors for aroma supremacy. The architecture was mostly done by the Turks as they occupied Nablus most of the time until the 1920s. The Great Mosque of Nablus had a tall tower and while nothing like the Dome, was still impressive.

I walked around and found the old Turkish baths but there were no Turks in them, however. This place looked more together despite how many times it had been hit with disasters both natural and manmade. I walked down Nablus Road. I got a picture of the street sign that looked like the Abbey Road sign on the back of the Beatles album with the same blue tile except for the large bullet holes. I saw vendors and the mosque there. I walked for a while, feeling overwhelmed with wanting go home while I was taking back with me a sense of completion of every past, every future.

It was sudden, as epiphanies could be and it dawned on me that I had enough enlightenment, death, and anger.

I grabbed another cab and went back to Jerusalem. This guy's English wasn't as good as Omar's and we even had a dispute over the cab fare. He went a little out of the way and I knew enough to know he was juicing me for more money same as in New York, the fucker. I avoided getting arrested by paying him. The soldiers would have gotten involved and it would cost me more than it would to pay this guy. I asked to be dropped off at the Dome of the Rock. The place was sacred because supposedly, Mohammed ascended to heaven from this spot, flesh and bone on a horse. Sacred didn't ring much with me much but it was interesting to know. I walked around the "campus," if that is what it was called. The back side overlooked the Mount of Olives and I stood there awhile and just stared at the Jewish graveyard. It was funny because there were homes right behind it, facing the Dome of the Rock.

But between us, was a rocky field, 150 yards long or so. It was a no man's land and was pretty close for being the burial place of your so called enemies. One couldn't choose these things any more than one could choose relatives. Why one fairy tale was better than another was beyond me. Lots of things were beyond me at that point.

The famous gangster Meyer Lansky could not be buried in the Mount of Olives per orders of the Israeli Government and Prime Minister Golda Meir. He was best known for being the cleanest guy in the American Mafia, their "accountant."

Charlie "Lucky" Luciano died in exile, in Italy. Benjamin "Bugsy" Siegel got his eyeball blown out in Los Angeles over a bad set of troubles founding Las Vegas as a young man. Frank Costello was able to die of a heart attack in his 80's. Alas, poor Meyer, he wanted so bad to be buried in the Mount of Olives. He loved the State of Israel so much and gave her so much money but it didn't matter. The Israelis didn't look at the Mafia like the Italians did, Catholics being more forgiving and the Vatican cashing those fat checks. Yet Israel cashed Lansky's check donations regardless and while Jews enjoyed the "right of return" as a rule, it was not afforded Mr. Lansky. He was allowed to visit, however. Even his last attempt with a million dollar check was too blatant to be accepted. He probably died the most broken hearted of the big four Murder Inc. bosses. Karma, as the saying goes, is a bitch, being a clean accountant notwithstanding.

It was weird to think as he stood in the Mount of Olives that he stared at where I was standing at that moment like a ghost. I wanted to be cremated in America and in the end, it wouldn't matter.

As I walked back to the restaurant, I came around the front of the mosque. I crossed the street which was full of people and sidewalk vendors and people buying food for dinner. The smells and sounds were everywhere. Corner falafel guys were selling their shwarma, ice cream vendors were pushing their carts, and people were bumping into one another, like pinballs in a game. The place felt like the rest of Jerusalem.

In the middle of the hustle, I saw a 12 year old boy get stopped by Israeli soldiers and I could tell that they asked for his shoes because they made the same motion they made with me but the kid yelled something at them in Arabic that translated basically, to "Suck my dick, bitch!" or the expletive laden equivalent. He was waving his hands like an old shop keeper, haggling with his customer over fig prices or soccer stats. The escalating of the tensions got the crowd to part like Moses and the Red Sea yet no one stepped in to break it up.

Two of the soldiers flipped the boy on his back and ripped his shoes off his feet, while the other beat his bare feet with a baton. It was fast and it was brutal and there seemed to be no concern for his age but he was just a boy.

Eddie and Abdul Lateef were uncovering the truck loaded with the heroin that they left in an abandoned farm house just north of Bethlehem. Lateef kidded Eddie about the events of the morning. Eddie did not find humor and warned Lateef to shut up.

In Arabic, Lateef asked, "Do you think he knows? He was in Bethlehem talking to Niven, right? If he knows then who else does?" Niven was the dead minister in Bethlehem.

Eddie told him not to worry, that he has it handled. Eddie looked over sternly and said, "Sam and Ali have no idea. That much I know and this morning only happened because my little cousin thinks he's a man. But Niven could have said something which maybe gave him some courage at my uncle's house. The Christians talked to quite a few people I think."

Lateef said, "If that's the case, well...I can fix this," he nodded solemnly as he got in the truck and Eddie followed in his car and they headed toward Lebanon. The Lebanese border was porous and the perfect place for them to make their drop. From there, it would go to Turkey and Europe, mostly France and Italy. Some would get sold by dealers in Lebanon and Turkey but heroin wasn't the big trade that pot was locally so it would be sold to further middle men.

As the kid's beating began, I ducked into a small dress shop and peered out the window between dresses. The frocks smelled new but the place was musty and probably no bigger than my aunt's living room, the cashier being right by the door. She was in back or something when I ducked in there. The dresses were mostly unspectacular knockoffs and factory seconds. She had a few of the embroidered dresses like my aunts had. A small crowd had gathered back from scattering as a fourth soldier stood guard and kept the watchers at bay with his rifle; stabbing at the air and screaming "Imshih," the same Arabic term for "get the fuck out of here"; Ayoub told Eddie that morning. The saleslady ran from the back and stood at the doorway, staring. Apparently, she didn't hear the little bell as I walked in.

The people seeing it was a beating as opposed to a shootout must have felt safer because they came back to watch. The boy screamed his fucking guts out as tears flooded his face and his friends and old ladies yelled at the guards. He was trying to reach up and punch the soldiers holding his feet but they had him at an awkward angle so he couldn't reach. It would have mattered little, anyway. He was about one hundred pounds. A couple of older cleric guys ran out of the Dome of the Rock and yelled at the soldiers to stop. But this failed dramatically. They stopped when they were done and not because they were chastised by Arabs.

I am ten years old. Eddie is visiting our house again, waiting for my mom to finish making dinner. I'm sitting on the floor watching a "Batman" rerun. Eddie is sitting on the couch, reading the paper, also watching the show, glancing up, periodically from the Times.

The show had a "Batgirl," who was some built for speed sex kitten in a tight, purple outfit. Eddie looks up from his paper and says, "Wow! Is that what you like, cousin?" Maybe it was, but at ten, I wasn't copping to shit.

"I dunno." I said. I hadn't even really admitted I liked girls yet and I'm fucking ten!

"Yeah, you do...or maybe you're a fag? Do you like it in the ass, cousin? Your dad know?" Eddie sneered.

It had been a year of this shit and even though he had smacked me a few times before, I still wasn't truly afraid of him. While possibly a lack of common sense, on my part, fear also involves a degree of respect and this was not someone I respected. Hate on the other hand, "Dude, you're a pig." I said without turning around.

"What did you say?" Eddie was incredulous.

So I repeated myself, "You're a pig, dude." Having got the term from my hippie, feminist, fifth grade teacher who said that all the time. She said both "pig" and "dude." She was also a built for speed sex kitten who wore tweed jackets, tight jeans and turtleneck sweaters. I caught her smoking a cigar once after school and it was sexy...

I heard footsteps and I thought Eddie was going into the kitchen but he walked over and flipped me on my back and started beating the shit out of me, screaming curse words in Arabic, using his fists. Sometimes kids cry for effect when adults spank them but this fucker was using his fists and knocking the wind out of me, hitting me in the ribs.

My father came running into the room, pulling Eddie off me. When Eddie, in Arabic, told dad that I called him a pig, my dad freaked! You don't call Arab Muslims "pig," ever, for anything! My dad then hit me too, my insistence that Eddie called me a "fag" fell on deaf ears and I was told to go to my room. Working to hold back sobs, the tears came anyway as I closed the door. That beating fucking hurt and I still couldn't tell which part of this debacle was worse. I was ten. I was supposed to trust these people, these adults.

Eddie smiled that day as he stood behind my father. Cocksucker. Maybe I was too nice that morning on the stoop. Maybe I should have dropped him.

When it was over, the boy's friends put him on their handlebars on one of the bikes to take him home. Another rode his own bike holding his friend's bike by the handlebars, balancing himself as best he could. The poor kid was sobbing badly, like my aunt at the funeral. His feet may even have been broken, they looked real swollen and he couldn't get his shoes back on so one of the other kids carried them under his arm as well. I couldn't imagine what ran through his father's mind as he saw his son come home humiliated like that. But shit, the kid stood his ground at twelve. His dad would have to be at least proud. Me? I was hiding in a fucking dress shop and reminiscing my own defeats. Shame on me but this was the Territories. It was the poet who said, "The sound of gunfire, off in the distance, I'm getting used to it now..."

My little victory that morning was sullied a bit so it seems my humility was for naught. I was still in the dress store and ten minutes must have passed as the sales lady just stared out the door, looking at the crowd conducting the post mortem with someone on the phone, the old, knotted up phone cord stretched to capacity. I don't think she even knew I was there.

I was numb.

And on it would go. Israel "protecting" herself from civilians was a bit lopsided yet they wondered why the Arabs called it "occupation." Jewish settlers attacked little Arab kids with clubs going to school and wondered why they were called religious extremists. Arabs attacked Israeli civilians, killing their kids, blowing up buses and hospitals and they wondered why they're called "barbarians" and "monsters." The Arabs wondered why their religion was so misunderstood when it was clear that on both sides of this shit God had little to do with humanity being human.

Again, this was for what? I had asked myself that question a lot. They say it was for religion but I doubted that more and more. Sure, to the masses, that was the sales pitch but the guys who ran the show could give a shit. The proof was in front me. This was for some to have more. The time had come to put away the bed time stories about 1947, 1982, last Sunday, who the fuck cares and move on.

I realized that in America we could afford the free press *and* the Mercedes. Other countries, who have to make a choice, always take the Mercedes. If things got that bad in the States, we would do the same thing. Americans and the West were so precious to think democracy was paramount to greed but it wasn't. Sad thing was I first heard that theory about the free press in a movie in college but I didn't take it serious. It was a comedy. Many a true thing has been said in jest but I was on the verge of a breakdown, suddenly, violently. I worked to keep the sales lady from noticing me as I walked out breathing heavy. Something went click and I think I snapped but I didn't know how. It wasn't visible.

Somebody benefits from all this shit and as sure as I stood in a fucking dress shop, hoping to not get shot, I knew it wasn't the people. I was to leave in a couple days. So there's that.

Chapter 6-The Road to Canaan

The commotion was quelled as I left the dress shop but one guy started to get a chant going. Others joined in and it started to look bleak as there was only one way this was going to go. As I walked back to Sam's place I had my hands shoved into the pockets of my Levis. I was strangely thankful that a Jew got to America in the 1800s, took a French fabric and made jeans out of them. This did not reduce my eagerness to get off the street or the shame I felt as I believed that every old lady and little kid were staring at me. They were staring because maybe I could have done something to help that boy and I didn't. I guess I could have also gotten shot or thrown in jail and we wouldn't want that. Maybe I was too selfish to think this also was not *my* fight, either. The street glided past me and it didn't feel like I was walking. I began to zone out a bit. Feeling like shit is never easy.

I got back to the Dome and it was busy which snapped me out of my stupor. Sam said we were shutting down, that curfew got called early because of the beating and the "students" were coming. I knew that chanting guy was trouble. I went downstairs and waited my turn to shoot pool with some of the locals. Sam wasn't kicking anyone out just yet but he was also not letting anyone in and sending his workers home in this situation may not have been a good idea.

 Even though I was in a funk, I was kind of hoping to run into Karly again, having returned to the scene of the lust but I imagine that train has left the station. These guys, playing pool, were cool. They were probably about 15 or so but they were trying hard to act 25. Both were smoking, one was wearing an overcoat, affecting a really bad mullet, attempting a version of Bono that hadn't existed for awhile.

Mullet man was wearing a t-shirt of some euro trash band that I sort of recall hating while the other was wearing a Creeping Charlie t-shirt, an American band I was familiar with and they actually didn't suck. I was quite surprised to see an American rock band on a t-shirt and not some crap assed pop group, Michael Jackson or Madonna. A real rock and roll band with a fan in the Territories was kind of a novelty. The kids themselves seemed like good dudes. I called to play the winner. Ahmed was the kid in the Creeping Charlie shirt, mullet man was named Samir. Both spoke decent English, in that I could understand them, and were giving each other a real hard time both in English and Arabic. I think the English was more for my benefit which was fine.

Ahmed, the taller one, shot his own two balls into two pockets at once but then the cue ball followed. This was a "scratch" in the parlance of the game which meant the person who scratched has to pull out one of the balls and lose a turn despite making the shots. His euphoria soured into a palpable disgust, "Ah...Fuck the shit!" Ahmed shouted with histrionic anger his right hand in the air. I thought he was doing this to show off his bad boy, American Attitude which I found humorous as I grinned, Samir just laughed.

I gently suggested, "Hey man, I don't think that's an expression." He looked a little embarrassed and Samir pointed and said something in Arabic that made his friend's face a little red.

I smiled, trying to coach the lad and said, "'Fuck' or 'shit' alone is good enough or you can say, 'fuck *that* shit,'" I thought the specificity would help clarify as to which shit it was that you actually prefer to get fucked, or be the focus of one's attention. Too bad I couldn't teach a class in this.

Ahmed smiled, "Thanks to you, my friend, sucran (shoo-krahn)" Then he turned his wrath on Samir, saying something like "shut the fuck up," in Arabic. Samir just looked down and kept laughing as it was obvious he has been down this button pushing road before. Success was his again as he giggled, holding out his hand saying, "Shubuck masaree," which was Arabic for, "give me money," apparently winning a bet. This struck me as being cute, oddly enough; like watching my younger brother and his friends. After watching a beat down, soaking in guilt and confusion, I could use a little comic relief.

Suddenly I was not in the mood for pool at all. It wasn't the kids fault, as I just got real anxious all of a sudden and felt like being outside. I went upstairs into the kitchen and it was slammed with orders going out and burgers frying with the pizza oven on full blast. I told Sam I needed a beer. I asked to go on the roof. Sam said I could but I had to be cool about it so he gave me a couple of paper bags. I walked in the cooler and took several bottles, putting a couple in my jacket pockets.

I sat on the roof and stared out over the ancient city, drinking. What was neat about this was the roof was surrounded by a wall so no one could really see me from the street but it came off like a huge porch. The overall cool of this was not lost on me as I was drinking an Israeli beer in the Holy Land. In the States, we got wet over the Liberty Bell or Washington Monument. This place was thousands of years old and was more or less, the same. There was no Homeowners Association to ensure that the apartments all looked alike. Here, it was the mayor's job to simply collect taxes, administer the bread and, for Chrissakes, don't get fucking shot. This was not so much a source of any real concern on my part. Not like I was planning on running for office or even knew the Mayor but it seemed like common sense. Looking over the city, I felt like the human race was never going to change and that suddenly saddened me. I was 23 and already thought the human race to be a conspiracy. Jews, Arabs, it didn't matter if it was there, in the Territories or back home with old fashioned red, brown, black and white racism as the same old shit was simply happening over and over. It had for an eternity before I was born and it just didn't look like it was going to ever get better in the next eternity. It's just what people do. Dying was easy, comedy was hard, and no one cared to be funny.

Dusk was settling on the city. The sun falling behind the Dome of the Rock was post card perfect; the golden Dome shone like a big, mystic bowling ball, rays of light sparkling and dancing along the edges like I was crossing over from the dark side of the moon.

I stood with my elbows on the wall and sipped my beer. It was my second. This would have been cooler if Karly was here. Why was I thinking so much about her? I was thinking more about this girl than I did about Shelly, *ever,* and we knew each other for over a year before we dated. She never got me and I had to explain everything I said but Karly definitely knew what was up. She looked at me the whole time at Sam's and I wondered if she was a virgin? She was raised in what I would call a pretty "straight" environment so how serious was she about all that God and Christian stuff? Where did spirituality and sex get separated anyway? How did controlling that come to determine my soul's salvation? I was beginning to believe they were one in the same, a joyous communion between two people, that errant piece of ass after a gig, notwithstanding. If love were involved that could be the religion of the two of us and our bed would be where service was held.

I heard trucks and shouting, stomping feet, marching feet, sticks beating on the cobblestone and trash cans, chants to egg the Israeli Army on in Arabic. It was loud. I peered over the edge of the roof and saw the students coming down the street as the pedestrians were clearing out, catching cabs and buses on the different corners of the block. Shop keepers up and down the street were closing up fast. Time to get the fuck out of Dodge or at least sit tight in your shop until Dodge went home. Through the trap door in the roof I could hear some of Sam's guys yelling in Arabic, chasing the customers out the back door into the alley so as to not shove them into the oncoming skirmish out front. I could see Samir and Ahmed in the crowd as they were all moving away and down the alley moving in opposite directions. The humor had left the eyes of these boys and their break was over, back on the clock, as it was.

The front door was bolt locked shut and I could feel the vibration of the security cage making its run along the roof coming down the front of the building at my feet. Sam stuck his head up through the trap door, "Hey man, you're cool here. Just don't get made, alright? This shit's no joke." The workers left in the restaurant were in there for awhile. May as well clean up.

I nodded, strangely calm as I pulled on my beer and looked over the edge of the roof. I could see the Jews coming down the other end of the street. An Israeli unit, in full riot gear, was followed by a troop truck that rolled down the street and stopped. They stared down the students who initially numbered around fifty but their numbers were increasing behind them. The students stopped yelling as the Israelis neared the middle of the block.

Most of the soldiers, except for the officers, were almost all in their teens and 20s. The students or protesters was more like it, seemed to range in age from 15 to 40. From where I stood, I was a little behind the students so I could only see the faces of the soldiers. Some of them looked scared, while some looked ready, real ready, and I'm sure the same could be said for the Arabs though they were seemingly unarmed and I could only really see the backs of their heads. I'm sure the same human qualities were exhibited by them as well.

The lead soldier said something in Arabic to the effect of "clear out" and that this was a matter being investigated by the authorities and all the other official shit people got used to hearing in these kinds of scenarios to the point of inoculation from any logic of the lie. Kid got his feet broken and everyone saw it, end of "investigation" really. There was an old saying that goes, "There's three sides to every story; yours, mine and the truth." I found that this was, more often than not, employed by lawyers, liars and assholes. In some instances, it was all three simultaneously.

The Arabs seemed to share this view as one threw a rock and hit a soldier in the helmet. Before the captain or whatever rank he was could keep his guys cool, many of them opened fire. Another soldier shouted out something that resulted in a formation of some of the troops moving toward the Arabs and firing their weapons. This got out of control fast. Their precision was scary and the situation was escalating. I could see that there was something about boots and guns that just made men move different and I was just watching.

The Arabs in front of the pack dropped like bags of hammers holding their legs or ribs, screaming, crying and cursing. Others, still standing, started screaming obscenities, hurling rocks and bricks, trying their best to dodge the rubber bullets ducking behind cars and trashcans. I grew concerned because rubber bullets bounce and I didn't want to have my eye shot out for being a spectator but my concern never turned nervous. The calm was almost disturbing me but I was too zoned out to care. Should I have been alarmed? I didn't feel near as bad as watching the kid get beaten by the Dome. These were adults walking into a fight. The kid was basically minding his own business. These guys did not need my help. That kid could have used mine. I had no sense of guilt or responsibility here as I was just watching and drinking beer like I was watching television. Maybe this was a uniquely American reaction that is, until someone loses an eye.

The troops moved forward in unison, firing their guns and dodging rocks and bottles. Some stepped on the necks of a couple of the lead Arabs, keeping them pinned, while some of the soldiers cuffed and arrested the other fallen and dumped them all in the troop truck, beating them with batons as they loaded them in. As the troops continued firing, most of the Arabs fled while the tougher, more seasoned protesters held their ground behind parked cars and the like. All they had were sticks, rocks and garbage and not one of them pulled a gun.

As the remaining students were rounded up and hauled off, I noticed a couple photographers that I assume, caught the whole thing on film. I was curious to see how this would pan out in the paper the next day. The proverbial smoke cleared while I sat on the roof and realized that I was on my third beer and that it all seemed to happen very fast.

Pretty buzzed and sure glad I was going home.

I was looking forward to Denmark. Looking forward to a mindless, mellow time which was something these guys, on either side, weren't really able to do. Violence and crime did have an effect on leisure. At the end of the day, that's all it really was despite any euphemisms like uprising or self-defense and both sides were guilty. I was just watching the whole time, with the feeling that this was not my home. Maybe it was a residual shock over Niven that left me numb to regular old beatings, I don't know. Should I have felt guilt over that?

I just wanted to get back into a rhythm, go back to work and band practice. I wanted to call Karly and take her out. Go to a cool seafood place I knew in

Ventura, on the pier where we could walk afterwards, make out and giggle and I could smell her hair again, just for starters.

Sam and I went back to the village after the ruckus and I got dinner at their house. Sam had offered to do the cooking and opened a bottle of red wine. He had a case of 1982 Larose-Trintaudon, Haut Medoc that he bought from a food vendor in Tel Aviv before the Intifada got going. Nectar of the gods that stuff, and tasted even better drinking it in my dad's village. We sat in the living room and drank as Sam got food ready. Nina and I had a nice little chat and laugh about back home in California and who was doing what to whom.

"How's your dad?" She asked.

"Well, you know…" What to say? He's a fucking prick but that's not polite conversation.

"My father said something once about your father that I have tried to take as a life lesson," Nina continued.

My father serving as a lesson to anyone made me curious, "Really? Well? What was it?" I grinned looking into my wine glass. Her father was older than my father by quite a few years.

"He said that your father was not capable of being happy, that you boys could be full blooded Arab, speak Arabic, practice Islam with little Arab babies and he'd still be miserable…that he'd been that way since he was little." Nina continued softly, "So what I'm trying to say is that I hope you don't feel guilty living your life. Your father's a battle you can never win."

"No, I don't. I'd feel worse trying to be like being like my father. Hell, he's not even like my father," I chuckled. I had not looked up at her but at that moment I felt like God was speaking through her even though magic tricks and burning bushes had not been his thing for awhile. I had to hear that and it was nice to know that someone outside was looking in and actually gave a shit.

I could tell that Nina was a little tense. She didn't bring up Bethlehem so I wasn't sure that was the issue and while she kept the conversation encouraging, something seemed off. I didn't know if she and Sam had a fight or maybe she did hear us talking about true love and Kelly the other night, who knows?

After dinner, I thanked them for the evening and Sam suggested we walk the road to Canaan the next day. "It's your last day here," he said.

"That'd be great, man." I really meant it too. It had been a sad few days...

****

"Out here in the perimeter there are no stars/Out here we is stoned/Immaculate."

The next day, we started off for the road to Canaan. I had a backpack with some lunch that my aunt made for both of us. Ali had begged off, he really wanted to hang out with his mom. I think it was more her, than anything but he was in no mood to argue. He knew I was leaving the next day and he was cool with it. He owned a small chain of parking lots that ran themselves for the most part, so he didn't have to get back right away. But I still had a job. Also, I think that while we all got along, he was still more Arab than American and not in some ignorant asshole way, either. He was a good man but Sam was worldly and could straddle the cultures with relative ease, despite his being too American for some Arab tastes, maybe Ali's. Naturally, I felt more at ease and could hang with Sam because he was more like my buddies and band mates back home.

Behind some butcher shop, Eddie and Lateef met with some Arabs in Ramallah who were known to ferret out collaborators and deal with them. Lateef grew up with one of the guys and he set the meeting up. Eddie was working to rat me out as a traitor. He never thought that, the bastard, but he was convinced that I was going to blow his heroin trade, nonetheless. I guess the episode on the balcony probably did little to endear him to the issue of my safety or survival but fuck him.

To the Arabs he was meeting with, things like facts or being real fucking certain matter little if you really enjoy teaching "evil doers" a lesson. These guys could get real creative as only psychos can. Not all the accused were innocent and that was understood so their duplicity was not lost on me. I get treachery, especially among your own people but these guys would find any reason to do this because they're fucking nuts and they actually enjoy this line of work. Using God and country to justify it is to be possessed of the paramount hypocrisy. Every army has guys who enjoy the job a little too much. Heads got broken and God didn't seem to mind. It's like watching a pastor do a sermon on hell and not get emotional or at least weepy. Watch out for that guy.

The Road to Canaan kept the same not-too-much-change-in-two-thousand-years vibe as most things did there. There were some paved parts of the road and that was about it as far as innovation went. The same hundreds of olive trees flanked either side of the road, same as when Jesus walked it going to Canaan. Farmers could let livestock graze and not get in any trouble whatsoever. This region wasn't necessarily owned and while it was still occupied the olives were up for grabs. There were some scattered folks picking olives to jar. There was nothing in the world like home made, pickled olives. They were just so goddamned amazing. Don't know if it's the whole garlic, chili peppers and limes or overall good vibe that they're made with but they ruled. It didn't seem to matter what kind of shit was going down because when people made food, things just felt a little better.

If this were the States, there would be no olive trees and mini malls would be up along with office buildings. Of course there would be the New Canaan Shopping Emporium, New Canaan High School, New Canaan Ford, in addition to a host of other New Canaan based things with a flood of tract homes and a home owners association. Why, I could see the commercial now;

"Hi folks, Asaluma Alaikum to you, in the name of the most Merciful, the most high, Crazy Abu Ali here, with a deal to end all deals!"

He's walking through the lot of cars with robes flowing, "This Mercedes 300 series convertible, fully loaded, yours for 3,000 dinars, this beauty of a Beemer 525i, yours for a song at just 5,000 dinars, this Peterbilt tractor was once owned by President Assad of Syria and can be yours for the low, low price of only 2,000 dinars! People ask me how I do it. Volume, volume and volume that's how! That, and I'm crazy like a desert fox but you can call me Abu Ali, Crazy Abu Ali!!! That's New Canaan Ford, located at 1477-8999-0 New Canaan Blvd, on the corner of New Canaan and City Drive. Come see me before I really go CRAZY and tell you I don't remember what I just said!!!"

And then as he finishes sweeping through the car lot, sitars wailing in the background, Crazy Abu Ali stands on his head with robes draping his face and we see that he is a boxers' man.

In America, the marketing would be, "Jesus walked this road, man! It's like famous and stuff! So you have to, like, live here and like, buy things." This would be the pitch for the over-priced studio apartments over-looking the patch of olive trees left for posterity in a square, "Look, that's the one Judas hung himself on!" There would be a plaque and of course, this was conjecture and supposition on my part.

We walked awhile and saw some kids smoking out under one of the olive trees. They saw us and stopped with some coughing up the fear of getting busted but Sam just waved them off, laughing and saying something in Arabic where the kids laughed back. They continued puffing and inhaling passing the joint amongst themselves. My dad, along with the New Canaan City Council would shit and die twice if he knew his precious homeland had given way to this sort of behavior and *haram* which was Arabic for sin or "it's sad." It was also used for "there but for the grace of God go I." Kind of like "aloha," the phrase had many uses. But I think this kind of thing has always been here. My dad was just so straight and prejudiced that he couldn't fathom what he would never do himself. Empathy was never really his thing anyway.
I was having a hard time being at ease and a couple of heavy sighs gave that away.

"Long stretch huh, cousin?" Sam asked.

"You know it, man." I said.

"Oh, I know…I know." Sam looked over at one of the pastures with cows, just grazing. "People are like that. Like cows."

"Really?" I was waiting for the elder statesman to make valid his point.

"Yeah…cows are cool as long as the basics are there, food and water, place to live. We are no different."

I thought about that for a hot second, not sure if the thought was deep enough to affect me.

Then he said, "Hey, and you don't have to, if you don't want to, but I brought some mushrooms. I haven't done any since college."

"You mean like 'shrooms?" I asked, my fingers in quotes.

"Yeah, ever try them?" Sam smiled. "They're fun. Not like acid at all."

I had not tried them. I had been curious but not sure I was in the right frame of mind, given the last several days. I had not tried acid either for that matter;

just the occasional joint and more than occasional beer and whiskey. Sam explained that they weren't as intense as acid but that they were more like pot with more color and laughs. You may have a thought or two, he explained but mostly we'd get the giggles and see some cool stuff maybe.

"Man, you're just a fucking drug addict, aren't you?" I laughed. "Aren't they grown on cow shit?"

"Well, yeah, something like that. That's where those falafel sandwiches come in…We stuff the sandwiches, eat and they kick in like in an hour. You won't even taste them in the food, man."

I thought about the cab coming to the house at 3:30am the next day, even though the strike had not been called. We left the time set as though there were a strike because it was looking shaky. Cabs into Tel Aviv were not happening after 8am anyway.

Then I thought "fuck it," mushrooms on the Road to Canaan? How many chances will I have? Long as Jesus doesn't show up and get pissed that I'm stoned *again,* what have I got to lose? Even still I might have offered him some and I bet he would have done them. There's no way you come up with some of the shit he did, unless you were real fucking high. People are not that introspective being sober. Well, maybe some. The enlightened and what not, of which I was not a member. We ate our lunch under the shade of an olive tree.

I was really looking forward to Denmark. I knew it wouldn't be near as intense as being here had been. I could use an easier time for a few days.

"So when you coming back to the States, man?" I asked in between bites of lamb and gulps of water. I could kind of taste the mushrooms as the yogurt and falafel were fighting a losing battle against the residual cow shit they were grown in.

"I dunno…a month I think. You wanna hang out when I get there?" He asked.

"Yeah but no Heather," I said, referring to Mike's secretary. "I don't need the guilt, I don't need to see, don't need to know."

Sam chuckled, "That's cool. I get it."

We just ate and sat overlooking the pasture. It was hills upon green hills with cows and sheep dotting them for as far as the eye could see.

114

A couple days earlier, I had walked my great aunt to where she watched the family sheep when it was her turn to do so. I don't know if anyone even kept track of whose turn it was but she liked to get out and get air. It was about a mile from the house and she had a walkie talkie, in case of wolves or whatever but their dogs did a good job. There was this big, dark green tarp set up on five posts, kind of like a small circus tent without walls. It overlooked the green hills like a painting with sheep just grazing, waiting to be killed and fed to the village. She had her little director's chair that she would fold up when she wasn't using it. She had an old wood burning stove, where she made her coffee. We sat there and watched the sheep. Actually, I watched while she fell asleep in her chair, the soft static of the walkie talkie picking up my uncle's shop sounds of chopping meat and laughing customers.

In 1998, she would be found there, having died in her sleep at 104 years old, all the while never learning to spell the words, "sick" or "ill." She was late coming back and didn't answer her walkie talkie. She never had a cell phone. She was found sitting in her chair with a magazine in her lap, overlooking the field and the sheep still grazing…

It had been some time and Sam and I were just talking about whatever. I could feel the mushrooms starting to kick in. I was used to getting high in some form so there was no anxiety because I knew something was going to happen so the startup felt kind of the same, at least psychically. My fingers were getting tingly and I could feel my cheeks get hot.

It was only around one in the afternoon but the sun was looking darker, prettier for some reason. I looked at Sam and he was sitting on a rock with his eyes closed. Without looking over, he asked, "You alright, man?"

I said that I was fine but I was really starting to come on. The tingly feeling gave way to a sort of buzz that was becoming consistent. I was really feeling it. I sat there too but I couldn't close my eyes. I didn't want to. I had the urge to take it all in. The pasture was so *green*. The sun was shining on it different too. What was a cooler breeze now felt like a soft, warm shower of air. The grass moved like light.

Sam looked over. "We should walk, dude."

"No, man I don't wanna walk…Not yet…Not yet, I'm cool like this for a minute…no, hang on…no time…Don't need a minute or time, man… I don't want to tell time… I just wanna look at this grass. It's so fucking green!" I was awestruck by the colors. Even the cows seemed more like they had purpose.

Sam looked on. He didn't answer but he didn't have to. Once he opened his eyes and saw the pasture, he got what I was talking about. He got quiet.

So whatever time it was, thirteen o'clock, I didn't fucking know, we just walked without a word. We just did. Sam had told me this story about how he saw Pink Floyd perform "the Wall" in L.A. Of course, I was wildly impressed by this. Those were hard tickets to get in 1980 because they only played the one night. No San Diego. No San Francisco. Just L.A. He talked about him and Kelly and how they dug the show and how they went home that night and fucked.

Sam was talking about the dresser getting knocked over, "We just drunk fucked, man. Balance was not coming our way."

As soon as he said, "coming our way," I asked, "Coming? Were you breathing hard?" I started laughing like it was the funniest thing in the world.

Sam started laughing too. I kept repeating the phrase over and over, in different ways but the laughs were still the same, "Breathing hard! Oh my God!" Sam had tears in his eyes, he couldn't control himself. I thought he was going to bust an organ.

We found this tractor. We started to play on it. I found a broken wrench and started banging on the steering wheel. Sam started singing some stupid song about sheep and ended every phrase with "Tractor Rock!" I started joining in on that part, too. I then stared ad-libbing some DJ part for each song explaining of course, how Tractor Rock was composed by Pete Townshend's tortured gardener, Nigel, because every tortured gardener was named "Nigel," naturally and how he got fucked because Jimmy Page stole his girlfriend. This would only make sense if your girlfriend was not into your horticultural career choice as much as she would be into Led Zeppelin's god of rock guitarist. Bitch. This led to Pete teaching Nigel guitar and Tractor Rock was born! But to tell these rock stories successfully or make them up, one had to have that classic FM DJ baritone that said you have lived a hard life yourself and were on the air while very, very fucking *stooooned*. Otherwise, you sound like any other guy with a nasal condition and a hyper inflated sense of self.

Sam was cracking up because he recognized the L.A. DJ I was trying to mimic and the radio show, too. The ultimate stoner show, called the "Seventh Day," as in on the seventh day "God kicked back, dude!"

There were these three DJs who all took turns but the main gist was they would play seven albums on Sunday nights, back to back, only to break for commercials in between whole sides of the featured record. Of course they would give you the run down on each song after the side was over as if this stuff was world history; lots of gravitas as they explained all the vital "facts," basically confusing real historical delivery with a session of "Fun Facts to Learn and Tell." But I bought into it when I was in high school and to a larger degree into adulthood. So our Tractor Rock bonanza was fitting in very well with The Seventh Day motif.

A piece of advice I always took to heart about getting high and recounting these tales was that I never did it at parties, because they have the tendency to rely on location humor. Sometimes conversation cheapens vision and often I found that these were things best kept to myself. This was probably why anti-drug purists would always seem to be justified and smug in saying "I just don't get it," when they would watch their friends get high or drunk. They could be so superior about it too. Of course you don't get it, you fucking dolts! The only people who know what it's like to be Superman come from Krypton and move to earth. The only people who knew how the president felt were other presidents. However, if they did the same drugs, at the same time as their friends, they'd have a fucking blast, thus making moot their posturing bullshit as well as suddenly having a desire for and believing in the possibility of individual space travel and becoming the President of Krypton.

I thought, "I can trump being famous. If I was the bastard son of Marilyn Monroe and the Pope, I'd never *not* be famous. I'd be more famous than John Lennon and John F. Kennedy, Jr. combined." It was weird how I could move my body and sing these stupid songs and think this other stuff at the same time. I thought of how the conspiracy theories would be crazy. Did the Pope kill Marilyn to keep his secret? Did he meet with cardinals or agents posing as ambassadors in the Vatican halls to plot her death to make it look like a suicide? That would be so wild!

She died before I was born so the timeline was a bit screwed but still.

Having spent what seemed like several hundred minutes or so with our musical creation, I was spent and the laughing was turning into a cool buzzy feeling again. I walked off into some trees. The air was temperate and

117

everything was vivid. I looked up and saw the daytime moon. I was so overwhelmed by its bright light in the daytime that I lay on my back so consumed by this odd, *loving* feeling. It was so intense that I couldn't comprehend hate or killing or death. The clouds were connected to my forehead with invisible wires and I could control their movements with my eyebrows.

Then it hit me that this is why we could never prove faith. What if religion, every fucking one of them, consisted of a bunch of *whomever* going out into the woods and doing peyote buttons or drinking wine, smoking weed, getting a vision that was uniquely theirs for *that* group on that day? Then because they believed so fervently that this vision was from God and thus true, they came down the mountain and told one hell of a story? Now, the ones that got it were cool. The ones that didn't would get their heads chopped off or banished to hell, which may have been invented because these guys were high in the first place for fuck sake! I mean what all knowing, all loving God creates a hell? What if Sam and I made a Tractor Religion? The Tractorians? We could totally do that! Think of the power, the cash, the chicks, the tax exemptions!

But I wanted none of that. I just wanted everyone to love everyone and at that moment I think I finally knew why. As I lay there in the grass, I knew I wasn't going to join or start a movement. I was just going to be me, love starts with me. God kind of always felt the same way since I was little, so that part must be true at least for *me*. This was already easier than I thought but I knew this wouldn't last.

That's where it was going to stay. I was going to stand in one spot and look up. I figured if I wasn't crazy or evil, God would tell me what's what. That intuition, that love I was feeling was God and I didn't have to chop anyone's head off or die on a cross to prove shit. I knew, in my heart, that this was not a unique or earth shattering view. I was 23. What the fuck did I know with the world being around so long? I figure there had to be at least one or twelve hippies who came up with that same humanist view before, right? But here's the thing I had to ask myself; if God was infinite then why did man give Him such petty human qualities making him a jealous God? "Thou shall have no other gods before me," what other Gods, man? I thought you were it? What we're dating, now?

Man, those mushrooms were awesome! I got up and Sam was sitting in a tree, looking at the daytime moon rise further with the set of the sun. He silently looked right at me, beaming with a glow that said, "We are airborne, man."

I only wished my Uncle Jacob had this much fun with his buddies, the day he died. I'm sure it sucked for my grandparents but it would be nice to think that those guys were all laughing their asses off the day they all went boom. Not knowing what hit them at all and they were having a fucking blast. God, I hope that's what happened.

We walked back home as the sun gave way to the evening. I could smell dinner from an abnormal distance. Was it my aunt's house or could I smell the neighbors food too? We got home and Sam sat with us and had dinner. We were laughing like idiots without the slightest provocation. My cousins were laughing with us or at us and I couldn't care less. This was too much fun.

I was to leave the next day…

Chapter 7-A Funny Thing Happened On the Way to Denmark…

"And I'll tell you this.../No eternal reward will forgive us now for wasting the dawn."

****

Even though everyone was awake anyway, I hated getting up at 3am. I was always kind of an early riser, usually existing on five or six hours of sleep, but there was no lonelier feeling in the world than 3am. It always seemed darker than the evening, kind of what I imagined the twenty-four hour Alaskan night to be like. It didn't matter if I got to bed at seven and woke up eight hours later, I always felt like I was the only person that was up in the whole world. It was ink black and isolated like that last night in the United States. I was in and out of sleep but heard my aunt rustling around the kitchen and that got me out of bed before I could slip into a doze again. All I wanted was 15 more minutes to dream one last thing but I didn't get it.

There was something about the noise my aunt made. It had an uneasy quality. It was as though she was trying to keep her mind occupied or fix something irreparable.

When I came downstairs, my aunt and uncle and a few cousins were up and some others had come over. My aunt had made some breakfast and even with everyone up, I still felt lonesome. I could see by the look on her face we shared that or maybe she was just tired and I was reading too much into it.

I told Sam not to come, but to just sleep in. He came anyway, "Yeah, I know what you said, but fuck it." He smiled as he came in the door behind Ali. The three of us did a bear hug like rugby players having just won a match. My aunt came over and mockingly pulled my ear to get me to eat. I could see she approved of the camaraderie.

We were all eating and chatting and I was wide awake when the cabbie got there and we invited him to have some food with us. Nice enough guy, his name was Saif. He spoke little English and I could tell he was in a hurry and for obvious reasons. Even though there was to be no strike, there was still a chance of something happening. Not for nothing, the last few days had created the atmosphere to call a strike. Saif and Ali exchanged some conversation

120

back and forth and Ali motioned for me to give him his $500. Saif's concern for safety was justified. These strikes were seldom logical and they could have landed us dead or in jail so being careful would be the smarter move. Saif also didn't want to be rude to my aunt so he sat down to eat but ate quickly. He was very polite, saying "sucran" (shoo-kran) which is thank you, a lot. Jamal told me he was from a poorer village which is why he probably took the fare and I also didn't get a "great deal". It was a big risk and maybe getting back as I wanted was foolish, but I had to get back. Strangely enough, I could sense a class issue at play that night. It was clear that Saif was self conscious because of where he was from. It's just everywhere, it's what people do.

Everyone was pretty cool about saying goodbye except for my aunt and uncle. They cried hard, both of them hugging me, I could feel Ayoub's four day beard scrape my cheek, wet with his tears. He was saying things in Arabic about being protected by the "hand of God" and that kind of thing while my aunt rattled in my other arm as she wept, her face pressed into my chest. They cried like they knew something I didn't. My feelings felt dead. I began to miss sadness, as at least that would be something but I sure as hell wasn't missing it at the same time. This would have been confusing to the casual counselor. However, that wasn't all of it. I really wanted to go home but I somehow knew that wouldn't feel the same anymore there either. My concept of home was gone forever. I knew that this place was part of who I was but it wasn't my home any more than Brazil was. I was an American, whatever that would come to mean when I got back.

"We saw a lot of shit, man." Sam smiled as he and Ali came down to the taxi with my bags. We all shook hands and did the three kiss/cheek ritual. It really had been some time.

After the cabbie loaded my bags, we were off. His "cab" was basically a rehabilitated gray Mercedes with a painted insignia in Arabic in yellow spray paint on the doors of the car.

The drive out was bleak as most parts of the road out there didn't really have street lights, so the headlights were about it. Dust kicked up behind us, highlighted by the red tail lights. Staring out the rear window, I couldn't stop watching the trails the dust seemed to leave, a residual of the mushrooms, no doubt. I was in the back seat, alert at first then I started dozing off, only to be jolted awake by some of the unpaved parts of the road. I caught Saif's eyes in the rearview mirror. He looked at me as if to say, "I got this." I was still tired, not having gotten much sleep and while the mushrooms didn't feel like a hangover, the laughing and staying up late did wear me out and I may have slept two hours total.

The night before, after dinner, Ali, Sam and I were up talking with the other cousins. Ali had no idea we did mushrooms. He was a really great guy but still pretty straight. Even though he didn't really drink, he'd have a beer or two to be social but not here. He'd never do that here. However, the mushrooms or pot would have been too much for him to handle. Moreover, he had two brothers with drug or alcohol problems and one was dead, so I think he'd fail to see the humor or hubris in all of that quasi rebellion. Actually at that time, everything had the effect of too much anyway and I just didn't want the drama of justifying.

Man, was I looking forward to Denmark. My eyes were closed as the cab came to an abrupt stop and I could feel its tires skidding in the gravel.

It was the Israelis. They had set up a check point and Saif said something to me about waking up in Arabic. It was the same thing dad said in the morning to wake me up to go to school. The familiarity of the phrase had my eyes pop open real fast, "Well, fuck me…" I said as I saw the now familiar military hardware.

Saif told me in English to relax and only speak when spoken to and that it'd be all good. "We are nice, go fast quick, OK…" he assured me in his broken English.

One of the Israelis came to the car and spoke to Saif in Arabic. Saif just threw his thumb over his shoulder pointing in my direction. I wasn't quite sure just how to take that. Thanks, dick!

The soldier peered into the back seat with his flashlight, which was one of the high powered military numbers, probably three hundred torches or something. He was moving it fast in wide circles inside the cab. The circles got big and purple, moving quickly before my eyes could catch up. I was still faintly buzzed. He asked me to step out of the car. As I did, two other soldiers had their guns trained on me. I saw some faint, purple streaks as my eyes focused in on the rifles, lit by the truck lights. I was not usually afraid of death, at least it never served as a preoccupation for me but pain is a bitch so I did as I was asked. "If I were to die, please make it fucking quick." I asked God that night, not terribly sure if He was up at this hour so this could get dragged out, before He clocked in, got His morning coffee and pastry, read the universe…

Again, the soldiers took my shoes and asked for my passport. These guys seemed a bit more intense than the guys from the other night with Sam. Maybe it was because of the bombing or the beaten kid in Jerusalem and the riots after. Maybe it was because it's early in the morning and they hated being out here too, dealing with the smelly shoes of tourists. It could have been something from a half hour ago. Maybe they were fresh from beating the shit out of the paperboy for refusing to give up his shoes or shot a barber smoking pot in an alley. This whole region was dictated by wild mood swings and these guys were basically cops without a lot of supervision running a derelict homeroom and that was as fucked up a situation as one could be in so they had to keep their wits. The Israelis had their own stories of soldiers who were "too nice" and paid with their lives. The current climate wasn't going to work in my favor so I was just working to get out.

"You fly out in Tel Aviv, eh?" the lead soldier asked, his accent thick, having seen my passport and tickets, "No Amman? Where you fly in? Why?"

"My cousin got me a cheaper flight." I lied, thinking what I would like to have said was, "If I get chased by Bedouins, you got my back, right Ari?" Did I say that out loud?

"Would you step clear from the car, to please?" English not being his first language, he meant away from the car. This guy was trying to be polite and I was trying to get on a fucking plane so we indirectly had a lot in common and I still wasn't sure if I said that last bit out loud which may have been why I was asked to step out of the car. Did I say it?

The solider yelled something at Saif who had his hands on the steering wheel and another Israeli pointing an M-16 at him through the windshield. The trunk popped open so that must have been the command.

"You only have for the two cases?" asked the Israeli.

I said yes and that one was gifts for my mom. He asked me if I packed the cases myself or if anyone else had touched them. Sam told me to say that no one even helped me take them to the car and that they never left my sight the whole time I was there which made no sense. Making sense or saying otherwise could land me in an Israeli jail until, well forever. The embassy would have to get involved and it could be a real drag, to say the least, if the embassy would even help at all. I worked with a lot of Jews at C.I.A. This was a stigma I didn't need there either. All the Israelis would have to say is I was under suspicion and that statement alone would add a month to jail. Frankly, I

123

was sure it was worse than an American jail. Like it mattered; I didn't like the idea of jail, never been and I wasn't planning on it. Going in is how one finds out why it's called the "pokey." I intended to keep my ass virginity intact so fuck logic, basically.

"Please. We have to inspect for your cases." The soldier politely demanded.

"Whatever, man. Do your thing…" I was resigned at that point. I let his guys open them up as if I had a choice. Maybe it was because I lacked an accent or they could tell that I was really a harmless American tourist, I don't know but they went through my stuff pretty carefully. After about 45 minutes, they had everything neatly together and had us on our way. The soldier nodded and said something friendly to Saif in Arabic but I could tell the tone was stern. Probably something along the lines of "What the fuck are you two doing out here with all this shit going on at three in the fucking morning?" or something like that. Saif smiled and responded humbly. I was so glad he understood that freedom was a good thing. Having been on the ass end of a rifle as often as it seemed began to wear on me. I knew if I looked the part or more like Saif, the Israelis would have had a very different chat with me and that was a fact. God bless freckles and green eyes.

We went through Ramallah and then hit more of the same rural roads that were common on the outskirts of these towns. Just a lot of highway and brush with no real woods or anything like that, just flat. It was still dark with light just barely breaking over the ridge as the moon mapped out its descent. I was falling asleep again.

We're playing a club in L.A. when all three of The Stray Cats showed up which I thought was weird since their break up, a couple years prior, was widely reported as being hostile. Anyway, we were "headlining," which only meant we were last on the bill but we had more people than the other bands that night so I guess that meant we were. Brian Setzer asked me and my singer if they could use our stuff to jam a couple of songs. Life is made up of moments so we all four said yes. Even though I wasn't a huge rockabilly fan, this was a story I'd milk for years to come. They played for about an hour. That made us look real cool real fast. Everyone in the club got on our mailing list that night with some even double checking just to make sure. We drank a round on Brian Setzer, the guitar player and we got hang out with Lee Rocker and Jim Phantom too. Tonight, I'm going home. My California…

The car stopped again with the jolting and skidding that woke me up as there seemed to be panic in the braking the second time. This road block wasn't the Jews.

"Yallah, Yallah!" I heard outside the cab. Another car pulled up behind us which Saif hit as he tried to peel out of there in reverse with stunt driving not being a strong suit of his. Saif's door was opened and he was jerked outside by the throat! Before I knew what was happening I was yanked outside too and rolled onto the ground. About eight or nine guys with AK-47s were standing around the cab with their rifles on us and while it seemed like forever, they did all this in about thirty seconds like a S.W.A.T. team or something.

At first I thought this was a set up but I could tell Saif was scared shitless as his eyes were real wide on the verge of tears, darting around and scanning the situation and he didn't seem sharp enough to be that great an actor. Maybe $500 wasn't enough to ask for. I was scared too but I had a pride problem, the couple of times in my life I was threatened with a gun, I didn't beg. I stood there waiting to die. In either case I was scared out of my mind but I just wasn't about to give any assholes the satisfaction. All these guys had keffiyehs around their faces, just like on the news when Arabs hijacked planes in the 1970s.

We were about a half hour away from the Israeli border…

Saif was begging and explaining in Arabic that we were cool. He was doing his damndest to have these guys let us go, trying to convince them that they made a mistake. They were screaming questions at him and he kept saying several things over and over ending with "*Americaniyah*" or American, meaning me. That made me nervous as I had zero idea where that exchange would lead. I mean American what? One of the guys rammed a rifle butt into his stomach and he dropped to his knees like a bag of hammers so I suppose he was trying to help me and they weren't buying it. I rushed over to Saif only to get smacked upside the head with the same gun, myself.

As I lay there checking for blood and feeling a knot well up, they got Saif up. As I was finding my feet, one of the guys he was talking to pulled out a pistol and shot Saif in the head! Point blank. Bloody pieces of his skull hit the hood of the cab like chunks of lamb fat in Ayoub's shop and I could hear them hit the metal of the car with dull thuds and splattering sounds. Saif dropped dead, graceless, face in the dirt, his legs almost flopping over his back. His blood splattered my sleeve but I felt the warm drops splash on my hand and saw the many spots that looked like motor oil in the light of the moon. I always had a thing for the moon and here it was lighting up the blood of another man on my hand.

I lost it, I didn't see that coming or ever in my life for that matter! I started hyperventilating, "What the fuck! Are you out of mind? He's a fucking cab driver! He didn't do shit, man! God damn it!" My eyes were still watering from the knot on my head, the pain started to blind me in my left eye.

Then I got hit in the stomach with a rifle butt from another guy. As I hit the ground gasping for air, clutching road side brush as a way to brace the pain, I heard, "Sorry cousin but the driver? He got off easy."

I look up and Eddie walks through the couple of goons right up to where I'm kneeling with Lateef right behind him. "Good morning, habibi. Sleep well?" He grinned and as he lit a cigarette, his face had a scary assed glow which would have looked corny in a b-level mob movie. At that moment between us, it looked grim and like I was a goner.

"What the fuck is going on here, man?" I grunted out through clenched teeth having thrown up in my mouth a little. I should have been stoked to see a familiar face in a situation like this even if I didn't like the guy because it was family, right? Eddie's grin said all I needed to hear. "So," I choked out, "...this about the other morning? You fucking cunt!" The energy to raise my voice was strangely absent as I groaned out my observation.

Two of his guys got me up by each arm, I felt a massive head rush and got dizzy, my feet caved. I hung by each arm as I tried to find my legs, my neck barely holding up my head as it lolled back, then forward. Eddie along with everything else started to seem curvy, out of sorts. I had a sinking feeling that these guys were going to take their time. Lateef was leaning against the cab, smoking a cigarette as if he were supervising. He didn't say much, just stood there, puffing away and grinning every now and then. I got concerned as I realized that he and Eddie didn't cover their faces. Maybe because dead guys can't I.D. anyone...

Eddie started, "No, cousin. This is haram, a shame and I hated to find that you were a collaborator and for that I am sorry. But you can't conspire with the Jews and then just go back to America like nothing happened. You have to pay."

"Conspire? What the fuck are you saying? Jesus Christ! What Jews?" Then it hit me; maybe Niven, the minister, maybe Ali said something about him in passing although I couldn't really make the connection at that very moment. Seems that's all Eddie needed to hear to round up a bunch of psychotic assholes. These guys would do this shit for free. Fuck country, fuck freedom and fuck haram. I doubt the average Palestinian looked forward to burning dudes alive in the desert. It seemed that was where I was headed.

If there ever was a Palestine, these motherfuckers would surely end up in jail for all the non-sanctioned shit they loved to do which would be illegal in a functioning society. These guys liked things the way they were. Saying they wanted a lasting peace with the Jews is like Al Capone saying he was against Prohibition. These guys weren't my grandfather and neither was Eddie. I should not have been surprised that Eddie would pull this kind of stunt.

But it wasn't just the fight we had and I would lose everything to find that out…

I spit in his face and paid for that with another gun butt to the head. Everything went white for what seemed like forever and the two guys let me drop. I think that last one cracked my skull but I was still with it as I rolled over on my back, "Fuck you, Eddie. You lying piece of shit…" I rolled over clutching my head, fighting back tears, coughing up spit or blood, I couldn't tell and I was trying to stay conscious. I was trying to see, to focus on anything but all I could see was white from both eyes now. Shit, was I going blind? Then I smelled gasoline, Eddie's guy started pouring it all over me. I tried to get up but got kicked hard in the stomach a few times. I couldn't get up anyway so I didn't need any help staying down.

"Yallah! Yallah!" Eddie commanded. I don't think these guys spoke any English but they understood "fuck you" or at least the tone. Spitting in Eddie's face was a giveaway to my inner feelings.

I was having the toughest time breathing and I was swallowing gasoline.

"Well cousin, 'the moment of truth,' as they say in the movies…" Eddie said quietly, lighting another cancer stick as my vision was fading in and out, "I'll make sure to speculate to your parents that this all had to be just a tragic mistake. You know, American kid being too friendly with the Jews. These things happen, this ain't Jersey." Eddie nodded in Lateef's direction. He walked over. I guess Eddie really didn't want to "technically" do this.

Eddie gave the nod for Lateef to flick his cigarette on me, make a bonfire out of me when his forehead exploded! At the moment of truth, truth came quick in the form of a bullet right between Lateef's eyes! He fell to his knees with his tongue hanging out and his head spinning back and forth as he dropped dead, face first with his teeth cutting off his tongue, blood spurting into the ground. Eddie's head exploded as I felt the chunks splash on me and he dropped dead too. Truth from the barrel of a motherfucking gun!

Two helicopters had flown in, hovered, and surrounded the immediate area. My ears were ringing so badly and I was in such a shock that I didn't even hear them. Israeli soldiers were rappelling down on ropes, two troop trucks had moved in real fast and covered the remaining Arabs! A couple of them had scattered into the fields and the Israelis shot them right in the back, night vision goggles making it easy to see. Yeah, I know, in the back? Oh well, to make an omelet, we have to break a few eggs and these fuckers were going to set me on fire, so how you like them eggs, assholes?

As I lay on the ground, choking for air, coughing up the most heinous matter, I hear, "You American?"

I look up and it's Liev, the New Jersey Jew from the check point. Eddie may have foretold something with his crack about Jersey but man, was I relieved. I start coughing up more gas and snot and tears mixed with some blood, I'm sure. It was still dark. He sits me up against Saif's cab and gives me water. "You good, man?" he asks.

More blood came back with the water, I threw up the great breakfast I had. I could smell the gas, wiping my chin, I answered, "I guess…How'd you know this was going down?"

"One of the undercovers heard something about this in Jerusalem. Sometimes we get there in time, sometimes we don't," he said shaking his head. "He heard your name and didn't recognize it as one of ours. Thought there was something wrong…Sorry about the cab guy."

I started crying. I felt embarrassed so I choked it back, "Thanks man…so, you good?" I asked.

"Better than fucking good, dude!" He smiled. "Today is my last day." He said looking like the cat that ate the canary with an awesome side dish. Then I don't recall the rest of our chat. I think I passed out.

****

"It's better to die on your feet/than to live on your knees…"

I woke up in a hospital room, not feeling well but not horrible either. Liev was sitting there. "That was a long nap, man."

"Shit! Damn it! I missed my flight!" I groaned holding my head.

"Relax, I took care of it. Denmark, right? I'm coming too." He smiled.

"What do you mean you're coming too?" I asked.

He explained that since he was an army veteran (all of a couple days) that he could get on any El Al or Israeli airline flight for free, anywhere in the world. Also, because of extenuating circumstances, he could get me on the flight too, even though I missed my plane two days before. Ordinarily, I'd be considered a security risk but it's about who you know. Isn't this a trip? The Israeli border guard and I are flying to Denmark! Random is too weak a word and if I wasn't already in a hospital on meds, I'd swear I was high.

So we got through security, they checked my bags real fast and we boarded the plane. Liev hooked us up with first class seats so the stewardess poured us red wine and we had appetizers as everyone else was boarding the plane. I quickly drank a couple of glasses and fell asleep. This had to be a dream and if it wasn't, it couldn't last, could it?

We landed in Copenhagen and I was glad to say, the security here was not the Mid East. They didn't even run the bags through x-rays. "Did you pack everything yourself?" As soon as I answered yes, the blond goddess said, "Welcome to Denmark" and stamped my passport. Done.

I had the address to the bed & breakfast that Jamal set me up with. So we grabbed a cab and headed to the city. Liev said he had a brother here that he was crashing with but we would catch up later. He gave me the phone number as we dropped him off.

"Thanks man. I mean it." I said trying to still be a "guy" about it.

"Don't sweat it, bro." he grinned. "We're Americans, right?" with that he hit the roof of the cab and it sped off.

129

The cab dropped me at my place and it was next to this gorgeous 16ᵗʰ century church, right on the Mollean River. I walked up the side street to the small lodge which was about two buildings down from the main street that bordered the river and left my bags. I had no patience to even check in right at the moment because I just had to walk. I went from the hospital to the plane and then a cab so I just had to get out, be outside and just breathe. I had never felt claustrophobic before but I was feeling deeply confined, all of a sudden.

The city was just breathtaking. Some of the bigger streets were paved but the smaller ones were still cobblestone. At a restaurant, on one of the back streets, I saw this guy rolling a huge barrel of beer up the ramp and into the second floor of a bar. One thing that was apparent was a near utter lack of fat people. Maybe a few pounds plump but no one really obese and the streets were packed everywhere I went as Danes walked a lot and Danish women were exquisite. I noticed a couple and they noticed me back and it was nice, given that I had bruises. Maybe they were afraid of me or just felt sorry for me but it was nice to be noticed.

After I walked around for the couple of hours that flew by, I decided to check in. The lobby had these old, almost greasy hard wood floors that were covered in old Afghan rugs. Everything was neatly ordered but old and not in the way of being antique but more threadbare. But still the place had that quality that one can't find anywhere in a chain hotel and Jamal got it cheap. It was small and off the beaten path so it wasn't where the high rollers stayed. I knew one day, I'd come back here famous. I ventured into the bar which was four tables in a converted old dining room and had a scotch. I don't even know what it was but it did taste heavenly. I sipped it slow, letting it sit on my tongue before each swallow. I could feel my chest expand like a campfire that just gets going.

The bartender was happy to have the business. I approached the desk and as I pull out my credit card, the owner, who was also the bartender, had a strange smile on his face. A pair of cold, slender hands wrapped around my eyes. I reach up and thankfully, they belonged to a girl, I could tell. It's in the wrists, "Guess who?" she says. I reach up and loosen her grip and it's Karly!

"As I live and breathe," she said excitedly throwing her arms around my neck. Her hug felt nice, more natural than I ever imagined, her body giving in completely. She whispered in my ear as she touched my cheek, "You're not staying here too, are you?"

"Apparently," I smiled, trying hard to not look stupid. God was obviously on the clock on that day.

She got self conscious, in the most adorable way. Pulling from me, setting her hair back from her face, she said, "Wow! It's so good seeing you here… How long you here for?" then finally saying something about my face, she asked what happened.

"Well, I had a mishap," trying to keep it light.

"Yeah, I can see that…" her eyebrows furrowed, pulling that exquisite nose into an achingly cute crinkle. "Can you talk about it? Was it Arabs or the Israelis?" Karly asked.

"I'm here a few days…we can talk later, right? Just much ado about nothing, really…How long you here?" I asked. I could feel the owner waiting on us to get us checked in. Even though it was slow, he may have had things to do.

"I'm here a week!" she smiled almost with a shriek. Her tone and gestures told me this little reunion was starting off well.

We chatted casually, going up the stairs as the owner of the inn went for my bags, I insisted on taking the other one. He was an older man, probably in his 50s, definitely world weary but he had a demeanor that said he was grateful and loved life. He looked over his shoulder a couple times, checking out Karly I'm sure. He wasn't that old. We walked up the stairs and it turned out my room was right next to Karly's. She just giggled, "What are the odds?"

"You good for dinner, tonight?" knowing she'd agree.

"Most definitely, I'd love to," she purred like in the dream I had.

We agreed to knock on the other's door in an hour and go to dinner. The rooms were like the rest of the place; old wood floors, old furniture and a big bed. I lay down and tried to nap but I was too giddy. I got up and showered and I stood in there for a long time, feeling the hot water down my back, what a sensation it was. The plumbing was old so the hot water would spit and pitch but I didn't care at all. To think I was almost killed three days before. Just 10 seconds later and I'd have been dead three days old. If only my Uncle Jacob could have felt as good as this shower does on me right now. I have never felt more alive than I did at that moment in the shower.

This couldn't last, bliss doesn't last.

Karly and I went to a little bistro right on the river. We were drinking wine after dinner and I couldn't stop looking into this girl's eyes. They were the deepest dark blue. We talked about her old high school, her prom, "I actually had to go with a friend," she said.

I was flummoxed, "How is it that you of all people didn't have a boyfriend in high school? I figured your dance card would be full."

"Well, they did try." She smiled. "I just didn't want to deal with it senior year. Me and my boyfriend broke up right before school started and I figured I was going away to school so why start something again only to get hurt, you know? Life is short and I knew I'd be dating in college." Karly reached for her glass took a sip and grinned. I was impressed that she had such worldly observations at seventeen.

I was more surprised at how forward thinking she was given the background; grandfather was a big time radio pastor, her father had a drinking problem as a kid but got scared straight and met Karly's mom who kept him in line. Her parents were very conservative but seemed very happy to hear her tell it.

"This chick gets me," I thought although I had no real clue other than flirting but I already knew I was ready to be fucking understood by her. Maybe the same way her father was gotten by her mom. When people get each other, no adjustments are required. We take each other pretty much as is, love the rest, and suddenly my "issues" fall away.

At that point, I was trying to not give away all of my smitten cards. After all, it was still a dance and I knew that much, "Well, it sounds like you have a different point of view."

"What? I'm some innocent little miss because I was on a Bible Tour? It's educational." She said sarcastically.

"Yeah, well, then why's school out so early, Miss Karly?" I asked, affecting a bad southern drawl which she chuckled at but I think it was with me and not at me, the age old conundrum.

"I was having a crisis of faith, I guess. My parents made me go on it. They thought it would straighten me out, get me more into church."

"Did it?" I said as I flagged down the waiter for more wine.

"Not really. If anything it had the opposite effect. It also didn't help that Tom kept trying to fuck me," she said solemnly. "He'd been after me for awhile and he can't take a hint." This would be the leader guy of the Bible tour who did not like me at all and may as well have joined our little jihadists on the side of the road, for that matter, taking turns helping me master my impression of a piñata. "So I cashed in some miles and came here to hang out...I'm so glad you're here," she smiled.

"Yeah, me too. Tell your parents about the Tom thing?" I quizzed; a little taken aback but turned on by her use of the word "fuck" at the same time.

"Oh no...no" she said shaking her head slowly, gently fingering the stem of her wine glass. "They don't need to know. I'm a big girl. No, I'll just go home, be daddy's little girl and say not a whole lot about the spiritual side of life. We'll talk family, the summer trip to Chautauqua, his Lakers, his politics, it's his house. Keep it light. How I raise my kids and live my life will be my own deal." Then, seemingly catching herself, "Mine and my husbands'." She looked up, "I don't have all the answers, you know?"

Shakespeare wrote, "Thou doth protest too much," and I say those with the biggest sin scream the loudest. Fucking Tom...It's an old story with no changes coming it would seem. Glad to be out of that nasty bit of business. Religion, I mean. At least in the music business, I knew who was trying to screw me. What's the point of saving the Great Unwashed if I can't be nice to the waiter or kick the dog when I get home? This of course is easy for me to say, as I bathe in this glow of beauty. This perfect, holy beauty.

I wondered how an eighteen year old Ayoub would fare here or in the States? Maybe he would have had the option to pick his own destiny instead of the other way around. I never heard those guys complain about arranged marriages, the women sure didn't. They were not allowed. Some men, though, did get violent when the perception of pressure was too much to bear and when you're stuck with what's essentially a stranger it's probably worse. Ayoub, however, seemed to be in love and it had to be that or he was just a really good man with nothing bad to say.

Karly and I chatted awhile longer, then I got the bill and we left. We walked along the river and as the city lights danced on it, Karly's eyes sparkled in unison. I took her hand and we stopped. She nestled her head under my chin as we hugged. She felt good, like home. This was going to be more than a flirtation.

"It's really good to see you here," she whispered as she looked up and kissed me. Lightly at first then after her lips pecked mine for a minute, I grabbed her by the small of her back and really kissed her back. I stopped and buried my face in her hair as I held her. I took deep breaths, taking her in. She sighed and cooed as she exhaled. She instinctually knew that I was drinking her in and she may have known that we were in love from the moment we met.

We continued on arm in arm. I told her about my background and conversion to Christianity then to what I was when I met her, whatever that was. I told her about my band and my job. Told her about my cousin dying and why I was there to begin with. I told her about Bethlehem and Niven, the minister and very little about the roadside and Saif, mostly explaining my face but still telling her that Saif died and left out the really violent parts but her eyes got wet anyway.

"Wow. That's a lot of death for one trip." Tears streamed her cheeks. "Thank God it wasn't you." She reached up to kiss me again. She buried herself into it, her arms flung around my neck so hard I thought it would break. "I would have been very sad if I never saw you again," she said.

I had a hard time admitting that I watched someone die. I actually did more than watch, clearly, but a man's dead because I hired him and I hired him because my precious little schedule couldn't wait a fucking week. Given how things turned out, I ought to cut myself some grace but I was never really good at that.

I told her about some spiritual revelations, which may not have been wholly original and I admitted as much. I also confessed to the resignation that one can only be so original, that the best one can do in this life is pick a certainty and defend it. In most cases, defending that certainty didn't require much more than actually standing up in the face of things, some of which were easier than others.

"Nothing about you is *un*original," she said, emphasizing the "un." She told me about school, she had a year left and was looking at grad school. She talked about her friends and not quite fitting in with them. "I always held a slightly different point of view as you pointed out," she smiled. "I root for the underdog, the dark horse and that bugs my father. Part of why senior year was a big blank love wise." She talked about her penchant for bad boys and rebels and she thought that of me.

"You have such a 'little miss innocent' look," I said.

"Well, I'm still a virgin so I hope that doesn't screw up your plans." She said as her lips curled into a naughty girl smile. She explained that her father never liked a single guy she brought home. She loved her grandfather, who was a Congregationalist minister, the one who had the radio show. I surmised that she may indirectly be a P.K. or "pastor's kid," rebels that had been straitjacketed their whole lives ready to explode and not just cut loose. We walked back to the hotel. We got to my door and she quietly stood next to me as I unlocked it. She wasn't going for her own door, "Can we lie down together?" she asked.

"Yeah, sure," I was quiet and while I could have assumed lots of things, I felt her need to not be alone that night outweighed anything else.

"Not like that." Karly shoved me, playfully. "I just don't want to sleep by myself tonight. Is that okay? I want to be near you."

I nodded and she came in. We made out a little and then slept as we both got tired. This was easy to do as I was buzzed and blissfully zonked so we just held each other. It was so innocent, so sweet. Her lips were amazing, like a bowl of crushed cherries. When I finally slept, I did so, deep as a tomb.

****

The next day we got up around noon, got breakfast and walked around. We got back late in the afternoon so I called Liev at the number he gave me.

The accented voice of a woman answered the phone, suspiciously. I couldn't tell if she was being sarcastic. I told her I was a friend of Liev's and she went to get him. I heard what seemed like live music in the background.

"Hey man, what's up?" he asked cheerfully when he came to the phone.

"I'm good, dude. You up for doing something?" I was quick to see more of Copenhagen with folks who knew their way.

"Yeah, man. There's this bar and they have live music and my brother and his wife want to go, you cool?"

"Sure, man. I ran into this chick, the one I met in Jerusalem. Can she come?" I asked.

Karly just looked aghast and mouthed the words, "this chick?" as she hit me with a pillow, giggling.

"Yeah, man! The more the merrier. What's your address? I'll get you at like 7. Get a little food, it'll be cool." He wrote down the address and hung up.

Karly was sitting there as I hung up. She was just beaming. "What?" I laughed. "You're tripping me out a little."

"Nothing," turning red, she said, "I just like your smile. It makes me a little melty."

"Is that even a word?" I asked, throwing the pillow back at her. She jumped me and tried to wrestle. I flipped her on her back, looking right into her, "Well my mother thanks you, and I like *your* smile too." Then I leaned in and moaned as I kissed her.

We started getting into it and I was drawing massive wood. I always loved the first wood of the day with a new girl.

"Hold on there, tiger. I have to get ready," she giggled, biting her lower lip. With that, she pushed me off and ran out of my room. This can't last forever, can it?

Chapter 8-Don't Harsh My Zen, man…

Karly knocked on my door and looked amazing with her tight blue jeans, snug purple sweater and little black ankle boots. This was the 80s but that is a look that does not tire, perfection with a capital "P." Food, hotels, cars, or whatever, the word was cheapened when used to describe such mundane or passing fancies; things that could never possibly deliver on this level of glory because they were mere *things.* Women, and dare I say, the perfect woman, are the only beings that the word should be used for, especially Karly. Even her name was poetic. I'm no Keats but he didn't get smacked in the head with a rifle butt either so I felt I had some license.

Liev had taken a cab and met us at our cozy inn. He was casually dressed; he had on jeans, boots and an old Israeli Army sweater, the one with the canvas shoulders that looked cool going to a club. With his buzzed hair barely growing back, he had that hipster sense of irony and didn't look at all like a soldier. His countenance told you he was already gliding toward a civilian life.

Liev definitely approved of Karly when we came down and I could always tell when a guy found my girl attractive. I was never possessed of a jealous gene, thankfully, so I always liked it when guys would check out my girl because it meant I had taste. What's more, she was going home with *me.*

"You must be Liev, I'm Karly," she sparkled. "Thanks so much for what you did in Ramallah." She knew the little bit about him from what I had told her and she knew even less about the roadside.

"No worries. It's nice to meet you," he said as he tactfully avoided any gory details because I gave him the throat slash maneuver, standing behind Karly, meaning to say nothing. He was a sweet guy. With that we got in the cab.

Liev quickly shifted gears, "Micah and Sherri are meeting us at the club. It's a cool place, you'll dig it, I know… It's called 'the Boom Boom Room'." Liev was excited, "Shit man, I'm just stoked to be out of Israel. Looking forward to hanging out, drinking, gettin' high and doing pretty much nothing." He smiled. "Hey man, not like it's a big deal but Sherri's Iranian and she's Muslim born so don't be too surprised when you meet her…She's super-hot, though and not real religious." Liev qualified. I guess with him and his brother being Jewish, this required some clarity on his part.

"Yeah, I'm cool, man. Whatever…Not like I care, you know?" I said, sincerely. "Why, does it bug you?"

He just let his face fart and rolled his eyes, obviously it didn't bother him.

"That sounds neat." Karly grinned. "How'd they meet?"

"Micah's band was on tour in Europe and they met in France." Liev answered.

"Which band?" I asked.

"Creeping Charlie?" He said, almost asking, with a tone that implied he wasn't sure if I had heard of them.

"No way! That's pretty cool. They must have done alright?" I asked impressed by anyone's success at that point.

"Yeah, they did great while it lasted. Too bad how it turned out, but he'll live…and well." Liev shrugged.

We cruised the streets of Copenhagen as the lights came on for the night. Those street lights have not been replaced since the invention of street lights. They were lanterns at one point, that much was certain. They were made electric when electricity came and were pretty, iron and ornate. We pulled up to the Boom Boom Room which was basically an old government building, built in the 1930s, converted into many things and finally a club so it was still very art deco which was cool. The outside corners had the intricate carvings of gargoyles and all that.

What's more was the Boom Boom Room had their pot license which was legal in Denmark at the time, just like it was in Amsterdam. There was a blue conga drum with gold trim with the red logo emblazoned across the middle, above the front door and all in blazing neon lights. We walked in and it was just instant cool with red velvet walls that had patterns embroidered in the cloth, dark wood and wall mounted lights that were intricately detailed by the passions of a bygone era. The ceiling was wood as well with big beams and carvings with old crystal chandeliers that were yellow from years of smoke. The bar was a big, old wooden number that I could picture a bunch of Vikings or the average touring funk band, drinking and carrying on at. The bar maids had on tight, black booty shorts, fishnets, thigh high boots and black bikini tops which were very cute. The bouncers all seemed pretty mellow, their hair was freshly slicked back, ready for any eventuality but we were early so the night was young. There was a band that was still setting up as were going in.

We get to where the tables were and from a dark corner we heard, "Lee!" Apparently, "Lee" was Lievs' nickname because he responded quickly so we looked over and Liev waved at a couple seated in a booth that was a step above the floor. It was Micah and Sherri.

Micah motioned to the seats they had saved for us. As we approached, the waitress was there and asked what we were having. We ordered beers and Karly got red wine. We sat down and I have to say Sherri was stunning. She caught me looking for a split second and right when I went to avert my gaze, she said, "Hi, I'm Sherri." Her accent was kind of French but I couldn't tell for sure. It sounded like some of the Iranians I knew in L.A. but her diction was better, classier. Maybe it was because Americans always thought Europeans to be smarter than we were, gave them a superiority. This was not necessarily true but we thought it anyway and I was as guilty as the next.

Micah smiled and introduced himself. "Hey, man. I'm Micah." He shook my hand and Karly's too. Cool guy, about thirty, longish dark hair and black leather pea coat, he definitely was the "big brother" as he moved into that mode right away. He was no stunner by any means but he had "cool." That's what being successful at love can do for you. "Hey Lee, I ordered some food already…should be here soon." He drank his beer.

Sherri was twenty or twenty-one and she was wearing a short brown plaid skirt, black leggings and dark brown boots, with a brown turtleneck and a dark blue scarf. She had these luminous brown eyes that searched yours immediately when you met her. Great body; very curvy, with a great ass and her boobs were a nice size. She was very aware and looked to connect quickly in an intense but charming way which was rather sweet. Easy to see why Micah would be into her.

We get to idle chatting and Karly asks, "So how long you guys been married?"

"'Bout two years," Micah said, holding up two fingers before pulling on his beer.

"Wow, that's pretty cool…Sherri, right?" Karly asked cheerfully. "Is it Persian or Iranian, these days?"

"What's the difference? I am so tired of that conversation…" Sherri sounded a little annoyed with a debutante's demeanor but also braced for ignorant questions about any "support" for the Ayatollah that she may have secretly harbored. What many Americans didn't realize about Iranians was that if they were in the States, Europe or *anywhere* that wasn't Iran, in the 70s and 80s then most likely, they were pro-West and not Muslim fanatics. This is not to say the Shah was a painting, far from it, he just killed the *other guys.*

Karly was far from ignorant but I could relate to Sherri's irritation. However, I also wouldn't call Iraqis Babylonians, either. So there's that.

"Is 'Sherri' short for Scheherazade?" Karly continued, nonplussed. She was definitely a "people person."

"Very good!" Sherri smiled, changing gears fast as well, her nose crinkling, "You have very good knowledge!"

Making friends quickly, Karly beamed like a fifth grader who won a spelling bee, "Yes, I do". Then she pinched my thigh under the table as her hand ran over the top of my leg. Her fingers felt good stroking my thigh and I drew wood again.

"Lee said you play drums?" Micah asked. "I play guitar and sing and Lee plays bass…so maybe we can do something here tonight, man. I've seen these guys before. Slip 'em a $20, and they'll let us use their equipment."

"Cool!" I answered, assuming that I was slipping the $20. "So Lee said you were in the 'Charlie's'? That's great…I bet it was fun."

"Hell yeah, it was. It wasn't perfect but what is, right?" Micah explained how he played in Creeping Charlie; the one and the same from that T-shirt the Arab kid was wearing shooting pool in Jerusalem.

"I played pool with a kid in Jerusalem who a t-shirt of yours, man." I said.

Micah smiled, "Yeah, we got around. Busted our ass in the States but as not much happened for us there, if not for the movie."

Their fans affectionately referred to them as the Charlies. These guys were huge in Europe but really couldn't break the U.S. even though they toured a lot, kind of like Oingo Boingo. They had a song called "Breakfast at Sunset," placed in a hit teen movie of the same name. It was their only real known song in the States and their only U.S. hit, per se but they had rabid fans in Europe who bought all their albums. I saw the Charlie's open for Camper Van Beethoven in 1986 at the Whisky in L.A. but I didn't remember Micah, even though I had definitely known of the band. I was more interested in seeing

Camper anyway and my friend got me in because he worked at the Charlie's American record label, Candlewax Records.

Micah went on to explain how they broke up in France over some crap that was building up, culminating with the drummer having had an affair with the singer's wife, "Pete was pissed that he wasn't getting his share of press or some shit. I was like, 'Dude, you're the drummer!' Jeez! We can't all be Keith Moon…Anyway, I guess it came to a head when he started banging Bill's wife and Bill found out because she did it to get even 'cause she found out about some errant piece of ass Bill had who got their address and sent her a letter with some pictures or something. Came to blows one night in Cannes, on stage. Drums everywhere, I just backed up off stage, fucking mess, man." Micah shook his head at the memory. "So that was that."

I remember reading something about it in Rolling Stone so it's weird how he turned out to be Liev's brother. That would explain why Liev was asking me about music so intensely when I met him at the checkpoint that day besides just being a fan but it was funny how he didn't mention the Charlies there. I guess there wasn't any time.

"So I hung out in Paris for a while and that's how I met this one." Micah concluded, throwing his thumb over in Sherri's direction. The music was loud but really good. Sherri was vibing on it until Micah said "this one."

"Well, it was more than that, my sugar," Sherri said, kissing his cheek with pouty, lingering lips then she turned to us and her eyes sparkled like the stars over the Nile. Cleopatra had nothing on this chick. Sherri went on to explain that she was actually being given away in marriage to her father's cousin, a wealthy Iranian industrialist who was forty years old to her nineteen to which she had concerns about. "He was a pig! I don't mind older men…Him? He was a pig!" she was practically spitting the words out but even the anger was charming.

Sherri grew up frustrated, raised in Paris from age ten. Even though her family escaped the new regime after the fall of the Shah-led Iran, it meant little as far as embracing a new culture was concerned. Being in France didn't mean her dad was open to it, but the options were to go there or be killed. France also didn't require an application for asylum as long as one had legitimate business there, which her father did have in abundance. It was automobile imports.

"I am happy for my family to leave," she said. "If I stay for there, I would be dead or raped everyday to punish my father because he sell cars to the Shah." Her smile had vanished by this point.

I didn't wince outwardly but I knew what she was talking about. Theocracies have little tolerance for strong willed women. However, in Paris, Sherri was so close to Western Civilization but so far from the same. "When I was a smaller girl, I wanted to try out for the gymnastics, but my father, he say 'no,' for because I'd be 'running around half naked,'" she rolled her eyes and shook her head. Obviously, this was one of many challenges in that household but we didn't have all night to compare notes and being a boy in my family meant none of those restrictions applied at all. I couldn't get pregnant and it was that simple. It didn't matter that I could knock a girl up. It wasn't fair but I didn't set things up that way.

Then Sherri's mood changed when the subject turned toward Micah. Mocking him a little, she said, "I meet 'this one' in for the night club. We would to sneak from the home. To go out."

Micah chuckled shaking his head. He actually blushed and it was obvious he heard this story a few times, in addition to living it.

"Who's 'we,'" asked Karly.

"Me and other girls for my school. We go but come back before the sunrise." She beamed, "So one night we go into nightclub and there where he was playing for guitar." She explained how the club choice was completely random as she had never even heard of the Charlie's or Micah but was instantly smitten by him and his vibe while playing. It was the classic "girl-sees-guy-do-something-bitchen-and-gets-wet" or something to that effect.

"Then I knew, I just knew." Sherri said, her accent making the story even hotter. "He was the most beautiful thing I had *everrrrr* see. I didn't give a shit that he was a Jewish when I find out and he did not to care that I was born Muslim. So I run away from the home and we get married...Not that religious, I believe," she smiled as she lightly tongued at her straw. I could see guys in our eye line salivating, most having never wanted to be a straw so bad in their lives. So much for my "equally yoked" theory. Chemistry goes a long way where love is concerned.

"What are you drinking?" Karly asked.

"Copenhagen Dream. Rum, 7-up, tequila and a little cherry flavor," Sherri said.

Karly flagged the waitress over and ordered one. I could sense that she was competing a little despite getting her fair share of attention and entertaining the male gaze as it were.

Knowing what I knew, I was intrigued; Sherri's family would want to see her dead and this, I knew for certain. "Don't you worry about or miss your family? Your friends? Are you scared at all?" I asked.

"My father called me a whore for even questioning that marriage process, his choice for me. But I think the life is for the living. I like the men and I love this Jew." She kissed Micah's cheek again, her arm around his neck and she was swooning as she buried her nose into his collar. I liked the way she said the word, "process." "So no, I do not miss *them,* but I miss my mother...you ask good question and they don't know for where I am, but I write letter to my mother once for the month, so you see," she smiled and said nothing else.

"So you see...what?" Karly asked, checking for clarity.

"Oh, nothing. Just that is all. Is that right?" she smiled.

"Well, babe we still have to work on that language thing of yours." Micah chided as Sherri grabbed his leg or cock under the table. I couldn't tell either way but the feigned shock on Micah's face cracked us all up.

This girl is 21? Man, when she's 30...Jesus! Confirming, yet again, that which is suppressed will erupt! This could have been one of those stories I read in the Jerusalem Post and it happened all the time.

"Dude..." Lee chuckled, "same fucking guy, man."

"So your parents were cool about it?" I asked Micah, thinking of my Sam's brother and his sentence to the Island of Misfit Toys.

Lee chimed in, "Oh yeah, man. Our folks aren't too hung up with this shit."

The waitress came by with another round and at this point I was feeling pretty good. The band was playing blues, old blues; like Willie Dixon and Lightnin' Hopkins, Little Walter, Muddy Waters, that kind of stuff with a little early Motown thrown in. Sounded odd with a Dane accent but they weren't half bad and you could tell they were fans. People were up and dancing, kind of like the slow twists you see in old films about the 1960s. Nothing trendy or anything, it was actually kind of cool. I never saw anyone dance to blues before as they didn't do it in the States at all, in those days, and while I have always listened I have never danced to it myself. I never really thought about it but I guess the Danes could teach us a few things about the care and feeding of American Blues.

Sherri grabbed Liev by the hand and led him to the floor. The dance floor was darker than where we had been sitting but the pot and cigarette smoke hung heavy in the air and could be seen surrounding her like she was in the clouds. She started shaking her hips and doing this belly dancer and washing machine hybrid move. It was very slow with her sweater clad arms floating above the mere mortals like perfect angel's wings. With her eyes closed and a bitten lower lip, she was snapping her fingers like she had bells on them. We were all very grateful for a Mediterranean heritage all of a sudden. Those boots and that ass in that skirt gave every man in the room an immediate will to live. While not a unique observation, I was sure God was definitely a man.

Karly noticed my buzzed gaze and gently put her hand in my lap, "Hey Mr. Man," she purred in my ear. Men can be such assholes.

"Hey back," I whispered. "Having a good time?"

A nibble on my ear was her response.

Micah was just grinning ear to ear, "That's my wife, man!" He said, with a pirate's gusto, smacking the table.

I thought he said "What a lie!" because I couldn't hear him. So I answered, "What's a lie?"

"No, man, that's my fucking wife!" He smiled. "Of all the clubs in the entire world, she walks into mine." He clarified, as we laughed. We both knew the Bogart movie.

He then pulls out a joint, "You don't mind, do you?" he asked.

"Nope, go right ahead," I said. My head was spinning. The smells of the smoke, carpet and booze were mixing and while it should have had an odor, I was having a great time.

"You go right ahead too, babe." Karly said, putting her chin on my shoulder, her dark blue eyes looking up at me, she smiled, "I don't mind."

"Really?" I was blown away as girls weren't usually that cool, unless they themselves partook. I'm getting high in Denmark with Micah Lowensohn from the Charlie's. That was a story you tell later. "Life is good," I thought. The smell of Karly's hair near my face was like oxygen to a dying man. This couldn't last forever, could it?

I was saddened by death and the passing of time and I saw fire.

Micah and I took a couple of hits and then Karly said, "Let's dance, my mister." She grabbed my hand. I was relaxed as Karly led me to the dance floor. She started swinging her hips, shaking that ass. Men at other tables stared in admiration. If this wasn't Denmark, I'd have had concerns for my safety. Then she turned around, looking me dead in the eye as she did this, slow, sands in an hour glass type of move, wrists crossed above her head, with each hip shake designed to put my eye out, one foot in front of the other. Kind of like hip, step, hip, repeat but she did it standing in one place. I guess she felt a little competitive push from Sherri. That's always a good thing because how else do we improve? But where do girls learn this shit? It didn't matter because this was the Boom Boom Room, man! So boom boom she went. She took her scarf off and wrapped it around my neck and pulled me close. She kissed me and then let me go. The music was ringing in my ears in a good way. She bumped that pretty ass away from me and then looked over her shoulder, flipping her hair around, with an expression that asked, "Are you looking at my butt?" Then she wiggled her finger to "come here."

I was her silly puppy and this went on for several songs; slow, grinding back beats designed to be fucked to. Allowing any woman in the world to make her magic happen and being a guy, it didn't take much. For this not being much, my weapons were useless against her…

We went back to eat our food and I was ravenous, the munchies. Sherri was sitting in Micah's lap, feeding him with her fingers and the food as I recall, was not exactly light; Danish meatballs, smoked pork, creamed cabbage with chicken. There were different plates as we were all sharing. Taking a cue from Sherri, Karly started feeding me meatballs, letting me lick her fingers after each small piece. She was really making her mark and it was nice not to do all the chasing. I think this was the first time in my young life I had that experience. Sherri became my de facto wingman or wing-girl.

I would have felt bad for Liev except that he'd been dancing with pretty much every gorgeous girl in Denmark since Sherri left him to his own devices, having been the good sister-in-law that she was. When they were dancing I saw a girl get bumped by Sherri and she smiled, inviting this girl in to their circle to dance with them. She introduced Liev to the girl and they started dancing. She was a pretty blonde, a local and she had on a black mini-skirt and boots with a tight tan sweater. They got into it a little as she started grinding on him a bit and that's when Sherri made her exit. Good looking girls make excellent wing men, I found and if I was alone that night, I may have taken advantage of Sherri's services. She already greased the wheels with Karly and me. Dancing with your sister in law only made one look more sensitive and evolved. Girls really bought into that. Liev's girl sure did.

"Lee never had a problem pulling babes..." Micah observed rather clinically. "Mom always said he was the charming one." I lost count of how many beers we had but he seemed to be endlessly swigging.

But Sherri didn't hurt Liev's chances, either. As she came back to our table, she had her thumbs up in front of her with her tongue out like she scored. We chatted for a while and lost sight of Liev. I took a couple more hits off Micah's joint. That was good stuff.

Liev finally came back to the table and he was pretty excited. I thought he just got laid, "Hey man, I just gave the band a few bucks and they're going to let us play a few songs after their break." We finished our beers and ordered some more.

"Cool! That's awesome!" I was kind of nervous but looking forward to playing.

"So Lee said it got kind of hairy outside Ramallah," Micah started. He sounded like he was speaking from experience having visited his little brother in Israel himself.

"Yeah, you know," I was right about to find a tactful way out of this conversation when...

The Danish blues guitarist comes over to our table and says we could play for thirty minutes and that it would be an honor to have Micah play with his "new band" as that was how Liev pitched it. He was so into it that he gave Liev his money back. He apologized about the drummer taking a payment in the first place. Apparently, the Dane saw the value of a good story too.

He asked Micah what the new project was called. Micah smiled, thought for a second and answered, "Zen Violation, man." The Dane smiled and nodded like he was handed the Ten Commandments. Rock stardom offered a level of awe and ass kissing commensurate with the level of actual success. In the States, Micah was popular, in Copenhagen, he was a god. I found humor in the exchange and a bit of a relief because I really didn't want to talk about the roadside at all. I was feeling good but suddenly pictured my mother's reaction to the news if Liev and his guys hadn't gotten there in time. I shook it off.

I had spoken to my mom in the morning before hiking the road to Canaan with Sam. This was the day before I left. She was glad I was alright and had a good time under the circumstances but was happy I was coming home. I was never going to tell her about the stuff that went down.

We get up on stage to set up and Micah said, "You're the guest, man…whatever you want to start with."

"You know 'Paint it Black' by the Stones?" I asked.

Micah nodded and smiled toward Liev, "You know that, right Lee?"

Liev grinned. Then I said, "After that, anything you want…I can handle it".

"So you're open to jam?" Micah asked.

Usually, I didn't like "jamming" because all that meant to me was useless musical riffing, noodling and guessing but Micah being Micah, I was going to roll with it, "Sure. Whatever works."

Karly was with Sherri in the crowd that was gathering, most recognizing Micah. I could hear some folks chatting with the Dane and looking over. We were setting up, adjusting the band's gear to fit our needs for the moment but there was a buzz as many folks in the club were as in awe of the Charlie's as the Dane was.

Karly was in front, by the stage squealing, "This is so exciting! I get to see you play!"

Karly and Sherri was our built in hot chick cheering section but this joint didn't need any help as there were plenty of those. Girls abound as the Danish blues group obviously had a healthy mailing list themselves, if they did that sort of thing at all. Half the magic of any gig was the male patrons feeling the fleeting, illusory promise of easy sex with hot girls. I didn't matter what kind of music it was because if good looking girls were there, the show just went better and followings grew. Chances were excellent if one was playing in a band in Los Angeles in the 1980s, you were after girls as much as art and money. College rock flannel flyers or metal head Hessians, it made zero difference, really. We could have been "Poison" or "Divine Weeks," while the music mattered, the girls made it fun and everything we did came off like a fucking magic trick even on a bad night if we knew ourselves. This was primal and not to be challenged and it was fact, not theory. While we weren't hunting for food, we were expressing an inherent dominance known better as showing off. We wouldn't have hunted at all if unfed women fucked us when we got back to the cave. This was simply a casual observation.

I just smiled, taking it all in, drank my beer and finished adjusting the drums so I could play reasonably well. Drums were weird that way, like driving a car. The Danish drummer alone should get $100 for the hassle this was for him. But I wasn't going to pay it as I was still out $500 for the cab ride that Eddied fucked me up on. God bless Saif, man. I'm drumming in Denmark with Micah from the Charlies and the dude who saved my ass in the middle of the Arabian night. I was more than humbled by this.

So the Dane guitar player got up to welcome us and says in his accent laden English, "Ladies and gentlemen, ve have a special guest *treeeet* for you tonight! Micah Lowensohn's newest rock combo, I give you...Zen! Violation!" The crowd of 300 or so erupted and it sounded amazing! They were drunk and rude or in awe, I couldn't tell but it was loud. Micah was bigger than even I had speculated, apparently.

We started playing. "Paint it Black" had this distinct Middle Eastern vibe, especially the drums and guitar line. Micah played the opening riff, stopped and as soon as I started that beat, Micah jumped in again with Lee and everyone started dancing. Micah was really fucking good. People in the States really didn't dance to the Stones or to our kind of rock for that matter. They just stood and watched, then cheered when we were done. They mostly wanted to see something they didn't see on American Bandstand or hear on pop radio.

Karly and Sherri were up front just grooving to what was happening and this was more than ample excuse for Sherri to work her signature washing machine, hip move thing and Karly was eating it up as they were dancing together for a dramatic, sensual effect. They seemed to really be getting off on the attention this was drawing from some of the guys in their vicinity who had cleared a small circle for them. Of course, some of the other girls were digging it too and they joined in. Those who didn't simply watched or scoffed at the "American" and "whoever she was." This was conjecture and speculation on my part but I could see the ladies' scowls and grimaces from where I was sitting so I'm sure it was noticeable from where they were sitting.

As we ripped through five or six more songs with a couple of improvised jams, I knew we were going to be much longer than the allotted thirty minutes but I don't think the Dane cared and I could see he was digging it. Jamming in public always felt way too self-indulgent, but this was an opportunity and Micah actually sang some cool shit over what we were playing, making it up as we went along.

Surprisingly, Liev was a really good bass player. Who knew? Micah called out, "Hey man, you know 'Breakfast at Sunset'?" This was that hit Creeping Charlie song that I knew from the movie. This was a cool, riff heavy song that bordered on trance or dance music. It was their only good sized hit in the U.S. but monster huge in Europe. In fact, their albums sold very well on the strength of that single and they enjoyed near Doors catalog sales because of it. It was a song about being hung over and sleeping all day and getting breakfast at well, sunset! It was kind of surreal; each verse was a weird dream that someone could have if they slept through the day with the TV on, invading their subconscious. Even though Micah didn't sing it originally, he did write it and as soon as he started that opening riff, the place went ape shit.

When we wrapped, Karly ran around the small stage and threw her arms around my neck, the applause in my ears. "You know? That had to be the *sexieeeeest* thing I have ever seen! Ever! I didn't know you were *that* good!" She cooed.

I thanked her with a kiss. As I hugged her I could see Liev chatting up a couple of girls, one was the one Sherri had set him up with. Sherri kissed Micah and led him back to our table and people were back slapping him, crowding him a little until they got to the table. It was pretty cool, he signed bar napkins or whatever fans could get in front of him. He glad handed some of the customers and was genuinely humbled by people's kudos. He was a cool guy.

Just playing with different guys in another country was an experience, much less who it was with. Moments, man.

I was feeling good...Zen Violation, cool name. Our fans could affectionately call us "ZV" or "the Zen," I chuckled to myself. "Hey man, you going to ZV at the Palace?" some dude would ask his buddies in L.A. "Nah bro, it's sold out…fuckers! But the new Zen record is epic! Fuckin' Micah's a beast!"And so on…

****

We hung out for a couple more hours before we stumbled outside and flagged a cab. The club was still happening but Micah had invited some friends to his house for a little after party. We were all pretty lit, feeling pretty good and while Liev was out of it, he had managed to corral some girls who were for sure coming over to Micah's. I even started calling him "Lee." Sherri told us they do this every now and again so they were used to the locals. Micah was popular but not Beatle famous so it wasn't anything too scary I hoped. John Lennon's murder was only a few years old at the time. In L.A. we had a following and some good write ups but this was on such a different level. Micah was a bona fide rock star. He could do this here, France, Italy, anywhere on the continent, basically.

Karly had her arm in mine and it felt good. It fit. Standing out front of the Boom Boom Room, I felt a strange sensation, a consistent feeling since the roadside in Ramallah, a kind of peace. I wasn't sad about Mahmoud anymore, I wasn't even angry at Eddie or the Israelis. The thought of the dead minister or the beaten kid didn't weigh on me. I didn't care when I got back to the States or if I would ever get back. I was contented but I was then overcome by a heavy fear that this couldn't last and may end badly but I shook that off. Why wouldn't it last? Why can't good things last or get even better? Why couldn't I get rich and be married 50 years and die old? Why do shoes come in pairs and why can't the other one mind its own business before it decides to drop and just move on to some other foot?

Liev and Micah were good guys and we relished what we had in common which was more than what we didn't have in common.

"That was a fuckin' blast, man!" Liev said. He was with the cool blonde.

"Yeah, it was." I could not have agreed more. "Where'd you get the name, dude?" I asked Micah.

"Just something I had brewing awhile. I got a bunch of names. I wish I could be in 100 bands just to use all the names I got." He was definitely happy with how things went and why not? It was fun.

150

This was our religion, our rite. This was as good as it was going to get for me and I knew my spiritual and musical life were one and the same. These guys weren't thinking about rabbinical school anytime soon, either, especially Micah with his hot Persian goddess of a wife.

We were in the cab which was more of a mini-van. I had been dozing in and out listening to the chatter. I was on a bench in the van and noticed the girl next to me, she was the one Liev had met dancing. She was pretty but I wasn't sure if her name was Ingrid or Mildred even though Liev introduced us on the sidewalk earlier. Karly had her fingers locked in mine and her head on my shoulder, dozing as well and bumping with the cab ride. The street passed by us like a dream, the buildings and lights were blending together with the palette of the end of the night. People walked to where ever they were going with the same plodding steps that folks have when you pass them in a car quickly. Were they going home, to work? Did they have a fight with a wife? Did that guy just quit his job? We charged along, our merry band.

Micah and Sherri's house was a condo in a converted castle or old university building or something but it was huge and there were nine or ten big units with four to five bedrooms each. We puffed on more of that weed as Micah gave me and Karly a tour. She didn't have any but I had more than a few hits. The place was set up nice and he had turned one of his rooms into a practice room, another into a studio with recording equipment, and he had an old twelve channel Neve board which ruled. He turned another room into a wine room which had a fridge for white wines and beer and three walls of red wine racks with some nice leather chairs in the middle and ashtray tables for cigars with ceiling vents to suck up the smoke. Money's a good thing and I just didn't trust anyone telling me different either. I thought they had to have a trust fund, be stupid, or simply mistaken.

Sherri got some food out, cheese, cold cuts, that kind of thing. Their kitchen was one of those huge Italian numbers, with a marble counter island in the middle. There were lots of open bottles of red wine as guests helped her open them. She had baskets of bread and fruit on the counters and the whole house smelled like home. This perked me up a bit and I started to mingle with some of the folks that were there. Some were American, but most were Danes.

"Great playing, man! Zen Violation? Cool name…" A patron from the club said.

"Thanks a lot. What's your name?" I asked as I shook his hand.

"Tajco but everyone calls me 'Taj,' like Taj Mahal," he said, smiling. "Where are you from?"

I told him and he asked, so explained how I ended up in Denmark as people were cutting through us, excusing themselves.

Taj got very taciturn, "You know, what is happening to the Arabs there is completely unfair and anti-democratic, I don't see how the Americans can condone such..." he began solemnly.

"No argument, there, none at all." I agreed, cutting him off and I was quite buzzed so I know I was weaving as I said it. I was self-conscious about the interruption, "But they're going to have to stop with the religious bullshit, man." I burped quietly, through my nose, excused myself and continued, "It's enough, they should have had enough by now and it's not important to what's really going on...so, done." Then I stopped myself cold. I'm in Micah's house and Liev's my friend. I certainly didn't feel gracious about where this was going and I wasn't up for a political debate. So grinning ear to ear, I said, "Taj, you seem like a good lad and I'm going to get a beer and some cheese...would you care for some beer and some cheese?"

Taj smiled and shook his head no. I could tell that he could tell I was buzzed. He had that smiling look that said he knew. As I walked towards the kitchen, I realized that I was really glad to be out of there, the West Bank. Glad to be going home. I felt like I was over the discussion for now, if ever to discuss it again. Shit, I wasn't going to fix it and especially not in Denmark. For some reason, what I was feeling was anathema to this kind of conflict or *any* kind of conflict because it violated my new Zen, man.

I wanted to hang on to this feeling for as long as I could...It wasn't bliss, just peace and the last time I felt this way was when I was nineteen and running track at my college. I remember having cut class that day and sleeping in. I was walking across campus to go to practice and the quad had these big pine trees. The sun was so bright and I felt good. I caught the warmth of the sun as it peeked at me through the pines. Simple as that. Good. Nothing special had happened. I wasn't seeing anyone, Shelly being awhile away. I just felt really good. That entire spring was the most peaceful time I ever felt and it had lasted around nine months...

I caught up with Sherri, Karly and Liev and his girl in the den, Mildred! That was her name! Goddamit, she was hot and since when did I develop the habit of forgetting names of beautiful women? Liev looked like he was doing very well. God bless him.

I nodded at Karly and she smiled as she cut through the people she was talking to excusing herself demurely. I took her hand as we went into the hallway and my boots clunked on the old wood floor. I had found some stairs that led to the roof. We walked up the stairs and I allowed Karly to lead the way. I was becoming attached to looking at that magnificent ass do whatever it wanted. We got to the big wooden door that served as an entrance to an attic that went out to the roof.

There's *nothing* like a Copenhagen night in the spring, clear, starry and the air is razor crisp. I could feel it in my nose and the street lights didn't invade the sky like they did in L.A. The stars could be seen for more than miles. I don't know why that was. It was like a dream.

I looked over to Karly and she had closed her eyes, took a deep breath and took my hand and as she did we started *elevating.*

We glided slowly above the city and I wasn't afraid at all. Once we got over the church by the hotel, she let go. "Don't be afraid," she said.

"I'm cool," I replied, calm as the Buddha, gliding around the bell tower of the church. It had an old brass roof that was tarnished and I could see that in the moonlight.

It was not really flying as much as it was floating but even that was too anemic a word. We definitely had control. When we started to come down, we just moved our arms *once* and gained altitude again. If we did it again, we went higher but when we descended it wasn't like falling because we gently came down, losing altitude by choice. We did this throughout the city, floating over the Mollean River between the cargo boats and the pleasure trips. I could smell the water as the spray from the boats splashed my face. My clothes got wet from the mist and it felt good. We waved at those who saw us and those folks were calm as well, like they had seen this a thousand times, Karly looked over and said, "Go higher, sweetie."

I moved my arms and went up and did it only a few more times. I was up so high that I got a little concerned. I could see the city and the river looked small but Karly was still below me, so I stopped and waited for her to catch me. When she did, she said, "Wow, you're good…I didn't know if you'd be able to handle this."

"I can handle anything, man," I smirked as we floated through the city. We owned the night and then she kissed me.

I woke up…

In my bed in the hotel, I sat up and looked around as my hands were still being filled in, like I was incomplete, or somewhere else during my sleep and only now was I coming together...

Remnants from the dream, the pot or the booze, I thought. And I thought it weird.

I got up and showered and went to Karly's room and knocked on the door. She opened it and let me in. "Good morning gorgeous," she smiled. "Sleep good?"

"Yeah, just had a weird dream. Still want to go to the museum?"

"For sure. Just let me get ready, I'll be by in a half hour." Her face searched mine, "We good?"

"Yeah, yeah, great! See you in a minute," I said quite unconvincingly.

"So you don't remember last night?" she asked searching my eyes.

"Um, not really? Had a trippy dream though," I said, voice still rough without coffee.

"That wasn't a dream, sweetie," Karly had gently pushed me against the wall. "This isn't either," she continued as she undid my belt and pulled the buttons open on my 501s. She kissed me passionately as she reached into my pants. With my hard cock in her fingers, she grinned, "Good morning soldier!"

"Hi," was all I could whisper. I could do nothing but whisper and let her do whatever she wanted.

With that Karly slid down on me with her fingers in my mouth. After a few minutes as I was holding back I said, "Let's do this!" I grabbed her and she laughed as I threw her on the bed. She rolled away, stood up and held my hand.

She stopped, "Baby, just because I haven't had the fire in the hole doesn't mean I don't know the right end of a cock." She smiled sweetly, her fingers keeping me stiff with her free hand. I could barely see with my eyes rolled to

154

the back of my head. She continued like a sexy interrogator, "A blow job is just what will have to do under the circumstances. But I want you happy." She twisted gently, leaning into my mouth so close to kissing, "Is that OK?"

I grunted some semblance of a response. I think I said, "OK." She had me.

She slid back down and finish I did. This girl was not only smart and beautiful, she was talented. And yes, fellatio is a talent or an acquired skill, not ever to be taken for granted. This is also fact, not to be challenged.

Chapter 9-This is the Best Part of the Trip…

Karly knocked on my door, smiling, "Time to get up…again!" she laughed. We took off, got some food and walked through the city. I could actually live there. Copenhagen is just cool. Some of the streets were cobblestone and some were paved but the overall vibe was just clean, quiet. The people were walking more than driving, it seemed, so the streets were packed but folks seemed busy in a good way whether headed for work or errands. We had fun the other night but no one in the club seemed too uptight. Not like L.A. Copenhagen was cleaner than Los Angeles and most American cities I'd been to and definitely cleaner than the West Bank, which really wasn't a statement of any substance. Despite the old buildings, everything seemed well preserved and not too musty or dank. The Danes didn't suffer from mini-mall mania like we did in the States. They didn't have this hard on to tear everything down.

We saw a cool record store and we hung there for a while. It was an older store, definitely not a chain. They had old Iggy Pop and Sex Pistols posters up which were pretty cool as they were promotional posters that you didn't see anywhere else and they were huge. Easily, four feet by nine feet, the posters were almost floor to ceiling. The clerk was playing "Eight Miles High" by the Byrds when we walked in.

We didn't have a lot of culture where I grew up in South Los Angeles. Even Pasadena where I ended up had more beauty. My hometown was what amounted to a steel town; General Motors, Bethlehem Steel, Firestone Tires and the like, was where most everyone worked. They had good union gigs that kept food on the table and as such there was no Rosenborg Castle getting turned into a museum but we did have the Allen Theater. My dad took us to the museum every now and again like we went to Disneyland but it wasn't part of the routine. The Los Angeles Coliseum had a cool park my parents liked and my dad liked to take us to the science museum but it sure wasn't Europe. Nothing's that bleak as long as it's sunny and L.A. had sunny to spare. Still, when something's missing, it's always missing. That will never change.

Our neighborhood had some interesting characters. Retired GM guys and a couple WWII vets populated our street. There were a couple of old timers who would weld our bikes when we broke the frames, doing an early version of

BMX. They had the welding tanks in the garage. The older folks treated us like their own grandkids and while I'm sure they couldn't tell a Picasso from a piccolo, they would be real nice about it, if faced with the conversation. They had a grace and distinctly Midwestern decorum that I felt rubbed off on me and was definitely not apparent in the Los Angeles I lived in as an adult. Most of these folks were transplants after WWII. They came out to California because of the jobs which were steady with pensions and benefits. We certainly were not part of the "business" which was the entertainment business. We may as well have been in Iowa. We grew up in a different part of L.A.

Schools were okay as far as public school went I guess. We had some gang stuff but nothing too severe, at least not *at* school, anyway. There were the movies and the park and the beach but one had to work a bit find anything artistic. It wasn't too hard; hop a bus to USC or go to the library…you did what you could, if you were at all inclined. Most people don't ask a lot of questions. It wasn't anyone's fault, really. It was just America, at least the one I knew till I got old enough to be on my own and perfect or not, it was mine.

Karly and I walked through the park which I think was a shortcut to the Rosenborg Castle that the innkeeper told us about which was converted into a museum in the 1830s. It was very gaudy, in a French classical kind of way but the art was supposed to be breath taking. Christian IV lost it after several battles or something. However, things were fine now and everyone seemed happy with this version of royalty.

What has always fascinated me was the temporal nature of things. One day you're King or Queen and things are going pretty well, after all, you're a fucking monarch and then one day…poof, all gone! Dictatorships do provide steady work but the retirement plan is sketchy.

The King wakes up and realizes that he's like an old Marx Brothers movie as his generals tell him in a panic, "Sire! The people are revolting."

To which he replied without a clue, "You can say that, again!" Except that wasn't a proper response.

But it didn't matter, not one little bit. The majesty of government was only ever going to do so much for the people. They're suckers to think anything more than keeping them alive just enough to work and pay tax is what they'll get. But think that, they do until someone gets wise and starts something but then the original reason for the unrest vanishes and the people are lorded over like so many pets. Wash, rinse, repeat.

"Meet the new boss/same as the old boss..."

But nothing really changes does it? And dictators die.

So the castle was great. We saw the Royal Family's permanent art collection and a comprehensive Picasso show. Now there was a guy as the song goes, who was never called an asshole. Best pick up line ever, "I am Picasso, I will paint you." This generated 11 wives and various concubines that gave him a ton of kids. This was very impressive for a man who was no painting himself. He was lucky to have made a lot of money while he was alive.

Poor old Vincent Van Gogh; he cut off his ear, frustrated, penniless and he had no good pick up line. If he got laid more, maybe he wouldn't have been so upset. I was always a firm believer that more money and more sex can fix a lot and if you have the love to go along with it, so much the better.

Karly had gotten away from me while I was reading one of the descriptions of a Picasso work entitled, "Le Rêve" or "the Dream." The model was some seventeen year old ballerina named Marie-Thérèse Walter. He left his wife for this girl, more like his fourth wife. I liked Picasso but one thing that always kept me curious was how he'd get girls to pose naked and then paint them like he was five with a coloring book. The geometric impressions got him laid a lot, apparently.

Karly was gone when I turned around. I walked over to the Royal Family exhibit and there she was in front of vases or something. I never really cared for that kind of stuff in museums. They always looked like stuff I could get at Sears with the Stephanie Powers Collection or something. I knew it was by hand and not a machine but I still couldn't be bothered. I usually kept this to myself because it would often turn into an argument.

I walked up behind Karly and encircled my arms around her waist. She gave me a rise, immediately.

"You better watch yourself, mister. I have a feeling that you're trouble," her whisper curling into a grin as I could see the side of her face.

"Oh yeah…and how do you know?" I nibbled her ear.

"I bet your pants fit different than they did ten seconds ago." She turned around, "Right?" Looking me right in the eyes. Something about her expression said more than a sexy pass ever could. This was not a young girl's flirtation. She looked right through my cool like she was prepared to care for me the rest of my life. She made that rare connection of the heart to the lust, and she'd be right if she had arrived at that conclusion.

I just looked into her eyes right back. "Right..." I wasn't playing or being sarcastic. I leaned my forehead against her head looking into her soul without fear. She was fun and for the first time in my life, I felt like I was home and she was the coolest, sweetest girl I have ever met.

After the castle, we found this cool little café which doubled as a deli. They served French food but they gave you a lot and it was delicious. The pretentious joints back home were thimble sized portions and they charged you a fortune. The smells of meats, sauces and cheeses wafted over us as we drank red wine. The waiter was also the owner and he and his wife were busy. They had a couple workers in t-shirts and black vests so it was very casual.

We sat out on the sidewalk and enjoyed the evening air which blew cool because of the river as the last of the sun sank deep into it. The stars were coming out to play and were so bright and so many, that I was briefly overwhelmed with the beauty and my emotions at the same time. We talked and laughed about everything that we had done: the Boom Boom Room, jamming with Liev and his brother, Micah and Sherri, their house and their life. How did I come to be here? Why was God smiling down me when he ignored us long enough to get Saif, the cab driver killed? Why would God rain down a blessing on me but ignore two million Armenians or six million Jews? I'm sure many of them were good people. Sadly, I knew just enough to know I knew nothing.

I am finite.

"I wonder what happens down the road..." Karly asked.

"What...which road?" I asked.

"You're going back to L.A., right?" Karly was stirring a sugar cube into an espresso.

"Yeah, aren't you? Ventura, I mean?" I know I had concern in my voice. I didn't want this to end and if she decided to stay in Denmark, that would not work out in the long run.

"Yeah, of course…I just mean you and me. That's all," she was searching for something concrete, I could tell, and lifelong decisions were made in these moments. They only took a moment too.

"Easy to figure out…I love you," and although I blurted it out, right away I tried to sound like I planned it. Immediately, I worked to control my face as to not give anything away in the form of panic. While exciting, the first time that word ever came up can be sometimes tough, no matter what the overwhelming feeling tells you to do. So far I was not wrong the couple of times in my life I said it. I always got a good response. But this was different. This felt like it was the rest of my life.

Karly's eyes were quiet. She looked right at me, leaned forward in her chair and took my hands, "I love you, too. I really do…Weird how it happens, isn't it?"

We sat there, stroking each other's hands as the stars completed their appearance. The lights of the deli shone on the water. Not much was said and didn't have to be. It was like all the women I had ever met led me here and we haven't even made love yet. I could never call it fucking with this girl. Not ever.

I'm twelve years old and I'm walking home from the fair at the city park, having been rejected by this girl in my homeroom, I was in the midst of a pity party.

I'm a couple of blocks from home and I see the prettiest little tanned blond girl wearing shorts and little white sneakers, standing on the sidewalk, looking up as she was about to cry. Her cat was stuck in a tree. I asked her if she needed help and she said, "Yes, please." It was her utter girlishness that got to me, sniffing in between her words, smiling through her tears and braces, happy that someone was there to help.

She wasn't from around here or at least I didn't recognize her. Her name was Peggy and she was visiting her grandmother for the week as her parents were in the middle of a nasty divorce. I heroically got her cat down for her. At least as heroic as a twelve year old boy can be. Harrison Ford, I was not, and I got some nasty scratches for the chivalry. We talked for a while.

She gave me the phone number to her grandmother's house and we hung out the whole week. I took her to the fair, making homeroom girl jealous, we went to the movies, and I took her to the beach. We took the bus.

On the second to the last day of her visit I hopped the wall behind the house, after walking through the used car dealership, as usual. The owner always yelled at me for walking through his lot like I was going to scratch a car or something and I'd just keep walking. Once I was over the wall and disappeared into the ivy, he shut his pie hole.

Peggy was sitting in the back yard. I was a little surprised because she was always in the house if she knew I was coming over. She was wearing shorts and sitting barefoot on a blanket, reading "Tiger Beat," a teen rag that covered the 1970s heartthrobs du jour. I said "hi" and lay on my side, feigning interest at her magazine. I made a joke about Leif Garrett and I was nervous all of a sudden. I looked up at her face, she smiled and I had my first kiss and it was perfect, and not as first kisses go either but worldwide epic.

She left the next day, back to New Mexico. We called each other a few times. Her grandmother had died that fall, so Peggy never came back. We never saw each other again after that summer. She was my first sense of loss. My first sense of something actually dying, without a body attached to it and I was only twelve…

Karly and I got up and walked back to the hotel holding hands. We passed a movie theater on the way. It was built in the 1930s and had an actual box office in the middle of the foyer. Selling tickets was a bored Dane teen who would have preferred to be anywhere but working. The theater posters for "upcoming films" were almost all classics as they only played old movies, American mostly and they were showing "Easy Rider."

"Oh my God," I said. "Have you seen this? It's the best movie ever," pointing to the movie poster with Peter Fonda's back to us, staring out into forever, like the one in my room at home.

"A man went looking for America but he couldn't find it anywhere…" The last time I saw it was that last night in Pasadena. So much has changed since, I wondered what I'd find when I got home.

Karly shook her head and smiled sweetly, "They play it at school sometimes but no I haven't…"

"We have to see this, you don't understand. After where we were in the West Bank, we have to see this." I explained the saga behind the making of the movie and that it wasn't just about bikers, it was about everything anyone has ever believed in that failed them. I even went so far as to draw the comparison to the Jesus story as portrayed by Peter Fonda as Wyatt or Captain America with Billy being the John the Baptist character, played by Dennis Hopper. Whether this was their intention making the movie, I don't know. It was just a feeling I had.

"Ok, babe…I'll see it. But it better not suck!" Karly chided, hitting my arm, laughing. I paid for the tickets and the bored box office girl actually perked up. "Easy Rider is one of my best favorites," she smiled in her broken English.

This took me aback for a second. Beneath all the black and death metal couture, it was nice to see someone care. The theater was still regal and quite full, surprisingly. There were an assortment of different folks; students, young professionals, art types and older folks who probably actually lived the 1960s. My generation had romanticized the era so much, that it was possible none of it was real. To those who lived the experience, it was and I had heard stories.

Karly seemed to really enjoy herself and laughed at the campfire scene where Jack Nicholson explains the Venusians and their meeting with key leaders on earth, while the three characters were stoned. Karly's acceptance of irreverence was important to me; not exactly the hallmark of a good mother, I suppose but important, nonetheless. The movie was subtitled in Danish, which was something different for me. Karly sighed at some of the heavy parts and was openly weeping at end.

Peter Fonda's motorcycle was on fire by a roadside in the south after he'd been shot. It was a wooded area. Was this a déjà vu I'd been having? I kept seeing fire and was getting hit with a sadness and grief that something was slipping away. I wondered if it was just the film having seeped into my consciousness, because I'd seen it so many times. Maybe that's what it was.

As the movie credits rolled, Karly was quietly wiping away her tears. I had seen it before but I never got weepy at the end, I always just felt a little angry. It made me want to take a stronger stand against anything that was going to trick me into standing down. While funny in some parts, the film got very heavy and was a dark piece of work. I just held her hand, stroking her thumb with mine, staring at the blank screen, "Cool, huh?"

"Yes. And you know what? You're cool. You are so very cool." She said, turning to me and kissing my cheek as though she was looking to lighten her mood.

"Well, you're pretty cool too, missy." I smiled.

We got up and left the theater. It was late. She had her arm in mine. "You know what?"

"Nope, what?" I asked almost sarcastically.

"I hope if we have kids, they have as much love in their life as we do right now."

I was surprised by how tranquil I felt. In the past couple relationships I have had, a statement like that would leave me wracked with convulsions. It would have been very run for the hills type stuff. It was all I could do to not run from Shelly when she said she loved me and that was an instinct that should have been heeded, maybe.

But not Karly, though. Not her. Not ever.

I could never imagined saying what came next, "I want to have Micah's life and I want you to have that with me."

"Babe, as long as we're together, we'll have that and more." Her eyes were closed and breathing in the cool night air, she said, "We'll have each other."

I could grow old with this girl and I *knew* it. In the last couple days, I actually fantasized about watching her turn seventy, sharing our false teeth in the same glass. I even pictured her arms plump and with sun spots, jowls heavy with experience and being a grandmother, just as long as she laughed at my jokes the same way she did in Denmark. For as long as I live, for as long as she can look at me that way, contentment was mine. I wanted to see her nose on our kids, her eyes on our daughters and sons. "Who fantasizes about that?" I thought. Not the stuff of erotic dreams, but it was deeper than sex, deeper than how I felt around her. Like watching my own kids, I wanted to see what this woman would become and I didn't want to miss a single minute.

I didn't have any bad or weird feelings since the roadside in Ramallah. Not last night in the club or at Micah's house party and that was fun. This was in that same space in my heart, pure peace in a world without it. Even though I felt that something was coming I couldn't control I knew "now" was all any of us had.

Enjoy the wine now. Enjoy the food now. Enjoy the love…

We got to our hotel and got a drink in the little bar they had off the lobby. It was kind of cheesy with fake plastic plants and tables and chairs that were mismatched like they were borrowed from different churches or halls that forgot to get them back. They had a couple Danish beers on tap and a few wines.

"Last night was so much fun," Karly smiled. "Too bad you don't remember."

"Well, I thought I made up for that this morning." I chuckled.

"Yeah, well…" she trailed off, then, "Let's go upstairs, right now." She grabbed my shirt, pulled me in and kissed me hard.

With that, my resolve had stiffened, among other things, "Sure!" Looking around, I said, "Innkeeper!" I always wanted to yell, "Innkeeper." I pointed to our drinks and motioned for him to charge my room. The innkeeper smiled and nodded. In L.A. yelling "innkeeper" just wasn't done without the hipster irony but here one could get away with it.

Karly led me by the hand. We walked up the creaky narrow stairs and turned the corner to her room, which was next door to mine. The hall had the smell of old, musty carpet. The old throw rugs were threadbare but there was no better place we could have stayed at. Without really looking at me, she unlocked her door.

"I want you to be my first," she said softly, not quite looking over her shoulder. "I want to make love to someone I trust and you're the one I trust. You're the one I love."

I said nothing. We walked into her room. She threw down her coat and turned around. I kissed her and laid her down on the bed. We started kissing slowly and then as it got more intense, more clothes came off. We made love for the first time and I still didn't think of it as fucking. I knew it was her first time, her oral talents notwithstanding. That night was perfect and I knew it could not last forever as is the way with perfection in an imperfect world.

I am saddened by death and the passing of time and I saw fire. Maybe it was more than the movie.

Later in the week, we flew back to L.A. I had a life to get back to and so did Karly with school. I went back to work and the band started rehearsing again. I was only gone three weeks but it felt like an eternity. So much had happened.

Still not sure if I was growing up or gaining wisdom and I believed there was a difference.

****

Jim was our bass player who quit not long after I got back. Said he had grown tired of the "4/4 rock n roll time signature construct and the popular cultural instinct of herd politics."

I was angry like the other guys as I had blocked out the rest which sounded like, "blah, blah, fucking blah." I tuned it out. I knew it was his fucking girlfriend, Lusha, a pretentious, Uber vegan, performance art asshole who thought that killing ants on stage with Raid, to recorded beat poetry was the height of expressing man's inhumanity to man and whatever the fuck else Yoko Ono pretension she subscribed to. I had a hard time taking "performance art" seriously. A lion's share of the time, I felt it was a refuge for hacks that couldn't write, sing or act for shit.

It always went something like this; some dude in glasses and a fedora would come out and recite some "poem" that went, "I'm leaf! And I have disconnected from the mother tree and I'm falling!" Then he'd wave his arms like a falling leaf, I guess, "Wafting, drifting, wafting, drifting, but WAIT!!! Solace. I have landed."

Something like that…

It was odd, that these girls came to the shows, would dig us, got us to love them and then try to change the very thing that attracted them in the first place. They'd want to us to "get a job" or they said things like, "you don't really think you'll make it do you?" Maybe that was Shelly's problem and I just couldn't buy into her doubt, which meant she couldn't have someone who didn't need her. I only ever wanted to be there and there is a difference between need and want. The more miserable people never quite figured that out.

At any rate, before I left, Jim was already starting to change into what Lusha wanted him to be. He was my best friend but friends are like race car drivers and you're only as good as your last race. We'll never stop being friends and I would always love the guy but the relationship had become something else. I just would no longer count on him for the Formula 1 stuff, that's all.

Derrick and Paul were at a loss when I suggested my new friend Liev to play bass. Jim and I had met them both while I was a college intern at the record company I worked at, C.I.A Records. As a band and friends, we had been through quite a bit, so Paul's trepidation was duly noted as we were basically in a company with each other, a business. As such, the money was a factor too, so being cool with who we played with next was important. I joked that being in a band is like being married to three people but there's no sex and someone always asks the musical equivalent of, "Does this dress make me look fat?" Musicians knew exactly what I was talking about. I had excellent judgment in people so Paul had nothing to worry about where suggesting Lee was concerned, I felt.

But this was a democracy (or at least a benevolent dictatorship) and we had been through a lot together, so maybe I was too quick to bring up a replacement. However, I thought it would be a great idea and we had to get going. Christ, we weren't dating, this was a business and Jim quit. Shit, don't people remarry? Does Bank of America have a stroke when a vice president quits? Fuck no! They get a new vice president and sally forth, that sort of thing. Besides, if Ringo could replace Pete Best, I thought, it just goes to show you that everyone's ass was up for grabs.

"So, who is he?" Paul asked suspiciously.

"Liev…or Lee, rather…he's this dude I met in the middle of fucking hell on the trip but he's cool and his brother's Micah from Creeping Charlie. I jammed with them in Copenhagen." I left out Ramallah and in fact, I never told the guys or anyone in the States about it right away.

Paul looked impressed, "You jammed with Micah Lowensohn?" He looked to Derrick who shrugged.

"Yes." I said deadpan.

"From Creeping Charlie?" he said like a cop, rephrasing a question.

"It's not like it was George Harrison, man." I sniffed, playing it off when actually, it was quite fucking cool. Then sternly, I continued, "Look, I know the guy, alright? He's from Jersey and he can crash at my place for a couple weeks and it's not in stone. Fuck, neither were we, in the beginning." I had no idea if Liev would even come out to L.A. or not. He had barely just got back home to the east coast. Maybe he got into something there or a cool job, who knew?

"Let's just be open," Derrick suggested. "We'll figure it out as we go and if it sucks, we'll can it." That was my songwriting partner talking!

Derrick and I wrote all the songs anyway, so I didn't really care what Paul had to say. He still got a 25% share for playing guitar without writing at all. Maybe he was insecure and maybe it was my attitude that made him so. Whatever, I was feeling too good to worry much at all about these things. It felt right so I called Liev and he thought it'd be cool to try it out, "What the hell else I got to do, man? I'm starting over in the States anyways…Besides, if Micah helps us out, it could be fun, right?"

Things at work took some time getting caught up on. After being gone so long it wasn't easy but I didn't exactly dig ditches or kill sheep for market either. That stuff's hard. I was on the phone a lot for my job as I basically worked in marketing, which meant I got the bigger record stores in the country to report our records the way we wanted them reported on the college and alternative charts. That way there would be a story or buzz to take to radio. That simple. In the record business, it was called "marketing and promotion." The traditional, more accurate term if we were ever investigated was "Payola" and it went like this; if I had to give you a box of uncut, not marked as "promotional" CDs by the Who just so we can make some asshole's cover version of "Spirit in the Sky" number one on the college charts? That's called something…The store then turned around and sold the CDs at full price. This was their payment in near full as it never ended with those people. They were like blackmailing junkies, jonesing for a cheap fix and there's no other name for it. You say *tomahto* and I will call it a fucking tomato.

There was no real science to it and it gave me access for my band, which hopefully would get to the point where some kid had our valuable art to give away so some other dickhead can go number one with a cover of "Louie, Louie" or some shit.

Some of my guys in the "taste making" record stores were impressed with the fact that I jammed with one of the Charlies. It was a great story to tell and bought me a little more credibility with hipster record store managers who thought that our label was "corporate rock" anyway. Working at a major record label, you had to earn "street cred" by inches, especially with the record store guys. They had their finger on the pulse as it were and we were locked up in our ivory towers, to hear them tell it. Basically, I was dealing with pretentious, frustrated rock critics and musicians who thought managing a record store was "working in the music business" and that being hip, in and of itself was a career and fuck all else. But the stores they worked in carried weight on the charts so they had to think I was one of them. In a way, I was with one big difference; I was not deluded into thinking I had arrived, not one bit, even if I got rich like my bosses and I did work in the music business. Anything short of my band being huge was death, pure and simple.

Jamming with the Charlies got around L.A. It was funny how it went from Micah to all of the Charlies so fast as if they were all in Denmark with me. When I went to bars and such the regulars who knew me, heard about it. This was a very long time before the internet and the like, as this was still 1988. Frankly it was a nice way to change subjects when the Mid-East part of the trip was starting to get heavy. That's what's funny about art; you do it as an escape of sorts, a way to attempt to fulfill pretty much every need you could have and then that pesky, real life creeps in. I was getting better and better at keeping the crap at bay.

Liev came out to L.A. and crashed on my couch. It was nice hanging out again and he even went to Ventura with me to see Karly. She had an older sister that she raved about and the two really hit it off. She kind of looked like Karly but was a redhead with big, green eyes. She was a bit of a goof but real cute and flirty. Her name was Kara. Karly had soft-balled the whole thing for him; she talked up the exotic adventures and what fun we had in Denmark. I'm sure their protestant father would be less than thrilled, but fuck him; he'd be lucky to have Lee as a son-in-law and besides, Karly's sister wasn't into being yoked just yet anyway. She may have very well invented the term, "sowing your oats" or it was invented in her honor. She was wild.

We had gone to see Elvis Costello at the Santa Barbara County Bowl. He was playing without the Attractions. The bass player, Bruce Thomas had left in '86. Despite the presence of the other Attractions, Pete Thomas and Steve Nieve, he still called the band the "Rude 5." Maybe the bassist was his best friend, too. We had a blast and Kara could tip back the ales as well as we could. She screamed a lot but I didn't mind. It wasn't as though she was angry, as much she was loud. Lee had a blast and the two got away from us while we were walking around State Street after the show. We only ran into them accidentally, later at a bar which was good because I was Lee's ride home.

Lee seemed excited to be in California and I couldn't understand how he got stationed on the border of Israel and Jordan. Not for the life of me. Life's funny that way and maybe that was his lesson to learn, perhaps some gratitude. Who knows?

I had sent Liev a cassette of the four songs we wanted him to learn so when he got to L.A. it wouldn't be cold. He had a warm vibe and breezy manner that made being around him cool; the classic bass player. This put Paul and Derrick at ease too. We jammed on a couple of fuck around songs. He knew "When the Levee Breaks" by Led Zeppelin, so we played that and while Derrick didn't really know the words, it's still a great jam. Then Paul started playing the riff to the "The End" by the Doors then "Pale Blue Eyes" by the Velvet Underground. We played some other stuff for half an hour then we got to the songs I had sent.

Paul asked, "So, Lee, you know these, right? You need the chords?"

Liev said, "No, I'm cool. I got it."

So we played the first song and it went pretty well. Paul still made some suggestions to Lee, being the control freak, he was but Lee was good with it, "It's your house, man." He answered cheerfully and without sarcasm.

We played it again and then moved to the next. Three hours later, the four of us were draining what was left of two 12 packs of Lucky Lager.

"Pretty cool, man," Derrick said swigging his beer.

"Thanks." Liev smiled. "You guys kick ass."

Paul grinned, trying not to betray that he really had a great time. I caught him digging the vibe a bit, but he always had one eye on the door like a Mafia don waiting to get whacked.

"Well, that's it then," I said. "Call you guys tomorrow." With that we left.

Paul and Derrick finished the remaining four or five bottles of the second 12-pack. "He was actually pretty cool and he can play." Derrick said. "And we have shows coming up."

"Yeah, I say he's in, for now anyway. He was in the army so there's gotta be some discipline, right?" Paul suggested. "Hell, it didn't take us that long to be a band in the first place. He's fine, for now, I guess."

Derrick drained his beer, "Yeah, man, it's bass. He can play and he doesn't write and he seems cool with that. It can't get too complicated. I say we do it. Who knows, maybe his brother can help us out."

"Cool," Paul agreed. "We'll talk details if and when we tell him its official." And that's how business gets done when you're twenty-three years old.

With me gone and then Jim leaving, we haven't had a gig for almost two months. Word got out that we were back and playing with Liev. I should say that *we* got the word out. I got pretty good at getting information out there that didn't seem like it came from us. I realized this in college; when people repeat gossip, they like to make it sound like they discovered it for themselves. They usually credit no one as there's no real blame with gossip because you can always say, "It's just something I heard."

This little network of busy bodies was used effectively to our advantage to create a buzz. I let it leak that Lee was Micah's brother. But we were cagey when confronted with it. "Yeah, we met him, can't help who you're related to, you know?" that sort of thing. We really milked the Arab and Jew thing as far as where we met because we thought it was cool. Frankly I was Arab as Liev but what are the odds? Meeting your future bassist at an Arab-Israeli check point? Saving my life? Rolling Stone, hello, are you home? Still, I didn't look at it as a gimmick as much as Liev was just a good guy who could play. We were lucky to have him but I also knew a unique story could be as good as the songs themselves, at least at first.

I bet my grandfather would have been fine with it, if he were in the position. Sure beats being in a Turkish prison.

We kicked the shit out of our previous momentum and over the next eight months, our gigs were getting better and more buzz followed us in L.A. Karly came out for our show at the Palladium with us opening for The Pixies and Jane's Addiction, our biggest show so far. Our manager did an awesome job of getting 5 or 6 key record guys out to the show. One of them was sent by Micah. He got excited by our demo and sent his old A&R man out to see us. A&R stood for Artists and Repertoire which I actually wanted to do at first. After a summer internship at another label, listening to hundreds of demos, I figured my own art would suffer. How could it not? After listening to 273 demos that summer, I found 4 bands worth sending along for consideration. A&R were the guys who actually find the bands for the record company. They usually got the biggest salaries and fattest expense accounts but had the shortest life span of anyone in the business. Three stiffs at one label and you were usually out, at least from that company. These guys would change jobs like socks unless they get lucky a couple times. One hit album could buy an A&R rep a minimum five years of goodwill.

We got signed a few weeks after the Jane's show. It was inevitable after that night. Los Angeles Times rock critic, Robert Hilburn compared our "fire and energy" to the Doors and wrote two more pieces on us, highlighting the charity work that Derrick did with Amnesty International.

There was what the business called a "bidding war." All these labels got lathered up, mostly because the excitement was high, they were at a few kick ass shows and they read the paper. We went with the Charlies' old label at the end of the day. This gave us a decent royalty advance and street credibility at the same time as they certainly didn't pay the most for us. It's interesting how we were so concerned then with public opinion and street credibility. Weren't we supposed to be rebels? But there is value and there is price. We knew the value of savvy and we also got more creative freedom with that label which was the main concern.

Wow. America. The opportunity. Dad's not the only one who's glad he came here.

Candlewax Records, our new label. The owner made a mint managing some elevator Muzak band in the 70s and 80s so he started a passion project record label, at which he made money too. He was just one of those guys. We got to pick the producer and I got to work with our manager in spending the money because if that's done wrong, we could massively fuck ourselves. It wasn't like we spent the money on cars or houses either. We had to make a record. While not Sting money, Micah got a nice finder's fee.

We were just fresh from our signing meeting when I got home to find Karly in my bedroom. She came down from Ventura, to surprise me. Already having a key, she got Liev to stay out of the house and she brought Kara along to make sure they went somewhere else. This wasn't necessary; he already had met more than his share of girls he could "visit." Karly and I had been seeing each other pretty solid since Denmark and it was going beyond well. I so loved that girl. A year travels fast...

There was a note on the door that said, "Congratulations, babe" with a smiley face that girls in their 20s always used, with the loopy, cursive writing. In my bedroom, she was in black thong panties, strappy 4 inch heels and wearing a wide red ribbon across her tits, sitting on my bed for me like a gift. "I sent the kids out for the night," she murmured, biting her lower lip. "I hope that's okay," she cooed as I undid the ribbon with my teeth. We made love in my room.

Afterwards we nuzzled; lying in my bed, she said with a fake little southern girl voice, "So now you're gonna be a big rock and roll star, does this mean you don't need me comin' round here no more? You'll have all those eager girls after such a handsome drummer!" she giggled, as she reached behind her ass and grabbed my cock.

A firm little smack on her ass was my answer. She rolled over and bit my chest. We were at it again...

****

The next day I walked into my boss's office to tell him what was going on. I figured it was best to talk to him before it hit the trades, so I made the appointment with his secretary before the signing meeting. His office was on the top floor of the company overlooking all of Los Angeles in the Executive Suites. He had a small hallway before you got to his assistant's desk. She was in her mid-thirties and was *the* requisite Los Angeles hot chick out of Central Casting; high heels, long legs, short skirt, no pantyhose and a snug sweater that didn't do much for cleavage but didn't have to. Her tits were fantastic and I believe popped without the use of a bra. Sharon was her name and she always dressed to please. I defended her to the office critics as I liked to say she was doing "the Lord's work." Her critics weren't men.

Walking in, I felt kind of guilty because my boss mentored me when I was an intern in college, making copies and all that shit but also teaching me the music business. Also, he gave me the time off to bury my cousin, with pay.

His name was Mitch Mann, the quintessential marketing guy. The name kind of just rolled off the tongue. Mann was not the original family name. His family was Russian Jews, his grandparents coming in through Ellis Island. His dad was an old-school union organizer in the garment business during the 30s and 40s. Mitch was one of the folks who didn't give a shit what I was. We just got along.

He was a tall guy, about six-two, waspy looking but with an attitude that screamed "south side." Mitch was a hard boiled club promoter and radio guy from Chicago who moved up the ranks at C.I.A. to Senior Vice President, North American Marketing and Promotion. That doesn't roll off the tongue as easy as his name but the money he made was biblical; a fat high six figures plus stock options. While this was 1980s money and therefore a fucking fortune, he was still the club guy from Chicago and not to be trifled with. Because he presided over a bigger practice, he rarely paid attention to up and coming bands. He only cared when they became ours.

"So, Mitch, how's it goin'?" I started nervously. "How's the family?"

"Oh, fuck me! Is this how you're starting this thing?" He asked. Eyeing me straight he said, "It's not like I don't know, man! I don't do the clubs anymore, but I got eyes and ears everywhere! And you're making an appointment to see me?" he said, waving his hand, seemingly annoyed.

"Oh...I figured that...Well, I don't want there to be any hard feelings or...you know... I really do appreciate everything you did for me, man." I continued, "You taught me so much about the business but look, we go into pre-production in May. I can only give you a month but I do have a guy that I think would be great at this gig." I was thinking of one of my college buddies who was working for Xerox and hated it and was actually thinking about teaching school. I could teach him the basics and Mitch could drop nuggets on him all day.

"Yeah, that's fine. You send him in, man. I'll talk to him...Christ, I can throw a rock in this town and hit any hundred fucking kids, come in and do your job." he laughed.

"Drink?" he asked, changing gears as he walked over to the bar in his office. That place was about twice the size of my entire house and many times bigger than my converted closet of an office with no window. "Makers, right?"

Meaning Maker's Mark Bourbon, I was flattered he remembered. "Yeah, two fingers, up," I said. "Thanks."

He motioned me to sit as he poured the amber liquid into a shaker with ice. "You like football, right? Sure you do. Everyone likes football...Did you see this year's Super Bowl?" he asked.

"Yeah, kind of a blow out, but it was alright, I guess?" I answered. In fact, the Washington Redskins had beaten the Denver Broncos 42-10. I treaded lightly, not sure if he was a Broncos fan.

His shaking completed, he poured my drink, "Yeah, well that's not my point...the point is that it's 1988 and it took this long for a black guy to start at fucking quarterback in a goddamned Super Bowl! You know what that means?" Mitch asked firmly. He was talking about a guy named Doug Williams who also got MVP in that same game.

"We've come a long way, baby?" I chuckled as he handed me drink. We clinked glasses as he sat down.

"Well that but he won it too, see? Point I'm making is we're all due, kid. You hang in there and you're due. Everyone's due if they work hard," he got quiet. "I'm proud of you. You came in here, did your job, no bullshit. You navigated the waters on your own time and got signed. Not my ideal outcome, to be honest but still, no easy thing." Mitch continued, "You know the ropes. The odds are not good, not one bit but you if don't swing for the fences, you'll never hit a fuckin' home run, you know what I mean?" Mitch made the sports references often but it was always when the time was right to hear it. I cannot recall an exception to that observation.

"Yeah, I know," I answered.

"Sure you do, you've always been a smart kid…Look, Candlewax? Good company. Good distribution. You let me know if you need anything, I'll do my best. This thing stiffs which it could, you call me and I'll make sure you're not waiting tables next year!" he laughed. "Remember the bass player from Blondie? I got him his A&R job after they schtupped his ass by the second album." This would be a guy named Nigel Harrison.

"Sure thing, man," I was doing my best not to cry. I was once told by a speech teacher that if you clench your ass cheeks, it kept you from weeping in public. With that, I downed my drink and slammed my glass on the table.

Mitch grinned as we stood up. I went to shake his hand and he hugged me. "You don't get off that easy, man," he said with some emotion. "Congrats."

With that I walked back to my office. I felt euphoric and I knew this could not last forever.

Chapter 10 - May You Get What You Want

My real concern with making the record at all was that we all had such strong personalities. Paul and I were already particular or control freaky enough as it was. Then we actually got two producers on the album with similar reputations and they really got paid to be that way, hence my concern. T-Bone Burnett and Prince Paul had distinct visions for where things should go. We were definitely open and absorbed everything like sponges and the four of us agreed to leave the egos at the door unless something really off putting was going down. It could easily have been an issue of too many chiefs and not enough Indians but it wasn't, thankfully. It wasn't as though they tried to replace our singer with a seventeen year old girl or something. That would suck. We four were awed by their talent but I think because Paul and I were especially humbled by who was working with us, we worked hard at admitting that we knew nothing.

Candlewax was really cool about helping us with who we wanted to get to produce by pulling in some of their own connections. We got both producers at a good rate because of the strong buzz on our band. They were intrigued that we wanted to work with both of them and were surprisingly open to it. We still gave them their royalty rate but we got them to cut their up-front fees in half. This was either going to work out amazingly well or be a fabulous disaster so there had to be a shared direction.

Burnett was an alternative minded country guy, along the lines of the Flying Burrito Brothers or late 60s Byrds, who really knew his rock and roll, while Prince Paul was one of the best hip-hop producers at the time, having just produced the hippie rap group, De La Soul among others. We wanted to do something different for a rock record. We sampled movie lines, changed up the way instruments sounded. Basically, we did a lot of cool shit that would bore the average listener to tears who could not care less, except for the result being cool. All the audience cares about is can they hum it? The record label is the audience too. Elvis Costello famously said, "Talking about music is like whistling about chickens." I believed him.

Liev got along with the guys. He and Derek had a lot in common, including a rabid enthusiasm for early Clash. We got better with our shows and practices. We had the record release party at the old Roosevelt Hotel in Hollywood and we used the room that held the first Oscars during the 1920s. It was a small room which only held about 300 people. It looked bigger in the pictures. The hotel was classic L.A. art deco architecture with the sign on the roof in big red lights over looking Hollywood Boulevard. It was only a couple of years since me and Derek would walk those very streets with shoulder bags like paperboys, plastering construction sites and lamp poles with our band's name. We had fingerless gloves and baseball hats to keep the glue spray out of our hair. I guess if we were some hair metal group, we would have been cool with it. We never put up a gig date, just the name. That way when the club we were playing at listed us in the L.A. Weekly, or Times, folks hopefully made the connection. We placed fliers everywhere we could and it paid off because people always "heard of you guys" when the name, Mayan Tango, came up and we had a lot of people to our shows who were not on our mailing list. They'd seen it on their way to work or dinner is why. Also, because we never put up a date for shows, other bands left our fliers alone so they were up longer than most. It was fun.

We had a great night at the party. Mitch came and Liev brought Kara which surprised me. They seemed to really be getting along. Paul and Derek came stag. After all, it was our record release party; between KROQ, and some other college stations, all the magazines that were invited and their guests it wasn't as if there'd be no girls.

We called the album "Garden of Starts." Surprisingly, MTV took to our video for "Flattered" quicker than we expected. I figured it would be two or three singles before the album got off the ground at all but this song went first and surprised everyone. The chorus went, *suicide is a pitfall of the examined life/the gates of hell won't be opened any wider than tonight.*" It sounded different with a choir singing back up so no one really noticed the suicide reference in a bad way, perhaps? Maybe they did get it and understood the pit falls of too much navel gazing and self-absorption, so they could relate. If Cheap Trick could get away with "Auf Wiedersehen" which was a song about suicide in different languages then why not us? However, if some idiot couple played that song at their wedding, I would have to wonder how soon after the wedding they would be in therapy.

The MTV reception for the video was strong which made sense because the single was popular. Within a couple more singles ("Lament [for the Modern Lover]" and "Babies in Bliss") and videos we got an opening slot on the last leg of the Rolling Stones tour after the band Living Color dropped out to headline Europe. The "Flattered" video had us on a street in front of an old mission and we played the song with about four hundred white rabbits hopping around. There was the black choir we got from First AME Church in L.A. They actually sang on the record, thanks to Prince Paul and they stood on the steps behind us and moved and sang the chorus. What this video had to do with the song was beyond me and they were my lyrics. We had this Italian commercial director and he swore he'd knock it out of the park so we trusted him and the result looked cool and it was a successful video so what did I know?

When we played with the Rolling Stones, we went on before the band, Guns & Roses. My friend played drums in a metal band and we saw them open for Guns & Roses at the Whisky 1986. It was weird when they got signed because when I saw them, they still weren't that good. But they did manage to get better. Still, their album had taken over a year to hit. It came out and did nothing and then MTV started playing "Welcome to the Jungle" and they just took off. However, even after 3 million records sold, Axl Rose was still a royal fucking asshole but that was a great band.

I still couldn't believe this was happening. The Rolling Stones, man! Yeah, they're in their 40s and Mick Jagger did say, "If I'm singing 'Satisfaction' past thirty, I will kill myself," but so what? It's the Stones! Thank God, Jagger's a man of unbridled hypocrisy and Keith Richards didn't really seem to care. Hell, ten years earlier, he was shooting heroin into his cock. Sure they were no longer "dangerous" but whatever. How long can one live up to a bad boy image especially after Altamont in 1969? Time does fly.

We played the Los Angeles Coliseum with both those bands. Getting in front of sixty-five thousand people, having them scream nice things at you and applaud is something I'd highly recommend to anyone who asks.

We offered Jim some tickets for the L.A. shows but he passed. He got Lusha pregnant and it seemed he was out of music entirely which was kind of a shame but I did hope he was happy. Every band ends up with a Pete Best or three. I even got Sam and Ali tickets for them and their wives. Sam was backstage after the show, smiling from ear to ear, "Not quite the Road to Canaan but it'll do, I guess..." He looked around, "This is fuckin' great, man!" he hoisted one of the many free backstage beers. He seemed genuinely happy for me. "Here's to getting what you want in this life."

Nina hugged me, "Nice job, cuz." She said sweetly.

I introduced them to Karly and she didn't really remember Sam from that day in Jerusalem but of course, he did. Ali was very gracious, and even though the backstage of a rock show wasn't really his scene, he and his wife Vera seemed to have a real good time. They chatted with Karly a little and Ali seemed genuinely interested in why she in the Territories. He asked about the Bible Tour and what she saw. He was always interested in people.

Mitch and my parents came to the L.A. shows too. Mitch teased, "Well it doesn't look like I'll see you at the office on Monday." He followed up with, "Good job, kid. Thanks for the signed Gold Album. I like what you wrote." With a loopy signature and goofy smiley face, I had written, "To Mitch 'the Man,' thanks for everything."

My mom was real sweet to Karly, "Oh my, what a darling figure you have!" she smiled as she kissed Karly on the cheek, hugging her around the neck then holding Karly's arms out as if to approve. My dad was always charming to strangers, like a wholly different person and it was to the point where I sometimes thought I was insane and possibly imagined my childhood. He would never say anything about mine and Sam's drinking to our faces and behind Karly's back, she'd be a "whore" but to her face, he'd kiss her hand and be as charming as Omar Fucking Sharif.

I wasn't surprised about my mom coming. However, my father showing up did take me aback; he only ever made fun of the entire enterprise and always thought rock musicians were "fag drug users." He would say that over and over like that was his argument for me to quit and just keep my job; "Oh my God, dad! Shit! You're right! I don't want to turn into a fag drug user! Look! I quit playing music! Allah fucking Akbar! Please love me now!" I came to discover that the only reason he came at all, was because his cousin told him how big this was and he wanted to make sure I was going to give him money, eventually when money was no longer an issue.

I didn't care. I won. I stayed true to a vision and I won. I was feeling too good for this shit to really affect me. I had been waiting for the other shoe to fall and it didn't. I felt peaceful. Time to work on our situation as adults, me and dad, and if he wouldn't, there'd be no loss because I had Karly and we were going to make it. We were going to last just like Ray Manzarek, like Charlie Watts, like Paul McCartney, and some other married rock stars who weren't assholes to their wives. What the hell, when this would be over, all I wanted was Karly anyway. All this will be cool but it was gravy because I had Karly. Dad even dug the show so there was no need to rub his face in it. My little brothers, my mom and I, and my cousins all got pictures with the Stones. My mom got giddy as Mick Jagger kissed her on the cheek. She loved the Stones when I was little; always had the radio on when she cleaned the house. My dad felt funny about intruding on their time. He didn't get that it's cool backstage to get pictures taken. It's what the stars do for their people. The Stones were so cool to all the guys and their guests. I introduced my younger brothers to Slash from Guns and Roses. Steve Jones from the Sex Pistols was there and he was cool to them too.

After the "family hour" a bunch of us went to an after-hours place called "the Second Coming." It was in the attic of an old church off of Alvarado that was rented out to some promoters for the night by an entrepreneurial janitor. I doubt the pastor knew. No one got there till midnight or later. Booze flowed until they closed at four in the morning. We walked in and a band we knew, Shiva Burlesque, was playing. We got tables, hung out and of all people Jon Landau, who managed Bruce Springsteen, came to our table, "Hey guys, congrats on tonight. I heard your record. Really, really loved it."

"I take it you weren't there." I grinned, feeling honored at the same time.

"Nah, sorry, man. We're catching them in New York. Bruce may jump onstage with them. Had some business tonight…" He said, shaking my hand.

Paul and Derek shook hands with him too. I introduced him to the girls and Liev, "Big fan, Jon, I'd seen Bruce a few times."

Jon grinned and said, "You want to meet him? He's at that table over there. We're checking out a couple bands I want to sign to my label. Bruce is a partner."

We walked over with our dates and Jon introduced us to Bruce Springsteen. Truth be told, I was not a huge fan but Lee loved him. It was also cool just to meet the guy; he was an American icon for Chrissakes.

"Don't rush off, stay, man." Springsteen stood and offered seats to the girls as I tried to make an exit and let him have an evening. I figured he got bugged enough. "Grab some more chairs and sit. Loved you guys' record, man."

Lee looked annoyed at me, raising an eyebrow, "Yeah, man. Sit!"

It seemed like I was out voted and "the Boss" trumped all our votes so sit we did.

179

Not quite the Boom Boom Room but we hung out with Bruce Springsteen and he bought us beer. We had a great night.

Our tour of Europe went pretty well. We got to play smaller theaters with Jane's Addiction, whose first album for Warner's, "Nothing's Shocking," was tearing up the European charts. Three years before, Derek and I saw them open for the band X at Cal State Fullerton and now they were huge and we were playing with them. Their problems with heroin were no real secret, even though the drummer was clean. Spin Magazine ran a cover story on their European adventures entitled, "Shooting Up the Charts" which some found to be in bad taste but I thought it was funny. In America, "Jane Says" was a rock and alternative radio hit but in Europe, it was a "Top of the Pops" kind of thing, fucking huge. Micah and Sherri came out to the shows in Paris and Micah even had some of the ex-Charlies with him. I felt like we had finally arrived. Lee and I introduced the guys around and it was like we had gained entry into what I had always known was our club for the taking. We all hung out afterwards and Karly and Sherri just had the best time catching up like they went to junior high together. Paul was chatting with Micah about guitars and Derek was having a blast soaking up the kudos of being the singer and rock star he was. Life was good.

Temptations were legion because people spent so much time kissing our ass that we could have gotten very full of ourselves if we weren't careful. Hubris is a bitch but we were never going to let it get to us or be pretentious assholes about it. I saw it happen at C.I.A. all the time; "one hit wonders" who thought they were the next Beatles, only to have the entire career fall flat by the second record and mostly because they were such dicks to everyone the first time around and mistook fame for art. Folks fester like boils to see you down when you're a dick. They're quick to kick you right in the kidneys when you're on the floor and your back meets their boot. It's just how people are.

I was always spinning these cautionary tales to the guys and I prayed it stuck. We busted our ass to get here and we're going to play in front of as many people as possible and enjoy it for the moment's sake which is all any of us have. We wanted to make art and reach as many people as would hear us. No band bragging that they're satisfied playing for a small cadre of fans is being honest. That or they have serious fucking issues with deserving great things. Me? I lived it, so I deserved it…no problem. I have suffered for my art, it was called breathing. Next Beatles? That job was already taken and we wouldn't have been very good at it. I'd have settled for gratitude and feeling peaceful.

We came back to the States and finished the tour. We headlined places like the Wiltern Theater and the Fillmore in San Francisco. The shows were sold out and we were playing two and three night stands, just like Echo and the Bunnymen a few years before so I felt we achieved a lot. These were smaller venues than in Europe but it was still incredible! One thing I learned, working for Mitch, was that it was better to sell out a small place than to under sell the Forum. The reviews would start out with the term, "sold out show" as opposed to "half empty theater." Even if the review was bad, the reader would still have a modicum of respect as we did have a sold out show. We took a chance; getting a smaller guaranteed fee but the promoters gave us more of the ticket sales so we made out because we did fill the places.

The album finally went Platinum which was one million copies. I sent another autographed trophy to Mitch, this time signed by the whole band. This one read, "To Mitch 'the Man,' without you, we're nothing!" He got a kick out of that. We ended up with three Top 10 singles on the Rock and Alternative charts. Not Top 40 or Casey Casem but still, a million's a million. We were getting along great. Paul, Derek and me missed Jim but that's why they're called decisions.

To think I was almost a dead man 18 months ago…

****

I had to wind down and for the first time in my life, I had cash, time and an amazing girlfriend simultaneously! After a couple weeks at my house, wandering Pasadena, having sex, going to the museum, having sex, seeing shows and having more sex, Karly and I flew up to San Francisco to see Lou Reed. Some of my friends teased, "Why bring sand to the beach?" Their argument was that we've made it so I can have any chick I want, so, why take my girlfriend? While that may have been true, what would have been the point? I was in love, she was my *friend* and I didn't fuck over my friends. Besides that, it was my fucking beach.

If I do anyone a favor it will be to help them *understand* the Velvet Underground. To say Lou Reed was that band was not completely fair but not wholly inaccurate, either. His solo stuff was mostly amazing and he was one of my all-time influences. I would joke that he was on my short list of my four favorite Jews; Lenny Bruce, Bob Dylan and Paul Simon were the other three. Of course, this was in no particular order but Lenny was first with the others tied for second.

Lou Reed was one of the main reasons I started writing songs even though I was a drummer. He was playing the Fillmore and I was stoked to see one of the greats play where I just played. This would be cool. We went backstage after the show and we met Lou Reed and got pictures with him. Karly was excited, even though she didn't really know who he was except for "Walk on the Wild Side" and even then it was because he finally licensed the song for a Honda commercial. Rolling Stone Magazine was there so we got some more pictures in the magazine, too. I planned on framing the page we were on with Lou, though.

"I really dug your record man…That sound was cool!" Lou grinned. "You want to work on some stuff later when we wrap the tour?"

After almost shitting my pants, I said yes and got his number. He motioned for me to come around a bar and he grabbed a pen from the bartender. Lou Reed gave me his number and wants to write songs together! Lou being Jewish, he didn't seem too concerned with my background, either. I would take a bullet for Lou Reed. Christ, I almost took one for a Palestinian cab driver I didn't even know who did not happen to write "Run, Run, Run."

After the show, Karly and I went to Fisherman's Wharf. We found an open bar and got some drinks and appetizers, walked along the pier. This was beautiful. For the first time in my life, I felt like an adult and while not very rock and roll; neither was living with your parents and fantasizing about getting a car. I was realizing my dream, I was in love and the band started off right. Everything was ours for the taking.

I am saddened by death and the passing of time and I saw fire.

"God said to Abraham, "Kill me a son"/Abe said, "Man, you must be puttin' me on…"

That night felt like that dream I had on the roof in Denmark but it was raining as we walked out of the bar. The rain didn't curb that feeling, though. It felt the same 5,000 miles away. I pulled Karly under the awning of an old closed up restaurant, scaring some gulls that were camping out for the night and we started making out.

Karly stopped kissing as she rubbed my cock, outside my jeans and chided me a little, "Too bad you don't remember Denmark, Mr. Rock Star Man! You're much too busy with Lou Reed."

"Of course I remember babe…How could I not?" My words were breathless as I nuzzled her neck.

"No, I mean on the roof? Don't you remember anything? The flying?" she smiled.

"That was real?" I was incredulous, "How?"

"I don't really know but wasn't it cool?" Her eyes searching mine in that way of hers.

"Well, yeah! Can we do it again?" I looked around.

"I don't know. But I'll tell you something…I want you right now." She looked up, "I want you to be my first in the sky..." She grinned. "Don't wait too long to answer, Tiger…supplies are limited."

My mouth must have been hanging open and flies were buzzing around inside of it.

"Let's see if we can do it from the end of the pier," Karly suggested.

****

"Let me tell you about heartache and the loss of God…"

We got to the end of the pier and some older Mexican guys had their fishing poles in the ocean. We stood at the rail and watched the shadows of the lamp posts dance on the white foam of the sea as it retreated back into the night. The Mexicans' buckets were half full of fish, most of which should have been thrown back. I don't even know if they were Mexicans, they could have been from anywhere. There was a frigid breeze as the rain became a drizzle. But as soon as Karly took my hand, the air turned tropical, the rain cleared up and the stars were plentiful. We started to rise again just like before and she let go just like last time but this time I realized a confidence. I knew what I was doing like a seasoned veteran. I moved my arms and glided up. Karly did the same and passed me. I laughed as I chased her.

She laughed as I caught her, held her. We were high in the air and I looked down and we were way above the Pacific and we could hear waves crash into the pier. I could still see the lamp posts reflect on the white, sea foam as the water pulled out from beneath the pier. I could see the fishermen and the tops of their heads and one seemed to catch the biggest fish of the night and I could hear him whoop and holler as his pier mates congratulated him. Karly breathed in the sea air, taking deep breaths that she held like a bong hit as to savor the flavor. I looked to the lights over the sea and as I looked back at Karly, we were naked in the sky. That did not bother me at all. It felt perfectly natural, just two random naked people in the air as we kissed. I kissed her neck and she started kissing my chest. "I love you," she whispered, her lips curling into a smile as she felt my hard on. "I want you inside…"

I got my fingers inside her and her legs spread as her pussy opened up like a flower in slow motion. She bit my neck, giggling. We started making love. "I will love you forever," she said as she sighed out the sea air. It got furious and intense. I opened my eyes and saw her head reeled back into the night's sky. My one hand stroked her tits and the other had her ass. Her nipples were hard and clouds were in front of me. I wanted to have all the sensations at once and I made a reach for the clouds, they were so close and I thought I grabbed one.

The moon lit her skin…

Then Karly looked back at me, startled, crinkling her nose and said, "I smell gas!"

"What?" I smelled it too as she evaporated right out of my hands! I was clutching dirt and brush and she was gone.

****

I was face first in the dirt, trying to keep strength on my hands and knees as dignity had long disappeared from this vicinity. I got kicked in the stomach again, hard. Apparently, this had been going on for some time. I got hit in the back with another club or bat. I saw white as I rolled over on my back and looked straight into the new dawn. Pain shot through my spine and I couldn't feel my legs.

I was still on the roadside outside of Ramallah, covered in gasoline and more got poured on me. I couldn't move and I felt like cement and the pain was so great, I couldn't tell where it began or ended. "That's it, then cousin." Eddie said as he gave a nod to Lateef who then flicked his cigarette on me and I caught fire! Eddie didn't want the ultimate responsibility and he had not laid a hand on me that entire time.

I couldn't tell what catching fire felt like but I do remember screaming so powerfully that I could no longer hear myself within the first few seconds that went on forever. All I ever wanted was Karly and to be seventy with her. She's all I'll ever truly miss. Everything else was just a bonus but it felt like how life should be. I think I screamed at the realization that she was gone.

I'm certain I was flailing like a freshly caught fish on a boat's deck, a natural reaction to being set on fire. This went on for a minute or so when Eddie ordered, "Yallah!" Then one of the others pulled out a .38 and shot me three times in the head to put me out of my misery. Of course, the flames set into my flesh before he did me the favor. My body burned like a leftover campfire as Eddie and his boys got in their cars and split. Saif was lying only a few feet away and he actually did get off easier, looking back on it. I regret the bad judgment but Eddie had this planned, regardless of when I left. I was never going to get out of there.

I never made it to Denmark. Liev and his men did show up, however but only to clean up after the fact. He failed to make any connection to who I was even when he found my passport a few feet away. The Arabs left it so that I could be made other than using dental records. Eddie knew my parents would freak. I bet that Liev may have remembered me if we ran into each other in a bar somewhere in New York City though, *"Hey, man! You were that dude from L.A...the checkpoint! West Bank? We talked Springsteen, remember? How you been, man! I see you took my advice and didn't move there!" He would have to be reminded of my name but never forgot a face or a good story to tell his friends. We'd laugh as we shared a beer and chatted about life and how to live it.*

But here there was no rescue, no connection, no truth from the barrel of a gun and Eddie lived. There was no record deal, no Boom Boom Room, no Micah, no Sherri. Well, Micah did exist, only I didn't have the pleasure of meeting or jamming with him and I have no idea if he's married or whatever. Creeping Charlie was a band but it turns out Micah and Liev aren't even related, not in this world, anyway.

I never saw Karly again after that day at the Dome. That was sad to realize, and it consumed me for a long time after I died. She ended up marrying a gardener. His name was not Nigel but Mike. I didn't write him a tractor opera with Sam but he's not missing out, he's got Karly. Seems to be a good dude and they now have three gorgeous kids. Good for her. She's a good girl with a good heart and I see her sometimes get misty and wistful whenever she sees a piece of news on the Middle East. Maybe I was the true love she thought had eluded her. She certainly was mine. That I do know, even if I only knew her in dreams as I lay dying. But still, it was me and her. I'm thankful I had that experience. I just wish it would have been the rest of my life.

She sometimes wondered what she could have done to have me not call and she would occasionally bring it up to her friends for another couple of years when she would get lonesome. My horrific end would never have dawned on her. She let it go once she met Mike and it wasn't like I was on the evening news so she never knew. "Collaborators" died every day in the Territories, like babies in front yards in South Central L.A.

The whole thing seemed so real and I still watch her exhibit the same traits with her husband that she did with me. I don't have anything close to that now. It's not here. Heaven or hell is down there so for now, I glide...

She's still the same chick, only not near as sexual or horny but she's kind. She was the same girl who told me I was "very cool," after watching "Easy Rider" and she meant it. She told me she loved me and I can see she is capable of deep, abiding love and she loves Mike and those kids unconditionally. Lucky bastard. If he ever writes his memoirs, that's what it should be called: "Lucky Bastard - the Mike the Gardner Story." Name a beer after him too and sell it in the Territories. I guess she loves the way I would like to think that God does, if I believed in Him when I was alive. He and I don't actually speak on this side of the aisle. My thoughts are kind of the only conversation I have with him but it's actually real. I didn't get banished anywhere, either, that was all man-made bullshit. It's different than talking to him or praying the way we do on earth. It's the best explanation I can offer anyone who would ask.

I watched as Eddie and Ali told my parents what they thought happened; Ali actually did most of the talking and it was speculative at best, fueled by Eddie's bullshit. I'm sure Eddie rationalized the whole thing by the time he saw my folks, before he told Ali, even. After all, his fingers were never on me, the coward.

It wasn't a robbery as the goons left all my gifts for back home so explained a story of mistaken identity that Ali just went along with. My mother wailed, biblically. I was the oldest, the first born, *her* baby. She wailed like Mahmud's mother did, even though she's Brazilian. My other brothers were only seventeen and eleven and they held her shaking body as best as boys could. They were crying, too. All grieving parents sound the same. My baby brother was six at the time and kept asking where I was and why was everyone sad. Six is still a baby, really. Poor kid, maybe I was his Custer, who knows? At the end of the day, everyone gets a Custer or two whether they like it or not. Just ask Mrs. Custer.

My father had tears running down his face and his throat was so swollen, spit built up as he asked Ali, in between slobbering sobs in Arabic, "Did he suffer? Was it quick?" I don't know if he was mourning me or if the situation reminded him of Uncle Jacob and the day he went boom as my father looked at my six year old brother.

He's a dentist now. Just turned thirty and gets laid like a Kennedy, God bless him. He has zero self-actualization issues whatsoever and can knock back the booze like anyone. My other two brothers are a doctor and a social worker. Sometimes I see the doctor guy cry in the car but I don't know if it's about me. It could be about my dad; they haven't spoken in the years since his marriage so who the fuck knows? Too bad I wasn't there to support his wedding because I would have.

My friends and my band grieved and gave me a great sendoff; Jim, Paul and Derek arranged it. Jim never did quit, actually. Loyal to the end, he helped my mom with the funeral arrangements. Even his parents came to the service as I knew them pretty well too.

The morning was overcast but it cleared up by the time the service started. It was clear and sunny. Everyone met at Point Dume, north of Malibu, which was always my favorite beach. It was so quiet. You could go naked and you were maybe 100 yards from the closest person. It was kind of a bitch to get to, while very well worth it. Now you can't get at it at all as they fenced it up. Derek, the singer organized the smaller points beautifully. I requested a jazz band which was comprised of some guys we knew in other bands and they played "One Flight Up" by Dexter Gordon, in its entirety. I always loved Dexter Gordon and we had finger foods and T-shirts that said, "Never Trust a Naked Bus Driver" on them. This was nothing more than a non-sequitur that I would say on occasion and I stole it from an out of print book of the same name. The t-shirt was to be a shared experience for anyone who knew me.

Great things were said by some truly beautiful people. People can be so kind and then turn around and amaze you with how quickly they can hurt others. My boss, Mitch, came with his wife Trudy. He whispered to her, "I shouldn't have let him go…" as he wept. That guy is truly a lovely person and his kids turned out pretty cool. One of them plays drums, too. He ended up playing in a Talking Heads tribute band and making his money as a day trader. He avoided the rat race of the music business entirely. Smart kid.

Much booze was had and a lot of people seemed to really love me, which was nice to see. Even a couple of ex-girlfriends showed up, including Shelly. She hugged my mom hard as they bawled their eyes out. She told my mom I was the best boyfriend she ever had and while obviously a little late, still real sweet. Imagine that.

Ironically, I was cremated per my wishes which I wanted and technically, already had a head start on. My Roman Catholic mother did not like it at all but she knew what I wanted. My ashes were spread there at the beach over the ocean off a cliff. My mom and brothers stood together as Jim did the honors. My father stood at the edge by the parking lot, talking to relatives and some friends. He was all cried out. Even still, they weren't talking about what happened anyway. They were more concerned about James Baker, the P.L.O. and a possible airport in Gaza. At least that's what kept their mind off of the service. I mean, like me or not, those guys knew me since I was a baby so that had to count for something.

I had no written will, but my friends recalled several chats on the subject of death. My mother had to threaten my father with divorce to carry out my desire as he wanted to keep me over there and bury me with his brother and parents. Can't say that I blame him; my grandfather was a great man but I was an American first. My mom, God bless her, knew that and as always, wanted "what's best for my boys." So there's that.

Years later, the doctor brother married a beautiful girl and they have two great kids. My father has not met them. He disavowed my brother for marrying a girl who wasn't an Arab. My death had zero impact on him generating any real love for my brothers after the shock wore off or maybe he got more hateful. Who the fuck knows? Maybe it's one too many family members dying violently that does that to a person. It's that or he develops a serious drinking problem and forgets to wear pants at social engagements.

Eddie is now a millionaire who owns several multi-unit apartment complexes in Las Vegas. He got away with it for now. But karma's a bitch that pays back with interest. His wife was blown up in a car bomb meant for him in L.A. when she was out to visit. That was tough to explain to the cops but he made it out to be a case of mistaken identity there too. The cunt. The Afghans don't handle anger or missing cash in very healthy or productive ways and they're not real big fans of talking it out.

I can see that Ali suspects something but as yet, hasn't said shit. I don't hold it against him. That's a lot to accept. Sam continues running business for the family and has developed his own chain of "the Dome" restaurants throughout the more stable parts of the Middle East like Turkey, Syria, Egypt and Tunisia. The concept wouldn't really fly in Atlanta, Georgia.

In the Dome in Jordan, my picture hangs right below the King Hussein's and in Iran, below the Ayatollah's. I find great humor in that. His boys are grown and he's still married to Nina and still has the occasional affair.

In my present condition I find that there just...is.

God is actually a lot more Zen than we give him credit for or so he tells me. He doesn't even care for the "h" in "him" being capitalized but we never really asked, so he really doesn't say. He got out of the burning bush and magic trick business a long time ago, for all the good it did us anyway. He doesn't even go by "God."

As for the guys who helped Eddie? No fucking clue, probably dead. I didn't know them so I draw a blank but I have an idea…

On September 11, 2001, Muslim fundamentalists hijacked planes and flew them into the Twin Towers, in New York and then the Pentagon as "martyrs." Of course, before they could go and collect on the 72 virgins, they enjoyed the services of several professionals the night before at a strip club. Allah Akbar, motherfucker. Maybe they were anticipating the ensuing ugliness that would be theirs for eternity. Maybe one of my killers was one of these guys? I really couldn't tell you.

The night of September 10, 2001, is fact but the eternal virgin thing is simply conjecture and supposition.

Nothing has really changed in the Territories in the years that followed and if anything, it's gotten worse. Both sides have taken to killing civilians and are pretty open about their contempt for human life as long it's the other side that dies. Those same two sides say, "God is on our side because we are right and just." But eventually, since only one side can win, God dodges out and while one side wins the other becomes a cautionary tale. God can't serve two masters and someone's always got it wrong. Kind of like that quote by General George Patton, "No bastard ever won a war by dying for his country. He won it by making the other poor dumb bastard die for *his* country." At least Patton was honest about it as well as practical.

What every sports team, warring faction or political party fails to grasp is that "God" can give a shit as to which side wins. They can pray all they want but his is a bigger practice. Now, I understand that from where I sit, I cannot prove this and from where they sit, neither can they.

In the West Bank, there is now a small, Christian village that has a brewery and yearly Oktoberfest's, which is amazing. It's amazing they haven't been over run. There's progress for you. They are surrounded by really pissed off, really wound up Muslims but don't seem to care because it's "Eat, drink and be merry, for tomorrow we may die." If anything, the rest of the region has gotten worse. The Israelis have gotten itchier and the Arabs have gotten more violent as they grasp at anything resembling hope and they'll take it from whoever gives it to them. They're all fucking insane and I'm dead so dying has earned me an opinion regardless of how long this shit has been going on.

The rest of the world doesn't seem to be doing much better; the countries who can afford both the Mercedes and the free press don't seem to screw their people like the countries that can only afford the Mercedes. People do it to each other every day and then wonder how dictators can be so ruthless. People will do what they do and that won't ever change. It seems the bane of humankind is to get a little more cash, more respect, more love.

If I am forgiving at all it's only because it is quite nice on this side. One can't get too hung up with your neighbor's pool when the water's warm in your own pool and not from pissing in it. Maybe that was my problem on earth in that I was minding too many pools and not my own. I would have liked to have known what kind of man I would have been in the flesh but it didn't turn out that way. I have some idea and at least I did die relatively quick and had a better life by 23 than most people ever do in 80 years.

The life I lived up to and including my death was real, all of it. It was real. I had love. Love from my mom, my uncles, my band, my friends, Karly, and even my dad. If only I could have lived for that instead of always trying to get ahead and worrying about some crap that wouldn't matter if I grew old. How cool would that be if mankind could do that without being superior about it or mistaking hate for "knowing better?"

The biggest mistake I made was to think people had to love me on my terms. Everyone loves even if they have a fucked up way of showing it. The only love to stay away from would be the kind that kills, everything else can be negotiated. If I had some patience and expressed love first instead of waiting for it to be expressed to me, I'd have had a different life, maybe. Maybe my

190

dad and I could have had a better time of it. Hell, I'm dead and we all do that eventually so no one person is that special. Human nature tends to the negative but it takes not an ounce more effort to love well. I did a lot of negative when I was alive. To change I would have had to make a bigger effort to love and to do so like a mother. Like my mother. People will never allow it to be that easy but it really could have been that simple, had I fought harder for it.

I didn't know these things when I was alive but I know them now. So there's that.